Run Away Home:
Tempered

(Run Away Home, Book I)

Catherine Manett

RhetAskew Publishing
United States of America

Interior Design

© 2022 — FLITTERBOW PRODUCTIONS

Cover Design

USED BY PERMISSION - GETCOVERS.COM

ISBN-13: 978-1-949-39877-9

for my forever friend, cousin,
and partner in imagination,
Christine Lang

PROLOGUE

Danny

"Another new boy? How many can we fit in here? There's too many!" I say.

"Should we go take a look at him?" Darren asks us.

We're standing in the living room, hiding behind the wall near the walk-in room. I want to know what the new boy looks like.

"I think we should go see," Andy responds.

I slide closer to the door, getting as close as possible without being spotted.

"HEY, DANNY, WAIT!" Darren whisper-yells. That's when you yell in a whisper voice.

I don't listen to him. I do what I want.

I peek around the door and into the walk-in room. The other boys follow. They stand behind me because they're all chickens, but I'm not. I feel like a secret reporter. I should let them know what I see.

"Oh wow. Oh my gosh."

"What?" Andy asks.

"He looks like he got the shit kicked out of him!" I tell them, then quickly turn back.

"Really? What's he got, a black eye or something?"

"No, worse! He's on crutches, and he's got a wrist brace thing, and...he's got a big bruise on his head! Oh! And one on his arm, too! Wait, no..." I squint. "The one on his arm is just a weird tattoo."

"Whoa."

"He must be tough. Maybe he got in a fight?" Andy asks.

"He doesn't look tough. He prolly lost a fight. He's all beated up. Also, he looks like a girl."

"He looks like a girl?" Darren asks.

"Yeah, he's got this really long, crazy hair. Like wavy, blonde hair, and...uhm, he's really small like. Like skinny and short. He just looks kinda girly."

Melissa turns around and sees me peeking.

"Come on over, Danny," she says with a smile.

Ugh. I've been found. Some secret reporter I am. Andy and Darren run away as fastly as they can. Melissa doesn't see them. Thanks, guys.

I walk over to her and the boy with my hands in my pockets and my chin down on my chest. I look him up and down with my eyeballs, but I don't move my head. He just looks weird, not like anyone I've ever seen before. Melissa's going to make me talk to him.

"Hi." I wave, then look back down at my feet.

He says nothing. I sneak another look. Really? Maybe he thinks he's too cool to talk to me because he's older. He must be fourteen, or fifteen, or thirteen, or fifteen. But so what? I'm eight. Big deal. Why do the older ones never talk to the littler ones?

"I'm Danny."

He just stares. Maybe he's shy?

"He doesn't speak very much English," Melissa says.

WHAT? But he's white! That's very, very weird. I never seen a white kid who doesn't speak English. They all speak English.

"Well, doesn't he at least know 'hi?' Everyone knows 'hi.' That's the easiest thing you could say."

"I think he does know 'hi,' Danny, but could you imagine how he must feel right now?"

"I don't know." I watch my foot as I move it around in circles, kicking my toes into the floor.

"Why don't we all sit on the couch," she says.

Melissa holds the boy by his arm and points to the living room. He walks past her. She helps him sit on the couch and puts his crutches against the wall. Her gray curls fall over her face, so she uses a scrunchie to tie them back.

"I have so many questions, Melissa," I say.

"Like?"

"Where's he from? What happened to him?"

"He's from Scotland. I don't know what happened to him."

"How'd he get all the way to Long Island?"

Melissa stares at the boy like she's confused. "I don't know that either."

"Where's his family? Are they coming back for him?"

"The police found him all alone last night."

This is really, really, *really* weird.

"What's his name?"

"Peter."

"I want to help him," I say, just like a superhero.

"You're a good boy, Danny." Melissa rubs my back. I smile because I know I am. "Why don't you introduce him to the other kids? Bring them out here so they can talk to him."

"He won't understand what they're saying, though."

"He'll understand friendship. Everyone does, trust me."

I guess that's true.

Melissa walks out of the room. I'm here all alone with Peter.

CHAPTER ONE

Melissa

"I never had children of my own, but I wouldn't trade what I do have for the world. You kids—" A new coughing fit interrupts me. I push the oxygen tubes farther into my nostrils and wheeze. "Can you hand me that water bottle, Peter?"

He lets go of my hand and turns to the side table. He picks up the bottle and untwists the cap. I take it from him.

"I'm proud of you."

He looks back, wide-eyed. "Really?"

"Yes, really. You've become a very responsible young man. Helping out around the house, working and taking care of me... The list goes on. I couldn't—"

"I want to take Danny." He doesn't look directly at me when he says it. Instead, he looks just past me. I think he's afraid of my answer, whether it's yes or no. I can't say I'm very surprised. Through the years, those two have become close—almost inseparable—but still... A child? Can Peter handle a teenager? When I took in my first foster child, I was forty-six. He's only twenty-one.

"I can do it," he adds. "Where else will he go when you..."

He doesn't finish his sentence. Is that what this entire year has been leading up to? One question? I really am proud. If that's it, he's worked very hard to prove himself to me.

"I already told him he can come with me. He wants to come with me. Plus, I'll have Hayley, and we... We can do it."

I still haven't responded. I don't know how I feel. The thought of *both* Hayley and Danny in the same home, and Peter being responsible for them *both*? Will he ever listen to me about her?

"How does she feel about that, Peter? Helping out with Danny?"

"I don't know. She'll be fine with it."

I don't agree with that. I don't think she'll like the idea very much at all.

"I'd think about it some more, Peter. You should speak with Hayley about your plans."

"Yeah. I'll talk to her."

He leans back in his chair. I examine him closely. The tiniest smile forms in the corner of his mouth. I know how he feels about her. He'll never admit it, especially to me. He calls Danny his brother, but her? He doesn't call her his "sister."

I clutch his hand again, tighter this time, and I look into his eyes. He's a man now, and he's matured a great deal. Maybe I should trust him?

Danny

"Did you send in the deposit?" Peter asks.

"No, I thought you were doing that," Hayley says.

Hayley's washing the dishes, and I'm drying. She kinda sucks at it. Maybe that's why she never does anything. Maybe she just sucks at everything. Almost every plate still has tomato sauce spots. I scrape them off with my fingernail. Nasty.

I lean my butt against the cabinets and look at Peter. He's sitting at the kitchen table, frowning at his laptop.

"Hayley, you said you would pay the security deposit."

"Hayley, you said you would pay the security deposit," she mocks him with a bad Scottish accent. Yup, she does suck at everything. *Especially* Scottish accents.

Peter rolls his eyes. "Knock it off." He doesn't sound as Scottish this time.

She stops washing, dropping the cup she's working on back into the sink. She turns around to glare at him.

"I don't have it."

"We need to pay it before we move in next week."

"Can you just cover it, Peter?"

"Yeah, I guess, but then can you do the first month's rent?"

I'm just watching and listening. I know why Hayley doesn't have the money. Peter thinks I don't understand, but I'm not dumb like he thinks I am.

Hayley turns back around and continues "washing" the dishes—if that's what you want to call it.

"I'll pay the first month, if I can come up with it somehow."

"All right."

"Even though you're getting everything," she says.

Oh boy. Here we go.

"I am not getting everything, Hayley. I'm getting a few thousand dollars. A few thousand dollars isn't everything. Do you—"

"You're the favorite."

"No, that's obviously Danny."

"She's giving you the money."

"Because I'm becoming Danny's legal guardian, not you."

"Then let Danny pay the rent with the money Melissa gave to you," Hayley says.

I stare at her, and she looks right back at me. Her eyes are as red as the freaking tomato sauce spots she left on the dishes.

"What?" she asks.

"Stop spending all your money on pot and pills, then maybe you'll have money." I turn back toward the sink and continue drying.

"You fucking brat."

"Where do you even get money from, anyway? You don't work."

"Stop it!" Peter says.

"Did you hear what he just said to me?" she asks him.

"Danny, you shouldn't have said that."

"But it's true," I say.

"It's not... Just don't," Peter answers.

I turn toward Peter again. "I'm thirteen years old. Do you think I'm dumb?"

"Danny, no, I don't. Just let me and Hayley talk about money. You don't need to be in this conversation."

"SHE DRAGGED ME INTO IT!" I point at her and throw my dishtowel on the floor. "Are you even listening?"

"Shh! Melissa is sleeping."

I walk out of the kitchen. I don't want to dry these dirty freaking plates anymore. I wish Peter would just tell Hayley she can't come with us.

Hayley

"How do we spell her last name?"

"M-A-R-C-E-L-L-O," Peter answers.

"Thanks. Tell me about what happened this morning."

Police officers are in our living room. When Peter told me that Melissa was dead, I made sure to hide everything that could be incriminating.

"I woke up and went into her bedroom. She was dead," Peter says.

"And you knew that for sure?"

"I know what death looks like," Peter answers. "She had emphysema. She'd been a chain smoker as a young woman. At least, that's what she told us to try and get us to quit."

I'm still in my pajamas, but Peter's fully dressed. He's wearing light-colored jeans and a checkered polo. His hair is up in a neat bun. He looks very put together. I don't. Fuck... That's okay, right? Whatever, I don't care.

I sit on the couch and rub my eyes, then look down at my hands. They're covered in black smudges. I forgot to take my makeup off last night. Fuckity, fuck, fuck. I really look like a hot mess, don't I? I'd be suspicious of me if I were one of these officers.

"And you're her caretaker?" the officer asks Peter with one eyebrow raised.

I grasp my hands together and place them between my knees. Peter doesn't answer quickly enough. The officer sees me gawking at him and peers back. I quickly look away. Is he still watching? I don't want to draw any attention to myself.

"Well, sort of. I was one of her foster children until I aged out a couple of months ago," Peter finally responds. "It's me, Hayley, and then there's Danny. He's upstairs. Technically, he's not a foster kid. She adopted him. He's her son, and...uhm...that's it. There were more kids, but all of them moved out already. I stayed to take care of her. Danny's still a minor, and Hayley...well—"

Excuse me? I glare at him. He knows I won't turn twenty-one for almost a month. Not technically aged out yet.

"She's here too," Peter continues.

I hear a lot of banging upstairs, then the two men carry the body bag down on a stretcher. I don't want to see that. I'm not good with death. Is anyone?

"Danny!" Peter yells.

Danny's following behind the stretcher, wearing a baggy sweatshirt and jeans. The black hood over his head makes him look like the grim fucking reaper. Fuck, even he got dressed?

Peter walks over to the stairs. I should have known this would happen today. My horoscope said someone in the office would be up for a big promotion. I didn't know what that meant, but now I see I should have dressed for the occasion.

"Didn't I tell you to stay in your room?"

"I wanted to say goodbye to her."

"I know, I know. Come down here and sit on the couch with us."

"I thought you said she wouldn't die until after we moved out. I thought I had more time."

"I was wrong."

The men reach the bottom of the stairs and carry the body out of the house. Danny makes his way to the storm door and presses his face against the glass. He finally pulls his hood down. His light blue-hazel eyes reflect the sunlight. His thick black hair is messy, like he slept on it, but that could easily be fixed with a set of hands. Mine definitely needs a hairbrush.

Peter touches him gently on the back. "Come now. Death is hard. I know it. I know."

Danny looks up at him. He's almost as tall as Peter now, not even an inch shy. I don't know if it's that Peter's very small, or Danny's very big. I think it's both. Danny thinks he's *so* grown because of his size, but he hugs Peter and hides his face on his shoulder like a child. Their hug amuses me. With Peter's pale white skin and Danny's dark complexion, they look somewhat like a yin and yang symbol. They finally let go of each other.

Peter leads Danny to the couch where I'm sitting. I haven't said a word, but the brat takes a seat and stares right at me. I stare back. He thinks he's *so* intimidating. I'm daring him to say something right now, but he looks away. Knew it.

"The hospital will help you set up arrangements."

"I won't be doing it," Peter tells the officer. "Her sister wants her services prepared in a certain way. She'll be taking it from here. I talked to her this morning."

"All right. I'm sorry for your loss, and good luck to all three of you."

"Thank you."

I yawn as the officers leave. Danny snarls at me. What? Now I'm not allowed to yawn?

"I'm tired," I say.

He covers his eyes with his hands and throws his head back. He sniffles a couple of times.

How am I going to live with these two? Peter and I have been friends for years now. Living with him wouldn't have been so bad—honestly, it should have been fun. No Melissa? We could've done whatever the fuck we wanted? But he's changed since he decided to become Danny's guardian. He's way more uptight and very...vanilla.

Moving into this apartment... What a way to kick off the new year, right? I guess I don't have too many other options. I wish I did.

I glance back down at my smudge-covered hands. I wonder if Peter will let Tristian move in, too.

Peter

Packing all of our belongings from Melissa's house wasn't too hard. We didn't have that many things. Just some clothes, really. All the furniture was Melissa's, and her sister wanted most of it. I mean, it is technically her house now. She's planning to rent it out. Too bad we can't afford it. I don't think Melissa's sister ever really liked us much, not even Danny, but there *is* some good news. I was approved for a credit card at a furniture store. I don't know how. I have no credit, but I'm not going to question it.

I'm proud of the apartment. It has one large main room meant for a living space and dining area. The room is covered with a soft, gray carpet—and there aren't many stains, either! I might be able to scrub out the few that remain, or at least cover them with something...like a plant. I think the furniture store had fake plants. I'll have to check again sometime this week.

A separate kitchen's just off the dining room. The tiling is black and white, which clashes a wee bit with the speckled countertops, but it's not *so* bad. I like the cabinets. They're real wood, not the sticker crap that peels right off.

The short hallway leads from the living room toward a bathroom and three small bedrooms, one for each of us—well, one for Danny. Maybe in the future, Hayley and I will share a room, kind of like a...a family! I would never say that last part out loud, but the thought alone puts a smile on my face. *Family.* Sometimes it seems like it could happen. Other times, it feels like the most impossible thing out there.

What I really like most about the apartment is that you're never too far away from anyone else you live with. If I'm in the kitchen, and I speak loudly enough, Hayley can hear me from the living room. Unless she has the TV volume all the way up, which is typical of her.

I'm inside the back of the small moving truck. I inhale deeply and watch as my warm breath leaves my mouth. I pick up another box filled with clothes and head toward the door. My keys jangle against my legs as I make my way down the sidewalk. Second floor apartments are just awful. Carrying boxes up and down the stairs can really make you out of breath...like walking up and down a hill—

NO, don't go there!

When I reach the top of the stairs, I drop the box and just look around. It's still kind of empty in here. I bought a couch, a coffee table, an entertainment center, and a dining room set. Melissa's sister let us take the TV, and I was absolutely donnered. It's a crappy TV, but still! She also let us have a small round table with three chairs and the beds. The apartment needs some sort of décor. I'll figure it out. I have a good eye for that stuff—no money, but a good eye.

I bend down and open the box. It's filled with Danny's clothes. I pick it back up and carry it into his new room. He's sitting on the end of his bed. Nothing's put away, but at least he put sheets on the mattress.

"Not too bad, right?" I ask, setting the box on the floor.

"It's a little bigger than my room at Melissa's, I think."

"That's good."

"Yup." He picks up his phone.

"Can you start putting some of your clothes away?"

"I don't have a dresser." He lowers his phone to look at me.

"Can you hang your clothes in the closet until I can get you one?"

"Sure, but what about socks?"

"Put them in one of those plastic containers for now. I think they're still in the truck."

"Okay. I'll go get one."

"Thanks, bud."

Danny and I leave his room together. He walks toward the front door, but I stop. Hayley's standing in her new bedroom. Her arms are folded, and she sighs loudly.

"Something wrong?" I ask.

She turns, acting surprised, but I'm pretty sure she intended for me to hear the sigh. She doesn't speak immediately. I want to fill the void, but she's so distracting. Her blue eyes are a perfect contrast to her light-red hair. She bats them, gently but swiftly. I can't help but marvel at her untouched complexion. No zits—no marks at all, in fact—just soft porcelain skin surrounded by a curtain of silky red hair. She's flawless. She's beautiful. She's—

"I don't know, Peter. There's not a lot of light in here. Your room has more light and a bigger closet." She keeps her arms folded.

Oh, yeah. The bedroom.

"Well, it's the master."

"Why do you get it?"

I smirk. This is a perfect opportunity to be really nice. I'll take it.

"You know what?"

I walk out of her room and into mine. I pick up one of my boxes and carry it into her room.

"You can have that one." I nod toward the master bedroom.

"Really?"

"Yeah. I don't need a big room. This one's just fine for me."

"Thanks, Peter!"

She hugs me, and warmth spreads throughout my entire body. Maybe I'll be moving back into the big one with her soon? Sounds like a plan to me.

"You're welcome." I don't want to let go, but when she pulls away, I know I have to.

"Can you help me carry my stuff into that room?"

"Of course." I pick up one of her boxes and move it into what was going to be my bedroom. I come back for the next box. Now she's lying on the bed.

"You're the best," she says, but she's looking at her phone. She's texting someone. Who?

"But not...not *the* best, right?" I lean on the doorframe. She sighs again. She doesn't need to answer. I get it. "I know." I pick up another box and carry it into the bigger room. When I return for another one, I stop in the doorway. "Can I just ask you, was it the sex? Was it really bad?"

She cracks up with laughter. How embarrassing.

"No, it was fine, but that was just for fun. No feelings attached, remember?"

"Yeah, well, I was hoping... I guess, if it was good enough, maybe you—" I laugh at myself because I sound so pathetic. "Never mind."

"Peter, you're great. You're really great. You know that, but... You're not my type. You're a really great friend."

"A friend? Friends don't have sex."

"Some do." She laughs.

"That's not funny. I don't want to do that."

She stops laughing. "I'm just joking around. Can't you take a joke anymore?"

"Sure I can." I grab the last box from her room and carry it to the master bedroom. When I come back, she's still plopped down on the bed. Jesus Christ, Mary, and St. Joseph. "Well, can you get off of *my* bed then?"

"Yeah, sorry." She stands, then bends down to look under the mattress. She pulls a small bag out from underneath.

"What is that?"

"It's nothing."

"Hayley, I hope it's not more Oxys."

"It's fine." She tries to hide the bag behind her back, but obviously it's too late for that.

"It's not fine, Hayley. You said you would try—"

"I am trying, Peter. I am. Okay? I'm trying. You don't get it. Leave me alone."

I stare at the floor. "I can't stop you."

"I know you can't."

"I'm just asking you, nicely, please do that somewhere else. Not here with Danny."

"He'll never see anything." She heads toward the door. As she walks past me, I turn and plant my fingers on the temples of my head.

"You know what? Let's get you into rehab. Let's get you into some sort of program. I don't want you to—"

"When I'm ready, I'll go. I'm not ready yet, but I can quit any time I want to. I don't want to now. Okay?"

"You can't be doing this here, Hayley. You're not listening to me, I just said—"

"What will you do, kick me out on the street? It was supposed to be just the two of us way before you dropped this whole Danny bombshell on me. There would have been no problem if you just—"

"Hayley, I—"

"It's settled, then."

She grips the bag tighter as she leaves the room.

I don't know what to do...again.

CHAPTER TWO

Hayley

I wake up in a new bed. The sun shines in, landing right on my face. There's too much light in this room. I'll have to hang curtains, or a sheet, or something.

What will I do today? Maybe I can buy some stuff for my room, like those curtains. I sit up, looking side to side while cracking my neck. My phone lights up with a notification. My daily horoscope is ready. I pick up the phone and unlock it.

Monday, January 10th

**Aquarius: right now,
you're hoping for a miracle.**

**Although it may seem far-fetched,
always believe that one is possible!
Faith could be the difference between
inaction and positive change.**

Positive change. Sounds refreshing.

Footsteps approach my door, so I stand. I guess Peter's already awake.

He knocks. "I made you breakfast," he says through the door.

"Thank you. I'm coming."

"Take your time."

I open the door and shiver. It's cold in here. I cross my arms while walking toward the kitchen. Danny's at the table with a plate in front of him. Peter's cleaning off the stove and counters.

"Do you think I'll like my new school?"

"Shouldn't be too much different from your old one," Peter says.

"All new people, though."

"Yeah, that's pretty scary."

I sit, leaning toward the table while squeeze-rubbing my arms. I hope Peter made coffee.

"How did you do it, Peter?" Danny asks.

"How'd I do what?"

"I mean, a new school is scary, but a new country?"

"It was a relief, actually. Getting away. A fresh start. You should be excited too."

"What's for breakfast?" I ask.

"Eggs, cheese, bacon, whole wheat toast," Peter answers.

"Coffee?"

"This isn't a diner." He smiles and brings me a plate and a cup of coffee. I smile too. He starts cleaning again.

"Anyway," Danny interjects, "you weren't scared when you left Scotland?"

"No."

"Oh. Well, you were all beaten up. Did you get into a fight?"

"No, Danny, and stop your fixation with fights. No fighting."

"Whatever," Danny says. "What happened to you, then? You never talk about it."

"Nothing."

"Something happened, Peter. You had broken bones."

"I'm clumsy. I fell."

"Your parents didn't take you to a doctor?"

"Didn't I tell you they were both dead?"

"Yeah, well...no one took you to a doctor?"

"No, Danny. I was on my own."

Peter's story is *so* strange. It really doesn't make much sense. I've come up with my own theories of what happened, but none of those make much sense either. I'm so curious.

It's my turn to talk. I'm hoping for a miracle.

Positive change.

"So, let me get this straight," I say. "You lived by yourself in Scotland because both of your parents died. You fell down and got really hurt. Then, you somehow came to the United States?"

"Bingo," he says. "You're so smart, Hayley."

He's being sarcastic again. I guess there won't be any *positive change* today, after all. Or maybe the change isn't for him? Who else might make a positive change today? I look over at Danny.

"Yeah. How *did* you get here?" Danny asks.

"What?"

"Like, did you take a plane?"

"No. No..." His voice is soft as he continues scrubbing the stove.

"Then how?"

"I mean, yes. A plane. I took a plane. Sorry, I wasn't listening."

I laugh out loud. "Peter, this story makes no sense."

He stops cleaning and presses both hands flat on the countertop, looking down. "It doesn't have to make sense. It's my story, and I'll tell it the way I want to."

"Okay..."

He takes a breath.

"Cool. Now that's settled," he responds, still keeping his back to us.

Danny and I look at each other and not in a vicious, "I hate you" kind of way. More in a "what the hell?" kind of way. I guess there's a first for everything.

I start eating. Maybe it's best I've never had any real feelings for Peter. I can't stand secrets, and he has so many.

Now Peter's wiping the countertop dry. He takes the rag, hangs it on the oven handle, and turns around.

I examine him. He's so domesticated lately, almost feminine, with that ballerina bun on top of his head. All I can see are his flaws. His crooked nose, the way one of his eyes opens wider than the other, the three freckles on his forehead. I never noticed these things until recently, but now, I pick him apart in my mind. I dissect every last one of his imperfections. I could break him—shatter him, if I wanted to.

He sees me looking at him and smiles. I smile back.

Man, are his teeth big!

Danny

I'm sitting on the bus, staring out the window. I can't wait for it to move. Luckily, the bus stop is in front of our apartment complex. It's freezing outside, but I actually like the walk to our building. I don't mind my new school too much either, besides the work. It's been a long day, though, and I'm ready to go home.

"Hey, Danny!"

That kid from my math class just came through the bus door. What's his name? I don't remember... Matt? I think that's it. I didn't make any new friends yet. It's weird being the brown kid raised by white people. No matter what school you go to, you don't really fit in anywhere.

Matt sits beside me. His backpack is bigger than he is. He takes it off and puts it on the floor between his legs.

"She's such a bitch, right?" he asks.

"Who?"

"Mrs. Roland."

"Oh, I don't know."

"What do you mean? She embarrassed you in front of the whole class!"

"She did?"

"You're funny, Danny." He laughs.

"I'm just not good at math. I wasn't embarrassed, though."

"Oh... Sorry, then. Hey, we should hang out one day."

"Uh... Yeah, sure."

Maybe this kid wants to be my friend? I don't know, that was a weird way to break the ice. I need a friend, though.

The bus starts rolling.

"You live in building ninety-three, right?"

"I do."

"I live in eighty-seven C. Not far. We should walk to our buildings together."

"How do you know I live there?"

"I saw you leaving your apartment."

"Okay..."

"You could come over and play *Call of Duty* with me."

"When?"

"Any day."

"Okay."

"Do you have a PlayStation?"

"I do. My brother just bought it for me."

"That's nice of him. My brother doesn't buy me anything. My parents bought me my PlayStation."

"Yeah, well... My brother is like my parent."

"Oh. What's your name on PlayStation?"

"DanMan4279."

He pulls out his phone and types. "If you're on tonight, I'll send you a request. What do you play?"

"I just bought *Rocket League*."

"I have that. Are you any good?"

I smile. "I think I'm pretty good."

"I guess we'll see. I'm sure you're not better than me."

Uh...What?

We're quiet for the rest of the bus ride. He looks at his phone, and I look at the stupid stuff people wrote on the seat in front of us. "Lana + Mike = 4 eva." Idiots... Someone else just wrote "BITCH" really big. That's kinda funny when you think about it, just "BITCH."

I put my knees up on the seat to cover the writing. I reach into my pocket, but my phone's not there. Shit. I put my legs back down and dig through my backpack. I hope I didn't leave it in the school. Wouldn't be the first time I lost it. I reach all the way to the bottom of the bag and fish around. *Got it!* I get comfy again and play some dumb free matching game I downloaded this morning.

After about ten more minutes, the bus pulls up in front of our complex. We both stand before it stops.

"PLEASE REMAIN SEATED UNTIL THE BUS COMES TO A COMPLETE STOP!" the driver yells.

We look at each other, sit back down, and laugh. When you get old, like the bus driver, you start caring about things like that.

The tires squeak. That means we can stand now. We get off the bus together and walk. It's snowing a little, so we hurry.

"Your name is Matt, right?"

"Yeah, Matt. How do you like Truman so far?"

"It's okay. It's basically the same as my old school. I don't really like school, in general. I'm not good at it."

"No one likes school."

"You don't like it either?"

He looks like the kind of kid that would like school: scrawny, big backpack, and thick glasses.

"I like gym and lunch," he says.

"Those are okay. My brother's obsessed with school. He wants me to do well, and I don't want to disappoint him."

"Everyone's parents want them to do well in school."

"I'm thinking about staying late for extra help on Mondays and Wednesdays. I don't really get the math. Do you get it?"

"Yeah."

Oh. I kinda wanted him to say, *No, I don't get it either.* It's better to not get it with someone than to not get it alone.

"Can't your brother help you?"

"You kidding me? He doesn't know how to do it either."

"Oh. Why?"

"I don't think he ever went to school."

"You don't think?"

"I don't know."

"What?"

"Hey, Matt? I don't really want to talk about that. Okay?"

"I'm sorry."

We approach Matt's building. He runs up to his door.

"*Rocket League.* Eight o'clock? You down?"

"Sure."

"I'll talk to you then, Danny!"

"Bye, Matt."

He goes into his apartment. I shove my hands in my coat pockets and keep on walking towards ours.

Hayley

I'm on the couch, and Netflix is on. Yes, I'm still watching. Why does it always ask me that? Do I really watch that much? I don't care.

Peter's in the kitchen, cooking dinner, doing his Peter thing. I can smell peppers and onions from here.

"Hey, Peter? Can you bring me a bowl of ice cream?" I call out.

"We're going to eat soon. Can you wait until after dinner?" He yells back, then peeks his head out of the kitchen.

"No. I want ice cream now."

He shakes his head. "But dinner is going to be *really* delicious. I don't want you to ruin your appetite."

Food's his "love language," even before he decided to adopt Danny. I read about "love languages" in a magazine. Different people show affection in different ways. For him, it's food. If he really wanted to razzle-dazzle me, he would just get me a damn bowl of ice cream.

"I just want ice cream, Peter."

He frowns and shakes his head some more. *Some more... S'mores...* That would really hit the spot right now.

"Can you put marshmallows on top of the ice cream?" I ask.

"No, we don't have marshmallows. Also, we don't have ice cream. All we have is frozen yogurt."

Ugh. It gets worse.

"Why did you buy that instead of real ice cream?"

"It's better for you. Still not great, but better. You know how much sugar is in those little pints you like? It's crazy. I was reading the nutrition facts in the store, and it absolutely blew my mind. I couldn't—"

"I don't care."

"All right, I'll bring you a bowl of frozen yogurt."

He disappears back into the kitchen. I pick up my lighter and cigarettes. He must hear my lighter click, because he comes running into the living room.

"No! No more smoking in here! Don't smoke in here!"

"Seriously? Why not? It's cold outside." I continue to click my lighter, watching the small flame live and die.

"The couch is starting to smell like smoke...and the carpet!"

"How often do you sniff the carpet, Peter?" I stop clicking.

"It sticks to the fibers and lingers in the air."

"Holy crap."

"Look, just— Just go on the balcony. Please? I've been smoking on the balcony."

"I'll just smoke later. Are you getting my ice cream?"

"I'll get it now."

I hear the door open. Danny's back from school. He walks up the stairs and into the living room, unzipping his jacket.

"How was your day?" Peter asks him.

"It was good. I think I made a friend." He throws his backpack on the floor by the dining room table.

"Please don't put that there," Peter says. "We eat there. Hang it on the hook by the door or put it in your room by your desk."

"Hayley doesn't eat there. She eats on the couch." He points at me.

Why does he always start shit with me? I ignore him. Ignoring him is important for my sanity.

Peter looks my way. "She shouldn't. That's how you get bugs. Anyway," he turns back to Danny, "you made a friend? Tell me about it."

"We're going to play *Rocket League* tonight at eight."

"No, you're not. *The Real Housewives* are on at eight." I shove my lighter back in my pocket.

"WHAT? No! That's so unfair! Peter, she's had the TV the whole day while I was at school!"

"Hayley, just DVR it. Let him play."

"Of course you'd say that," I answer. He always takes Danny's side.

"Just let him play tonight, please?"

"Yeah. Why are you watching *Housewives,* anyway?" Danny asks. "You're not anything like a housewife...Well, maybe the house part. At Melissa's, you just sat around the house, but you didn't do anything else. Nothing's going to change here, right?"

"DANNY!" Peter yells. "Apologize now!"

"I don't want to, Peter!"

"Do it. We don't talk to each other that way."

"Sorry," he says, but the big baby doesn't mean it. He stomps into his room and slams the door.

Peter groans and walks into the kitchen. After a few minutes, he comes back with my bowl of ice cream. He sits next to me, holding it out with his head down like it's an offering. I take it from him.

"Can you please let him play tonight? First day of school is hard enough."

"Sure, no problem," I say without looking in his direction.

"Great. Dinner's almost ready."

"I'm not hungry for dinner."

"Well, I'll leave it on the stove for you and Danny. Just please do the dishes when you're done. I'm tired after work."

"Yeah. Okay."

"I'm going to finish up cooking and take a shower. Then I'll be ready for you to take me to the bar." He stands and stretches.

"I'll tell Danny he can play tonight. Happy now?"

"Very. Thank you."

Peter goes back into the kitchen. I put my ice cream on the coffee table and walk down the hall to Danny's closed bedroom door. I don't want to, but I knock.

"Who is it?"

"It's me." I cross my arms and look up at the ceiling.

"What do you want?"

I walk into the room and close the door quietly behind me. I lean against it. Danny's lying on his bed, staring at his phone.

"I wanted to talk to you about your game."

He doesn't look up at me.

"What? That I'm playing it? I know I'm playing it. Peter said I can, so I am."

This fucking brat. I don't say anything yet. I take a breath and close my eyes. He continues with his little shit fit.

"You don't do anything. You always just sit around and chew on pills and smoke. You've never helped out at all. I help out more than you. So why should you get the TV? Give me one reason." He puts his phone down and sits up.

That's it. He can't talk to me that way.

"Nope. Peter will be at work. I'll be watching my show. You can sit in your room. I don't care."

I yank the door open again and slam it as I leave. I'm surprised he doesn't follow me, shouting like the overgrown baby he is. So much for "positive change." No one in this apartment changed at all today! I wonder who my horoscope could have been referring to?

I go to my room, open the bottom drawer of my nightstand, and find my plastic baggie of kickers.

I could quit if I wanted to. I just don't want to, right? Now's just not the right time. I'll know when it is. My horoscope will say something about it, for sure.

CHAPTER THREE

Peter

"Job number one, done," I say to myself as I get out of the car. My legs are throbbing already. Waiting tables isn't so bad. I've only been doing it for a few days now, but I'm already wondering if it's worth it. When there's no lunch rush, I barely make minimum wage.

It's time to get ready for my second job, bartending at McAlister's. I've worked there for a while now. I make way more money there than at my day job. I need two jobs and government benefits to afford all the bills, and that's still just getting by.

I walk toward the apartment, rubbing my hands to warm them. My skin feels like it could peel right off.

What do I want for lunch? I'll just have something easy. Maybe a granola bar? I think we still have one left.

As I open the front door, I hear talking. Is someone here with Hayley? Who?

I walk up the stairs quickly and hang my keys on the hook. Hayley's sitting on the couch with a man. He has greasy brown hair, a few straggly curls on his chin, angular cheekbones, and a long, sunken-in face. He's wearing a stained wife-beater which looks like it hasn't been laundered in weeks. One of his bare arms has a poorly drawn tattoo of some *Mario Brothers* characters. Bowser's holding Yogi in the air with one arm, and his other hand is a fist, like he's going to clock Yogi in the face. What a clatty basturt. The more I examine him, the more afraid

I become to breathe in through my nose. God only knows what he smells like.

"Peter, this is Tristian."

"Oh. Hello," I answer politely.

"Hey, what's up." He doesn't look at me. His voice is monotone, so his greeting doesn't even sound like a question.

"Not too much."

I can't help but look around the apartment. There's garbage everywhere. Empty chip bags and napkins. Is that spit in a plastic cup? I finally take a deep breath in through my nose, but I instantly regret it. The room smells like skunk. There's a half-eaten sandwich on the coffee table, no plate. Who eats straight off of the table?

"I'll get you a plate," I say.

"Don't need one. Thanks, brother."

"Okay... Well, in my house, we eat on plates."

"It's an apartment, not a house."

Who is this guy?

"I know, but that wasn't the point. I've been trying to keep it clean in here, and I—"

"I'll put it on my lap." He picks up the sandwich and places it on his dirty jeans. The bread crumbles, and pieces fall onto the carpet. I guess I'll need to vacuum tonight.

"Well...I'm going to go to the bathroom now." I stare at Hayley. She knows, but she doesn't look back.

"Cool accent," he says.

"What?" I ask.

"You have a cool accent. How long did it take you to grow all that hair?"

"I don't know. My whole life, I guess." I start walking away.

"You didn't say thank you."

I stop and turn back around. I place my hands on my hips and raise my eyebrows.

"I'm sorry. What exactly am I thanking you for?"

"For moving my sandwich and for complimenting your accent."

"Thank you?"

"You're welcome."

"Okay. Great."

I head towards the bathroom. What the fuck was that? Complete rocket. I hear Hayley follow me. Suddenly, she grabs my hand and pulls me all the way down the hall.

"Can you be nice to him please, Peter?" she asks as we reach my bedroom door. I turn around and put my back against the wall.

"What did I do? He's such a fucking rocket."

"Rocket?"

"Like a crazy person. Who is this guy?"

"He's my boyfriend."

My heart falls. "Boyfriend?"

"I told you about him at Melissa's, remember? He knows Ryan. Remember Ryan?"

I do remember that...

"Well, that didn't stop you from fucking me a few weeks ago. I assumed it was over then."

"We were taking a break."

"Well, take another one. A nice long one. I don't like him."

"Of course you don't." She laughs.

"No, not just because... It's not just because of how I feel. It's..."

"Then why? You didn't even give him a chance."

"He's eating straight off the table. He's made a mess in my living room," I say as I tally the offenses on my fingers. "Are there plans to clean the mess?"

"*Your* living room? And it's not a mess. It's a few crumbs."

"Also, he's really weird. Did you hear that conversation? Am I the one being weird?"

"He's not weird. He's chill."

"Yeah, because he's so fucking high. Hayley, this guy is no good for you. You need someone who will help you get clean, not someone who is...who's—"

"Who's what?"

"Also an addict," I say, resigned.

She releases one laugh, an "I can't believe you'd have the audacity to say that" kind of laugh. She folds her arms and looks up at the ceiling.

"How do you know he's an addict, Peter? You just met him."

I roll my eyes. "First of all, have you seen that tattoo? That's it. That's all I needed to see, and my mind went straight to 'he's a drug addict.'"

"His tattoo is not that bad!"

"It's fucking Bowser beating the shit out of Yogi, Hayley!"

"That green thing's name is Yoshi, Peter, and it's from a game called *Super Smash Brothers*!" She rolls her eyes and shakes her head, like she's a video game expert.

"I don't know, you need someone more like..."

"Like you?"

"Not like me. Maybe just like...someone smart, and thoughtful, responsible...and blond...Scottish...maybe a man bun."

She laughs again. "Not into man buns."

"I'll cut it off," I respond eagerly. Probably way too eagerly.

"No, you won't. Also, I'm looking for someone who's a little, uh...taller."

"That's not fair!" I reply.

"It doesn't have to be fair. Get your ass in the shower. You need to go to work." She walks back toward the living room.

"All right."

"HAYLEY, CAN YOU BRING ME A DRINK?" he calls out.

"Sure!"

"Wait. You're going to bring him a drink? You never bring me anything!"

"Stop it, Peter." She doesn't turn to face me and walks out of sight.

I enter the bathroom and close the door, leaning against it while taking a deep breath. I stare into the mirror. I take my hair out of the bun and let it fall on my shoulders. What would I look like with short hair? I might like it. I stand on my tippy toes.

Danny

"How are you today, Danny?"

I look up from my notes and see Mrs. Roland standing by my desk. The bell hasn't rung yet. What does she want?

"I'm good," I respond and return to my notes. Maybe if I don't look at her, she'll walk away.

"Will you be staying for extra help today?"

"Yep."

"I spoke with your dad."

I sigh. "No, you didn't."

Really? She honestly thinks a dude with a Scottish accent is my dad?

"I promise you I did. He called me."

"I don't have a dad."

"Oh... I'm sorry, Danny. I spoke with—"

"Scottish accent?"

"Yes."

"Peter. He's my brother. I know he wants me to stay after school. He told me he called you."

"He said you're struggling with the homework." I don't answer her. "We'll go over it together after school. Did you have a hard time with math last year?"

"I've never been good at math."

"We're going to change that."

Matt runs through the door. His treads are very hard and loud for someone his size. Maybe the huge backpack helps. Everyone stares at him. The bell rings just as soon as he steps into the classroom. He laughs.

"I'M ON TIME, MRS. ROLAND!"

"Matthew, please take a seat." She steps away from my desk and heads toward the front of the room. Her heels clack against the tile.

Matt walks to the desk right beside me. I push the tip of my pencil into my desk, running it back and forth until it makes an indentation.

"This seat taken?"

"No." I put my pencil down and pull my textbook out of my backpack.

"Cool." He drops his backpack onto the ground. It sounds like a boulder hits the floor. What's he have in there? Doesn't he know lockers exist?

Mrs. Roland turns around and raises one eyebrow at him. "Everyone, please look at the whiteboard for your do-now. It's called a do-now because you do it now." Her eyes don't leave Matt. "You have ten minutes."

"Why'd she look at me when she said that?"

I glare at him. "Probably because you don't have your textbook on your desk."

"Whatever. I'm getting to it."

He reaches into his backpack and pulls out his book, flipping to the correct page. Everyone is working quietly, including me.

"Mrs. Roland, this is too easy. Do I really have to do this?" Matt announces to the entire class.

Why would he say that? I told him I have a hard time with math. I feel the blood rush to my face.

"Not another word, Matthew."

My cell phone vibrates in my pocket. Mrs. Roland is sitting at her desk now, grading papers. I pull it out quietly and place it on my lap. The text is from Matt. I look over at him and he smiles weirdly. I read the text.

```
r u gona to be able to
play tonite?
Or does ur friend want
the TV again
```

                                        Not my friend.
                                          I hate her.

```
7:00 gd?
```

                                                   Yep.

Mrs. Roland looks up from her desk. I stuff my phone back into my pocket and stare at my textbook. I don't understand. That's so embarrassing. Matt thinks this is so easy...

CHAPTER FOUR

Peter

It's hard to believe we've been in the apartment for two weeks. The days are melting into one. Didn't I just do this? Oh yeah, yesterday.

Every day is the same. The monotony, it's killing me already. Waiting tables, serving drinks, waiting tables, serving drinks... Bussing tables, cleaning the bar... Cooking dinner, cleaning the apartment. I'm a professional servant. Don't think about it! Thinking about it is what caused—

NO! Don't think about it.

Maybe monotony is better than excitement.

I get out of the car and walk to the apartment. The front door is unlocked, so I go right inside. The TV is very loud, typical. I walk up the stairs, hang my keys on the hook, and...

There he is again, the clatty basturt. *Tristian.*

He's sitting on the couch with the remote in his greasy fingers. This time, he has his feet on my coffee table, wearing muddy sneakers, and... Cheetos. They're spilt all over, in between his ankles, and the bag is on the floor! I still haven't paid off that coffee table!

This guy is fucking with me. I can't let him.

My chest puffs out. "Turn the TV down!"

"What?" he asks, still staring at the TV.

"TURN THE TV DOWN!"

"I really can't hear you, Paul."

I stomp toward him, enraged, and rip the remote out of his hand. As I bend to face him, he looks confused, like I'm the rocket. I glance at the table, then pick up a handful of Cheetos with one hand. With my other hand, I knock his feet off my table—hard. I'm not playing.

"My name is Peter, not Paul." I hold the Cheetos up to his face. "And in Peter's fucking apartment, we don't put our feet on the table. We don't spill crap all over the place." I throw the Cheetos onto his lap. "That's where you like them, right?"

"Yo, calm down."

"I will not calm down until you show me some respect in my house!"

"Apartment."

"Where the fuck is Hayley?"

"She's smoking."

I stand upright, forcing myself to calm down. I brush the Cheetos dust off of my clothes.

"Outside?"

"Yeah..." He stares at me.

She's smoking outside? She actually listened to me.

"Oh. Okay."

"What's your fucking problem? Haven't gotten any in a while?"

"What did you just say to me?"

"Sex? Seems like you're not too good with ladies. I mean, she tells me you pay for everything. You clean and cook, but she still doesn't want you."

"Get out of my apartment." I plant one hand on my hip, and the other signals to the door.

"What?"

"Get the fuck out of here. Get out. Get out!"

He stands. "You telling me what to do, little man?"

"Yeah. I'm telling you to get out."

He walks toward me. I shove him with all my strength. He stumbles but doesn't fall. He just looks angry. I probably shouldn't have done that. He's much taller than me, by at least half a foot—maybe more. Perhaps I could take him strategically, but he has something in his pocket. The outline looks like a knife. I decide I won't fight him and back away.

The sliding glass door opens. We both look to my left. Hayley's coming inside from the balcony.

"Tristian was just leaving," I say.

"Because he's kicking me out."

"What. Why?" Hayley asks.

"He's disrespecting me," I answer.

"Why? Because there were Cheetos on the table? Calm down, Peter," Hayley responds.

"More than that."

"What, then?"

"I... Nothing. I just want him out of here, and I don't want him back. Ever. I need to get ready for work. Just...please. Give me some time."

I walk down the hall and into my bedroom. I can hear Hayley say something to him, but I'm not sure what. The next thing I hear is the front door shut.

She's listening to me. She's actually listening to me.

Danny

Matt and I walk from the bus stop to his apartment. He talks the whole time. I say close to nothing. If he was a real friend, he wouldn't constantly be saying how easy the math work is. He's such a show-off.

"Yeah, and my cousin has this huge house! They're basically rich. His mom works for the railroad. Do you know how much they get paid? It's a lot. Probably ten times more than what your brother makes at both of his jobs combined."

What is wrong with this kid?

"Oh yeah? Probably ten times more than what your parents make too, since we *both* live here."

Got him. I'm celebrating my comeback in my head.

"Well, I'm going to his house this weekend," he says. "They have the biggest TV I've ever seen. Maybe you can play *Rocket League* with us from home."

"Yeah. I have other things I like to do more than video games."

"Like?"

"I'm going to try out for the lacrosse team tomorrow."

"Really? Maybe I will too."

Great. I should have kept my mouth shut. One more thing he can try to beat me at.

"I didn't know you liked sports."

"I love anything competitive."

Of course.

We reach Matt's apartment. He opens the door. "Come inside. I want you to see my set-up."

"What set-up?"

"I have a PlayStation in my room, with my own TV and everything. It's epic!"

"Okay." I follow him inside.

He has a first-floor apartment, but other than that, Matt's place looks just like ours: crappy and small. I guess all the apartments here are laid out the same way. They have more furniture and stuff, though.

Matt introduces me to his mom. She asks if we want a snack, and Matt suggests pizza rolls. She smiles really big and says she'll make some, then tells us to do our homework. I don't want to do my homework with him. He'll be such an asshole about it.

"Let me show you my room." He walks down the familiar hallway, and I follow.

His room is the same size as mine. He has some cool car posters hanging on the wall and a bigger bed.

"Ta-dah!" He points to a TV on a small table with two beanbag chairs in front of it.

"Yeah. Nice."

"Isn't it awesome? I told my mom I want to get a mini-fridge in here too. She said next week, probably. Want to play something?"

"Okay, but I should text my brother and let him know I'm here."

I pull out my phone and send Peter a text. I don't want to see his response. He's overly excited about the thought of me having a friend. I never should have told him about Matt. Who needs friends when they're like him? Why am I even here?

I shove my phone back into my pocket. Maybe Matt's mom feels the same way Peter does. Maybe that's why she seemed so happy to make us a snack.

"Let's play *Call Of Duty*," he says as he sits on his beanbag chair.

"Matt?"

"Yeah?"

"Do you have any friends other than me?"

Wow... That was kinda harsh. I didn't realize till it came out of my mouth.

"Of course I do!"

"I just never see you with anyone else."

"Do you have any friends other than me? No! Because you're the new kid." He picks up the controller.

True. I pick up my controller too.

"I was just thinking," I say. "Maybe we'll get more friends if we both make the lacrosse team."

"I'm not trying out for the lacrosse team to make friends. I'm trying out to kick ass!"

I scratch my head and squint my eyes.

"Why are you making that dumb face, Danny?"

Oh my God.

"I'm not making a dumb face. I'm just scratching my head. Chill."

My phone vibrates in my pocket. Once...twice...three times. Nope. I refuse to look at it.

Peter

It's a mild day. Heard it's going to be a nice evening too. Danny's at a friend's place. Too bad I have to work. It would be nice to sit on the balcony and have a beer or two...or more.

Who am I kidding? I laugh to myself. I can squeeze one in before work.

I unlock the door and walk upstairs. No sign of anyone around. Nice.

I walk into the kitchen and open the fridge. Where's my six-pack of Corona? No one else drinks beer...or do they? Danny wouldn't touch it, would he? He did say he had a new friend... No. That's ridiculous. Maybe I should ask Danny for Matt's mum's phone number, just in case.

I close the fridge. Maybe I just left it in the trunk of the car. No, it was in here this morning. I clearly remember seeing it in the fridge before work.

What if it was Tristian? Would he take an entire six-pack of beer? If he drank it, there would be bottles all over, for sure. It doesn't look like anyone was here. The apartment is clean. It's just like how I left it this morning.

Oh well. I guess I'll just jump in the shower.

I walk into the bathroom. The toilet seat's up. I never leave it up. Danny hasn't been home since I left for work—at least, I don't think he has. Someone was in here, but it doesn't seem like they stayed too long.

A crusty looking bowl is sitting right on top of the vanity. Not a bowl you eat out of, a bowl you smoke out of. I pick it up and examine it.

Would Hayley let Tristian in here to take my beer and leave?

Hayley

"We need to talk," Peter says as soon as I walk through the door. "Where were you?"

I really don't want to have this conversation. I mean, I'm not really sure what conversation we're having, but I know I don't want to have it. Plus, my horoscope told me to "chart a course that has no limitations." This conversation seems very limiting, right?

"I took a walk," I respond. He's standing at the top of the stairs holding a dish and a rag. "What do we need to talk about?"

"Christian."

I can't roll my eyes far enough into the back of my head. He always does this. He's so tit-for-tat.

"I know you know his name. Is this because he called you Paul? He told me about that."

He smirks because I caught him.

"No. It's because I think he was in here today. After I specifically told you I don't want him here."

"Excuse me, but don't I live here too?"

"Melissa left me to be Danny's guardian. I promised her I would take care of him. I don't think Tristian is someone I want around Danny—or you, as a matter of fact."

"Shouldn't you be getting ready for work?" I walk up the stairs and meet him face to face.

"I called out."

Great. We get to spend the whole night together.

"Why?"

"I needed to talk to you about this. Danny will be home shortly. I trust you, Hayley. Not Tristian. I don't trust him. I don't want him here, especially when I'm not home."

I walk past him and sit on the couch. Peter really needs to get over this whole Tristian thing. He's really not a bad guy, and this is my apartment, too. I lean back, close my eyes, and run my fingers through my hair. If I want to get my way, I need to convince Peter that Tristian is harmless, not argue with him. I can do that.

"Oh, come on. He wouldn't hurt Danny."

"Doesn't matter if he wouldn't hurt him. He's not a positive person for a teenager to be around."

"And why's that?"

"Because I know he's on the same shit you're on." He reaches into his pockets and holds up Tristian's bowl.

"Oh, wow. Marijuana. Yikes. That's some serious shit. Don't act like you've never smoked it. I remember. It wasn't that long ago."

"I don't want him or anyone smoking marijuana in my apartment when *we* have a teenager!"

Uh. No. Wrong. Wrong. So, so wrong.

"We have a teenager? I don't think so. You have a teenager, Daddy of the Year. I've told you this multiple times. I'm not a parent to Danny. I am not his mommy."

"Doesn't matter if you're his 'mummy' or not. I'm telling you not to smoke marijuana in this apartment. Also, I know the both of you are doing way more than marijuana."

"And? You have something to say about me?"

"I just want you to know, if it comes down to it—between you or Danny—I'd choose Danny every single time. Don't press your luck."

"What the fuck is that supposed to mean?"

"You're a smart girl. You know what that means. I'll do what I have to do to make sure that Danny is safe. If that means evicting you from this apartment, don't think I would hesitate to do it. Okay?'

"You can't evict me!"

"I didn't say I was going to. I said if this continues, I have the power to and I will. It's a fair warning."

"Because I've had my boyfriend here a couple of times, you would kick me out on the street?"

"You still don't get it. It's absolutely incredible." He walks back into the kitchen.

"Get what?" I jump up from the couch and follow him. "Get that you're trying to sabotage my relationship because you want me for yourself? Because you're a manipulative, controlling little man?"

He stops what he's doing and turns toward me. "So that's what he says to you about me?"

"What? No..."

"Really? Because he called me a 'little man' not too long ago, and I don't like it. Think what you want, though. I won't stand here and be insulted. Keep pressing your luck." He begins wiping down the countertops.

"Fuck you!"

He sticks his middle finger up. I storm out of the kitchen. I don't want to look at his ugly-ass face anymore. I grab my phone and head to my bedroom. I slam the door behind me so he knows how mad I am. I'm shaking from anger. He can't treat me like this! He can't threaten me!

I flop down onto my bed, belly first, and hold my phone out in front of my face. I have to tell Tristian what just happened.

> Im freakin the fuck
> out. U were right.

Y?

Peter said he'd kick
me out if u ever come
back her again.

Here***

Im so mad. He just
wants me for himself.

I no what u meant.
That motherfucker!

Can I stay with u if
tht happened?

I been sleeping on
ryans floor.

Can I sleep there 2?

It won't happen b/c
ass face won't even
know I'm there anyway.
I only come when he's
at work.

He'll no...

trust me.

I cant get anything
past him. He new u
were here 2day.

That's what started
all of this.

What? How?

u left ur bowl

Shit
I was wondering where
that was

I grab my headphones off the end table, plug them into my
phone, and lay back. I close my eyes. I need to get out of here,
but on my own terms.

Tristian

"Surprise," I say when Ryan opens the door. I hold up the six-pack of Corona with my right hand and wave my left hand beneath it.

"Hey."

"Told you I'd get you back."

"Okay, but why would you buy Corona? You know I drink Budweiser. Is that Peter's?"

I brought this guy beer, and he's not thanking me? Everyone is so ungrateful these days. Sad.

"Looking a gift whore in the mouth?"

He laughs. "Dude, that's not the saying."

"Close enough. Are you going to let me in now?"

"All right. Come in, gift whore."

He walks into the living room, and I follow. I take my jacket off and drop it onto the floor. I put the six-pack on the table and slide a beer out.

"You got a bottle opener?" I ask. "Fucking foreign beers, right? This is America!"

Ryan takes the beer from my hand and opens it with his key chain. He hands it back to me. It's still cold. That's what the winter is good for. Otherwise, winter is such bullshit.

"Thanks." I take a sip. "Lime?"

"I don't have lime, Tristian."

He's in a fucked-up mood today. I wonder who pissed in his Cheerios.

"It's cool, it's fine."

"Do you have my stuff, man? Yes or no."

"No."

"Fuck! You're the only dealer I know that smokes all of their own product."

"I didn't smoke your weed."

"Then where is it? You said you'd have it today."

"Hayley smoked your weed, but I brought you beer."

"You're such a turd."

"Hey, I thought we were friends? Give me a fucking break."

I lean against the wall and fold my arms.

"You're lucky we're friends. I never should have paid you before I got my stuff."

"Just chill, I'll get it. I'll have it to you next week."

"I hope you still have the money."

"I do, I do."

A piece of my hair falls in front of my eyes. I blow upward to move it out of the way. Ryan grabs a beer and cracks it open. I continue blowing, but the hair isn't going in the right direction. Ryan watches me. I move it out of the way with my fingers. Ryan picks up my jacket and "tsk tsks," then walks over to the couch. He drapes my jacket over the back of it and takes a seat.

Ryan's pissed. That weed would make him feel better. I'll get the money for it. There's got to be some cash hidden around that apartment somewhere. He's a bartender. I walk over to the corner of the living room where my pillow and blanket are, and I sit. I try to relax, but the Corona in my hand reminds me of that fucker.

"You friends with him?" I ask.

"With who?" Ryan side-eyes me.

"Peter. You know what he drinks?"

"I haven't seen him in over a year."

"So, you were friends with him? He's such a piece of shit."

"I only knew him because of Hayley. We hung out a couple of times. That's it. So, you did steal this beer from him?"

"No! No, I didn't! I like Corona too, okay?"

"Whatever, man. You know, Jillian is getting real fed up with your shit. We said you could stay the night, not the month."

It's not like they gave me a key or anything. They just let me in here to sleep. I don't bother them. They don't even let me sleep on the fucking couch! It was her grandmother's or some shit. Blah, blah, blah, give me a break. Fuck it. I'll be out of here soon with my own key. A key to my own place!

"I'll be out of your hair in no time, man. Just need to get back on my feet."

"Do you have a plan?"

"Uh...Yes. Hayley is working on getting unemployment. That'll be extra cash. We're going to apply for Section 8 housing too. We have it all under control."

Ryan laughs. I don't understand why. He doesn't think I can handle my shit? Fuck him, man. I'm done playing nice.

"Fuck you," I say.

Ryan sips his Corona. He looks so entertained by my struggle. One day I'll be the one laughing.

"Well, anyway." He picks up the remote and puts last week's football game on. I lean forward.

"Our team really fucked up this season," I say.

"Because they repeatedly tried to throw the ball all the way down the field and kept getting intercepted."

"Well, if someone would fucking catch it... They just suck. I'm rooting for a different team from now on."

"You would." He laughs.

"What?"

"Where's your loyalty, dude?"

"It's football. Fuck off."

He's being a real dick today. I don't want to talk to him, not even about football.

I close my eyes and clench my hands. It probably looks like I'm making a fist, but really I'm imagining Hayley, and me, and the key to our very own apartment in my grasp.

CHAPTER FIVE

Hayley

I'm sitting in the living room. It's been a whole day, and I still haven't said much to Peter, but he's still cooking all of my meals, so I don't care.

The door opens. Danny runs up the stairs.

"Peter! Peter!"

"What's up, bud?" Peter asks as he enters the living room from the kitchen.

"I made the lacrosse team!"

"What? That's brilliant! I'm so proud of you!"

"I need to get a bunch of gear! Oh! I have something in my backpack!" He puts his bag on the ground, pulls out a folder, and hands Peter a paper from it.

"We'll go to the store this weekend, okay?" Peter says as he examines the sheet.

"Matt made the cut too. He's going to have a party at his apartment Saturday night for a few of us on the team!"

"Wow. That sounds like a lot of fun. We'll go shopping in the morning, then."

"I already looked online and found a bunch of gear I like. Let me show you." Danny pulls his phone out of his pocket. Peter's face drops just a little as he stares at the screen.

"What, it's too expensive for you?" I ask. I'm being a total bitch, but he deserves it. He's such a little weasel fuck.

Peter's mouth props open, his eyes focusing on me.

"Is it, Peter?" Danny looks very sad, all of a sudden. "Matt's getting the best gear. His mom—"

"Nope. It's not too expensive. I'll make it happen. I have room on my credit card." Peter nods at Danny, then confidently sets the paper on the dining room table.

"You're the best!" Danny yells and hugs him.

"Yeah. He's wonderful," I add.

"You know what, Hayley? Just remember what I said yesterday," Peter says.

"What did you say?" Danny asks.

Peter looks back over at him. "I said that I'll always be here for you. *Always*. No matter what."

Danny smiles.

"Okay. I'm going to my room. Matt and I are going to plan the party for Saturday. We're gonna FaceTime."

"Just let me know what you want to bring to the party. Dinner will be ready soon."

"All right."

Danny runs into his room. Peter looks at me and sighs, then walks back into the kitchen.

Peter

Ding. I hear the bell, but I'm on the phone.

"What side did you want with that?" My accent is stronger than usual. Maybe when she comes to pick up her food, she'll say, *Who was that dreamy man on the phone with the Scottish accent? Here's a great big tip for him!* It sounds stupid, but sometimes it happens!

"What sides do you have?" the woman on the phone asks.

Not the most enthusiastic response...

"Fries, onion rings, mashed potatoes, vegetable of the day, salad," I say.

Ding. Ding. He rings the bell two more times.

I prop the phone on my shoulder and turn to look at the cook, Ralph, through the kitchen window. I throw my hands up at him and signal to the phone.

"What's the vegetable of the day?"

"Green beans."

"I'll just take fries."

"Anything else?"

"This food is sitting here and getting cold, you stupid mick," Ralph yells.

Did this motherfucker really just say that to me?

"Your total is twenty-one dollars and forty-five cents. It'll be about twenty-five minutes."

I hang up without saying goodbye to the customer and head to the kitchen window. He's already back at the grill flipping burgers. I pound on the bell furiously. He looks over at me. I keep pounding. He walks to the window.

"What the fuck do you think you're doing?" he asks.

"How does it feel? To be working while someone is ringing the bell over and over, demanding your attention? It's frustrating, huh?" I ask, hiding my accent again. I try to turn it on and off as best as I can at work, but people can still hear it a little. It's impossible to get rid of it completely.

"I'm the one that rings the bell, not you," he says as I pick up the two plates.

I put the plates back down and ring the bell with emphasis. "Don't." I ring it again. "Ever." I ring it a third time. "Call me." One more ring. "A mick."

"Go back to your own country. Then you won't have to worry about that." He returns to the grill.

Fat, hairy basturt.

I pick up the plates and head to my table. All the shit I get for being a foreigner at this job, and I'm white! Imagine if I was Black or brown?

I hope Danny doesn't have a hard time later on in life. I don't know if he's ever experienced racism before. He's never said anything to me about it, and I don't really want to have that conversation unless he brings it up. I don't want to be the one to point out to him that he's different. I'm sure he knows, but, hell! Just the thought of it makes me sick to my stomach. I fucking hate it.

I approach the table with the two plates.

"California wrap with a side salad, and one cheeseburger medium-well." I put the plates down.

"Can we get some ketchup?"

"I'll bring it right out. Anything else?"

The two women at the table look at each other and shake their heads.

"I'll be back in a moment."

I get the ketchup out of the fridge, but I'm distracted. My boss is talking to fat boy by the grill. He looks in my direction and signals for me to come over with one creeping finger. Great.

"Yes?" I ask as I approach the two.

"Are you bothering Ralph as he's trying to cook?"

"Yeah, after he called me a mick."

"I called you that because the food for twenty-one was getting cold," he retorts, as if he's so rational. Yeah, right.

"I was on the phone taking an order, and you knew it."

"Don't touch his bell again, okay, Peter?"

"I won't touch it." I turn around and throw my hands in the air.

I grab tightly to the ketchup bottle, walk back to the fridge, and look up. There, I find the little porcelain ramekins we're supposed to use for serving condiments. I get on my very tippy toes and reach, but I'm a little too short. To get the step stool, I have to walk past Ralph. I do just that, set it beside the fridge, and climb. Ralph snickers and goes back to cooking.

I hate my life.

Hayley

Who knew that you needed to be employed before you can get unemployment benefits? It kind of defeats the whole purpose, am I right? I am definitely right. What am I going to do?

I turn the knob and find our apartment door's unlocked. Tristian must be inside. I enter quietly and tiptoe up the stairs. Maybe I can surprise him. Scare the shit out of him. I giggle quietly at the thought. He's not in the living room. I hear some noise coming from down the hallway, from Peter's room. Maybe it's not Tristian. Maybe Peter's home early?

His bedroom door is open. I stand outside, unable to believe what I'm seeing. It's Tristian. He's taken everything out of Peter's closet. Why?

"ARE YOU CRAZY?" I yell.

He jumps and holds his chest. "Fuck, Hals, you scared me!"

"What are you doing?"

"I was looking for cash."

"So, you're stealing from us?"

"No. Stealing from *him.*"

"You do realize he uses that money to pay our bills, right?"

"He's hiding way more than you think!"

He lifts a round box off of Peter's bed and opens it up. It has about eight rolls of cash.

"Each of these rolls is one-hundred dollars! I counted!"

"I can't believe you, Tristian."

"You can't believe me? Meanwhile, this guy is hiding money from you!"

"Our rent is over two thousand dollars!"

"Oh...What? That's so much money for this dump!" He puts the box back down on Peter's bed.

"You need to put everything back in his closet the exact way you found it. He's going to be so pissed. Fuck!"

"I will, I will."

Tristian picks some of Peter's shirts up off the floor. As he does, two rolls of cash fall out of the pockets of his jeans.

"Are you serious?"

"What?"

I pick up the rolls and hold them in front of his face.

"Oh, so you *were* taking money from us?" I stuff the rolls in my pocket.

"I was borrowing money."

"You had no plan to pay Peter back, Tristian. Stop lying! We wouldn't be able to pay our bills if you kept this up."

"I was only going to do it once. I owe Ryan product. Product that *you* smoked. So technically, you owe him!"

"You didn't tell me anything that I smoked was supposed to go to Ryan."

"Well, it was."

"That is not my problem, Tristian!"

I pick the rest of Peter's clothes up off of the floor and place them on his bed. Tristian's watching me, like he's judging me. I should be judging him!

"Can you just leave?" I ask.

I go to Peter's closet and pull some hangers off the rod.

"What?"

"I asked if you'd leave. I have so much to put away before Peter gets home."

"So, you're mad at me?"

I laugh sarcastically. "Yes. I am. I trusted you with a key. I was out trying to get an unemployment check for us, and you're here stealing. I told you Peter said he would kick me out. Then where would I go? You said I can't stay with you... I don't know. I have to think!"

I put one of Peter's shirts on a hanger and brush it off. I walk over to the closet and hang it back up on the rod.

"Oh, come on, Hals. I thought you said what's mine is yours."

"That does not include what is Peter's. FYI, Peter and me are two different people! I really don't see where the confusion is coming from."

"I don't know. You sure are acting like him."

I knew he was judging me. I knew it!

"Can you please leave? Really? Give me your key."

"Seriously?"

"Yes, seriously, Tristian. Give it to me!"

"Fine." He reluctantly pulls out his wallet and hands me the key. "Good luck sobering up. I'm not giving you shit."

"I'm quitting, anyway."

"HA!"

"Tristian, LEAVE!"

He gives me one last dirty look before walking out of Peter's room and slamming the door.

Peter

When I get to the apartment, Hayley's sitting on the ground outside with her back against the wall. She's holding a can of cheap alcohol. I get out of the car and stare at her, perplexed.

"What are you doing?"

"Don't go into your room," she responds in a monotone voice. She doesn't look at me.

"Why?"

"Peter, just don't. Okay?" She takes a sip of her drink.

"What are you, fifteen years old? Even at fifteen I wasn't drinking that crap."

"It's cheap."

I sit on the ground beside her. "Hayley, trust me. I understand not wanting to talk about things, but...can I know why I shouldn't go into my room?"

"Tristian tore it apart."

She looks stressed. I won't stress her further. At least she knows it was wrong.

"Oh. Okay."

"That's it?" she asks.

"What do you mean?"

"That's all you're going to say?"

"You already look upset about it, so why would I make you more upset?"

She smiles just a little and looks away, like she won't admit that I made her smile. How did we get to this point? We used to make each other smile all the time. It wasn't a big deal or a problem. It was just natural.

"Thank you," she finally responds.

I sigh. "Can I ask why he tore my room apart?"

"You can't."

"Got it. Well, good enough." I stand back up. I don't know if there's dirt on my ass, so I brush it off just in case.

"I tried to clean it as best as I could."

I pause. "You what?"

"I tried to clean up your room, but it doesn't look as neat as the way you normally keep it."

"Hayley..." I turn toward her. "Thank you for doing that."

"You're welcome."

"Stand up."

"I don't want to."

"Let's go inside. I'll make you dinner."

"You still want to make me dinner?"

"I do. I want to make you the best dinner."

I offer her my hand. She grabs it.

"One, two, three."

I pull her up. She stares at my face for a little while. I stare back at hers.

"I'm just surprised you're not mad," she finally says.

"I'm not mad. I'm really not mad at all. I'm the opposite of mad."

We walk inside together.

CHAPTER SIX

Danny

"Hey, Danny. How was extra help?" Peter asks as soon as I walk into the apartment. Hayley is plopped on the couch.

"Boring, like Scotland." I drop my backpack on the floor.

"Put that in your room and drop the attitude."

I roll my eyes. Oh, yeah. How could I forget that backpacks can't go on the floor?

"I'm just saying, it was so boring that I left, and I don't plan on going back ever."

"Very funny, but you are going back."

I pick up my backpack and roll my eyes again, but harder.

"I still don't get the math. Mrs. Roland is a really bad teacher. Plus, she thought you were my dad."

Hayley laughs.

"Hayley, are you any good at math?" Peter asks.

She laughs again, louder. What would make Peter think Hayley is good at math? She's bad at everything. Math is a given.

"I'm assuming that's a no," Peter responds.

"I'm never going to be good at math, Peter. Can we just drop it? Matt keeps saying how easy the work is, and that just makes me really pissed off."

I sit down on a dining chair and hold my backpack on my lap. Peter sits in the chair next to me.

"Wait. Your friend Matt thinks it's easy?"

"Yes."

"So why don't you see if he can explain it to you?"

"Oh my God." I moan and put my head down on the table.

"What?"

I lift my head up and squeeze my backpack as tightly as I can. "That's embarrassing."

"Why is that embarrassing? Isn't he your friend?"

"Yeah, my friend, not a tutor."

"I would ask him."

"You didn't go to school."

"What makes you think that?"

Peter's weird, and he doesn't even realize it. That's why I think he never went to school. If you're weird at school, you realize it because people pick on you. Not Peter. He wears weird clothes, he has weird hair, and when he first came to Melissa's, he was scared of the TV. What kind of kid is scared of a TV?

"I don't know. I just feel like you didn't go to school."

"Okay... Well, anyway, just because I didn't go to school doesn't mean I didn't have friends."

I stop.

"We're talking about in Scotland?" I ask loudly so that Hayley can also hear. She sits forward on the couch and gives me a half-smile. I smile back. I know she wants to hear this, too.

"Yes, but I had friends here too, didn't I?"

"Who were your friends in Scotland? Why don't you talk to them anymore?"

"I don't want to talk to them."

"Why not?"

"I don't want to live in the past."

"This is monumental!" Hayley shouts sarcastically.

"What is?" Peter turns to her.

"You told us something about Scotland!"

"I'm sorry that there's not much to say about it."

"When did your mom die?" I ask.

"What are you talking about?" He turns back to me.

"Your mom. When did she die? You said she died, right?"

"Oh... She died right before I came here."

"What did she die from?"

"Pneumonia."

"And your dad?"

"Pneumonia."

"Both of them?" Hayley asks.

"Yes."

"At the same time?" I ask.

"Nope. My da first, then my mum almost a year later." Peter appears nervous, like he's being interrogated on one of those detective shows. "Okay, story time is over."

"It was just getting good, though," I say.

Peter laughs and stands. "Okay. Haggis for dinner, it is."

"Haggis?"

"Yup. You two want to experience Scotland so badly. I can help you do that."

He walks into the kitchen. I pull my phone out of my pocket and look up "haggis" on Google. What the hell? There's no way he's making that for dinner. He's just being an ass!

"That's nasty!" I call out.

"I know!" he answers.

Hayley

Danny is sleeping, and Peter's in the kitchen making tea. It's official, I've seen every episode of *Here Comes Honey Boo Boo*. I pick up the remote. I'm sad the show was canceled, really. I wonder how they're doing. Probably better than I am.

I turn the TV over to cable and put on the news. Another arrest in Patchogue, and a whale washed up in Mastic Beach. Any good news? I turn the volume all the way down and listen to the sound of the teakettle whistling on the stove. Peter should be taking it off the heat any second...

But the teakettle doesn't stop whistling. The whistling just gets louder and louder until the kettle is screaming. What the fuck? I get up off the couch and walk over to the kitchen, but I freeze in the doorway. What the fuck am I seeing right now?

Peter's standing by the countertop. His left hand is flat on the cutting board. He's holding a knife right above his own fingers. The tip of the blade is digging into the wooden board, just above his pointer and thumb.

"WHAT ARE YOU DOING?" I yell.

He drops the knife and jumps backwards as if he had just woken up.

"What? What?"

"The teakettle. It's been going off for a long time, and... Oh my God, were you going to cut your own fingers off?" I put my hands up to my head and tug the roots of my hair. "What's wrong with you?"

"No! Sorry, I... I phased out. I was going to get the kettle, and I stopped. I don't know what happened."

"Oh, okay. Great. So, you're walking around with a huge knife, and you don't even know what the fuck you're doing? What the fuck!"

I walk over and pick the knife up off the floor. I put it back in the drawer.

"Hayley, I..."

I grab the teakettle off the stove to stop the loud whistling.

"Are you having tea or not?"

"I am," he responds quietly. He backs up into the opposite wall and stares at the cutting board. He lifts his hands to his ears and covers them tightly.

"What the fuck is wrong with you?"

"I don't know. Thank you." He slowly takes his hands off of his ears. He grabs both sides of the long blue robe he's wearing over his pajamas and pulls them tightly around his chest.

"What the fuck are you thanking me for?"

I hoist myself onto the countertop. It's the only way I can reach the top cabinets. I grab a mug, close the cabinet, and jump back down. He doesn't say anything about my feet being on the counter. Something is really off. I hand him the mug.

"I think I need to lie down." He lets go of his robe and grips the mug. He takes a tea packet from the drawer and throws it into the cup. When he picks up the kettle to pour, his hands are shaking. He's spilling hot water everywhere.

"What's happening?" Danny appears in the doorway, rubbing his right eye.

Peter's eyes dart directly toward me. They are big and wide. They're telling me to shut the fuck up.

"Nothing. I just...spilled something," Peter says. He grabs a spoon out of a drawer.

"Hayley was screaming because you spilled something?"

Peter looks at me again... Fine, but only because I have no idea how to explain what the fuck just happened.

"Yes. He spilled boiling hot water all over. See?" I signal to the counter and the floor.

Danny's eyes dart back and forth between Peter and me. Peter puts his elbow on the counter and rests his head on his hand. He inhales and exhales.

"You want the TV, Danny?" I blurt out to break the silence.

"Now I definitely know something's up. You're asking me if I want the TV?"

"I'm done with it. I finished every season of *Honey Boo Boo,* and...Peter's going to bed." I look at Peter in a demanding type of way. Feels good to be in charge for once.

"You bet I am." He walks past Danny and out of the kitchen, mug in hand.

"Is Peter okay?" Danny whispers.

"Yeah. He's...stressed out, but he's fine." I take a seat at the small table in the kitchen and put my head down.

"Yeah, well, I don't want the TV. I'm going back to bed." I hear him walk out of the kitchen.

"Good riddance." I don't lift my head up.

After a little while, I rest my chin on my forearm and push my hair out of my face. It's quiet now.

I look over at the kettle, then at the cutting board. I'm not high, am I? No, I'm not.

Peter

My eyes are open. I cover them with my hand and close them tightly. They spring open again. I rip my palm from my face.

Are you gone yet?

No.

Stop watching me. Please, leave.

I need to go to sleep. Just go to sleep. Just go to sleep. Just go to sleep...

Every home I've ever lived in has been haunted. Or is it just me who is haunted?

Danny

I was going to go back to sleep. I really, really was, but I just can't. I'm awake now!

I'm sitting on my bed, looking at stupid Snapchat filters on my phone. There's this one that makes you look like a dog, and when you open your mouth, a big dog tongue comes out. It's so freaking stupid, but all the girls use it. It's kinda funny, I guess. Matt uses it a lot, too. I stare at myself on my phone, with the floppy dog ears, and it gets me thinking. What am I? I mean, I know I'm a human and not a Snapchat dog, duh...but Peter is Scottish, so what am I?

I take the filter off and look at my face closely. I have white people hair, I think. It's a little curly, but not tight curls. Just big, thick curls. My hair isn't like Peter or Hayley's hair, though. Mine stays in place and doesn't move around as much in the wind or when I walk. I have dark skin—way darker than Peter's—and I have a few freckles across my nose.

I have brown eyes, but sometimes they're kind of blue. What does that mean? It's pretty cool. I like my eyes. They are my favorite part of me because I've never seen anyone else with eyes just like mine.

It's not fair. All kids know what they are, but I don't. All kids know if they're Black, or Spanish, or Italian, or Scottish. Well, not a lot of kids are Scottish, I don't think...but if they were, they'd know it! I can't think of one other person who doesn't know what—

I put down my phone and stare at the wall in front of me. Maybe there is another person.

I open my door a crack and walk down the hallway. Hayley's on the couch now, looking at her phone. She's slumped all the way back and seems pretty chill. I guess she doesn't care about the spilled water anymore.

She looks up. "I thought you were going back to bed?"

"I was, but then I started thinking about something."

"Okay..." She looks kinda nervous. I get it, we don't really talk a lot, and when we do, it's not really nice stuff.

"What are you?" I ask her and quickly look down at my feet.

"What do you mean, what am I?" She drops her phone onto the cushion next to her.

"Like, Peter is Scottish, so...what about you?"

Her eyes open wider. She sits up straight and grabs her hands together. Her face is rosy pink now. She looks embarrassed, like she just farted or something.

"Uh... My mom was German. So, I guess I'm part German."

I breathe out loudly and feel my shoulders relax. "So you know what you are?"

"Sort of, I guess."

"Oh."

I should have known I have nothing in common with Hayley. Not even dumb, weird stuff like not knowing what you are. Absolutely nothing!

I turn around and start walking back to my bedroom. I close my door and lock it.

What if I never know what I am?

CHAPTER SEVEN

Hayley

I'm lying on my bed. It's been almost a whole day since I've spoken to Tristian. We've gone through rough patches like this before, but each new patch is rougher than the last. It's especially rough knowing that when I run out of kickers, I don't know where to get more.

Peter looks into my bedroom from the hall. Ugh. Why does he do this?

"You can come in, you know," I say, aggravated, still staring up at the ceiling.

"I like to make sure I have permission first."

I roll my eyes. "Well, you just standing in the doorway and staring at me is creepy. You might 'phase out' again like last night."

"I'm not going to phase out again. How about next time I'll ask, 'Permission to enter you room?'"

"If you say that, I'll say 'Access denied.'" I laugh.

"So, what should I say, then?"

"Peter, just walk in! You're staring at me, anyway."

"Okay, okay!"

He creeps in slowly with his hands in the pocket of his old beige cardigan. I think that piece is something he brought from Scotland. I sort of like it on him, actually.

"What do you want? What's going on? You're acting weirder than normal."

He sits down on my bed. "Your birthday is coming up."

"I know." I sit up. "Good time to break up with your boyfriend, right? Your twenty-first birthday is supposed to be the best one, too."

"Perfect timing, actually." He's serious.

I laugh. "You're such an asshole."

"Oh, am I?" He reaches eagerly into his pocket and pulls out his wallet. He grabs a folded-up sheet of paper and hands it to me.

"What is this?"

"I don't know. I just thought maybe I would show you Long Island has much better alcohol to offer than that crap you get at convenience stores."

I unfold the paper. It's a voucher for a full day wine tour out east.

"Peter, I don't know what to say. I mean—"

Hmm… I know this is another attempt to convince me to be his girlfriend, but it does sound like a good time. I've never done anything like this before. Tristian would never do anything like this, even if he could afford it. I look back down at the paper in my hand. Maybe it would be like the old times. The good times Peter and I used to have together, before Danny.

"It will be a lot of fun. A coach bus will take us to five different wineries. Please join me, Hayley. I want to show you how you should be treated. How you deserve to be—"

"When is it?"

"Tomorrow. We have reservations to get dinner afterward."

"What about Danny?"

"He's going to Matt's for that lacrosse party, remember?"

Why not let someone take me out for once? Somewhere other than fast food.

"Okay. Thank you."

"So...it's a yes?"

"It's a yes." I hand him back the folded-up paper.

He smiles. I look into his eyes. They're beautiful and kind. Wait... Did I just think that? About Peter? Crap! This is exactly what he wants.

"Get out of my room now." I flop back down on the bed.

"Sure thing." He sticks the paper back into his wallet.

Ugh! I wish he would stop with that goofy-ass smile!

Peter

I have to stop spending money. I pick up the package left in front of our apartment and rip up the envelope. A small, square box is inside. I flip it open. It's her birthstone. I move the box back and forth, watching the light reflect off of the gem in the center of the necklace. Jesus, Mary, and St. Joseph... Thank them all that it came today.

I close the box and stuff it into my front right pocket. I hope she likes it. I never see her wear any jewelry, but it might just be because she doesn't have any... Not that she needs it. She's beautiful without makeup or jewelry, anyway.

I walk into my room to change. My outfit's laid out on the bed. I ironed my shirt and trousers last night. Maybe I shouldn't have. Tristian's clothes are never ironed, and she really likes him. Maybe she's into messy guys. The kind of guys who are daring, adventurous, and don't think things through. I used to be more like that... Anyway, maybe I should crunch my clothes back up. Also, maybe I shouldn't have showered. She seems to like those mink fellows.

I face the standing mirror. Is my bun too neat? Maybe I should mess that up, too? Or I could cut it off. She said she doesn't like man buns. I turn to my side table and open the top drawer, grabbing a pair of scissors. I face the mirror again, rip my hair out of the bun, and hold the scissors up.

"Are you cutting your hair?"

I turn quickly. It's Danny. What's he still doing here? I put the scissors down to my side.

"No. Yes. Maybe. I don't know. Aren't you supposed to be at Matt's?"

"Eh. Later. I'm going to be fashionably late."

"You know Hayley and I are leaving in about an hour?"

"Yup. I get the apartment all to myself."

"Do not make a mess. Do you hear me? And if you turn the oven on, don't forget to shut it off."

"Oh my God," he moans. "When have I ever left the oven on?"

"I'm just making sure. Also, text me when you head to Matt's, and text me when you leave Matt's. Let me know where you are at all times. Got it? And if anyone knocks on the door, do not answer it."

"I'm thirteen years old, Peter."

"I know how old you are."

"Why are you cutting your hair?"

"It, uh... It gets in my face sometimes, and it's annoying. Anyway, I'm not cutting it." I put the scissor on my bed. "Is there something you wanted? What's up?"

"I'm supposed to be bringing Buffalo chicken dip to Matt's party."

Are you fucking serious?

"What? Didn't this party start—" I look at my watch. "Fifteen minutes ago? You're telling me now that you are supposed to be bringing a very specific dip? Why didn't you tell me this yesterday? Or this morning when we went shopping? Where the hell am I supposed to find Buffalo chicken dip right now? I'm leaving in an hour."

"You're not supposed to find it somewhere. You're supposed to make it."

I stare at him blankly. "You do realize it takes more than an hour to make, and I have none of the ingredients."

"Oh."

"I'm going to Applebee's, and you're getting spinach and artichoke dip."

"What? No! I said I was bringing Buffalo chicken dip."

"That's not an option at this point, Danny. If you would have told me this sooner, you would have had Buffalo chicken dip."

"You'd rather go out with Hayley than make sure I have what I need!"

I freeze. Is that what this is about?

"Whoa. You do not *need* Buffalo chicken dip."

"I'm going to look so stupid!"

"I wish I had these problems when I was your age. Jesus, Mary, and St. Joseph..."

I tie my hair back and pick up my phone. I search online for the number of the Farmingville Applebee's and dial. A man answers. He tells me they don't have Buffalo chicken dip, which I already knew. I ask for three orders of spinach and artichoke dip instead.

"Peter! Noooooo."

I put my pointer finger up to my mouth to shush him.

"Can I have three orders of boneless Buffalo wings too?"

I cover the part of my phone that I speak into with my hand. "Just rip up the chicken and put it into the spinach and artichoke dip, okay?" I whisper.

"That's so nasty!"

"Then eat them separately! You're driving me crazy right now!"

I uncover the phone. "Twenty minutes? Okay, thank you. Bye." I hang up. "Now I have to speed to Applebee's."

I walk past him and exit my bedroom. He's following me and complaining. I try to tune most of it out. I grab my keys from the wall in the living room.

"And they only give you crappy tortilla chips with it. I told the team I was bringing bread, not crappy tortilla chips. Not to mention, *unhealthy*. We are *athletes*! I thought you wanted me to eat less fried food. Do you know those chips are deep fried? Also, no one likes blue cheese dressing. Everyone only likes ranch. Did you ask for ranch with the wings? I didn't hear you say ranch—"

"DANIEL MARCELLO, YOU ARE GETTING APPLEBEE'S, AND THAT IS FINAL!"

He's quiet for a few seconds.

"God. You don't have to yell."

"Where are you going?" I hear Hayley ask.

"I have to run to Applebee's to pick up some appetizers for Danny's party. It will just—"

I turn around and find she's standing in the living room with us. She's wearing a red dress. I've never seen her wear a dress before. Is she wearing a dress for me?

Jesus, Mary, and Joseph...she's wearing a dress for our date together. She's even got lipstick on! Maybe this is a turning point for her—for us! I can't help but smile. The dress accentuates her figure perfectly, and God, does she have a figure. It looks as if the dress was made for her. I don't think anyone else could wear that dress and look the same way. It's revealing up top, but not too revealing. It leaves enough to the imagination. The bottom touches just the middle of her thighs.

"It, uh... I just... Danny..." I don't formulate a full sentence. Fuck. I sound like a love-drunk moron.

"What?" she asks.

"I'll be right back." I put my shoes on as quickly as possible.

"Why are you all dressed up for?" Danny asks her.

"Because we're going out."

"You never dress up," he says.

"Well, I had this dress, and I never get to wear it—like, ever—so, I decided..."

I look toward Danny. He rolls his eyes and stomps to his room. I hear his door slam.

"Why is he angry?" Hayley asks.

I'm staring at her...and not at her face. Oh my God, that's so rude! Women don't like when you stare at their chest. Also, it's possible that I might be drooling. I mean, my mouth is gaping wide open. I close it.

"Because he wanted Buffalo chicken dip, but he's getting spinach and artichoke dip and ripped up boneless wings."

"Ah, okay."

"Yeah, anyway... Happy birthday. Uh...I'll be right back."

"Thank you."

I take one last look at her and her breasts... STOP IT! I run down the stairs, trip, and almost fall. She probably thinks I'm a real, genuine ass.

As I start the car, I pray the food is ready when I get there.

Danny

I ring Matt's doorbell. I feel my eyebrows pointing inward. I can't make them stop pointing inward. I thought she didn't like him? Why was she wearing that dress? I hope she still doesn't like him. I hope she breaks his heart. I don't want Peter to be sad and stuff, but it's for his own good.

Matt opens the door. I hold up the two big bags of Applebee's.

"I know I said I was bringing Buffalo chicken dip, but I had this plan to get my brother to miss this date he was going on with that bitch, and—"

"APPLEBEE'S? YES!" Matt snatches the bag and walks into the house. I pull my phone out of my pocket and text Peter.

> Everyone is so pissed
> at me 4 bringing
>
>
> now I'm goin to have
> 0 friends on the team
>
> thanks a lot!!!!!!

I put my phone back into my pocket and walk into Matt's apartment. There are three other guys here from the team. They're all sitting in the living room eating snacks. There's potato chips, onion dip, and chocolate chip cookies. These snacks are crappier than what I brought.

"DANNY BROUGHT APPLEBEE'S, GUYS!" Matt yells as he sets the bag on the table.

"SWEET!" Preston says. "What did you bring from Applebee's?"

"Uh...I think it's spinach and artichoke dip and boneless wings."

"Dude, I can eat like twenty of those boneless wings. I love them."

"Well, my brother got three of everything, so..."

"Nice!" Matt says as he starts unpacking the bag.

"Have any of you guys ever played lacrosse before?" Reese asks.

"No," I say, "but I watched a lot of YouTube videos on my phone. We went to the store this morning, and I bought all of the equipment that was on the list. I got these really nice cleats. I have a picture. Hold on."

I pull my phone out. There's a message from Peter. It's a GIF of a crying baby. Asshole, asshole, asshole!

Oh yea?

well that's prob bout
2 be u when Hayley
tells u for the 10000
time she doesn't like
you!!!

OK. Bye.

Have fun at your
party. Text me when
you leave. I should be
home no later than
8:30.

Love you.

"Are you showing us that picture or...?" Reese asks.

"Yeah. Sorry. My brother was texting me."

"It's all good."

I pull up the picture of my new cleats and hand the phone to the guys. I sit in a chair across from them.

There's no way I'm going to enjoy this party thinking about Peter and Hayley being on a date. I hope their day is just as miserable as mine's going to be.

Hayley

The room we're in has glass walls with a beautiful view of the vineyard. A band is playing. Peter's coming from the bar area with a bottle in hand. He's dressed so nicely today. Not that he doesn't dress nicely every day, but he's dressed *extra* nicely today. I wonder what Tristian would look like if he ever wore a button-down shirt and khakis. That would be the day.

"They said this is a favorite here. You have good taste," he says as he approaches the table, and pops open the bottle. He's about to pour me a glass, but instead pulls his phone out of his pocket.

"Danny?" I ask.

"Yeah." He types something quickly, puts his phone away, then makes the pour.

"Can't you just ignore him for now? What's he saying?"

"Oh, nothing. Just that I ruined his life with Applebee's, he has no friends. Thirteen-year-old drama. I'm sorry, I won't look at my phone again."

He pours himself a glass and sits down across from me.

"I don't know. I like Applebee's."

"I think it's more than that." He swirls the wine in his glass.

"Like what?" I take a sip.

He smiles and leans back. "I'll just say it. I think he's mad that we're on a date."

"Probably. He can be such a brat."

"I don't blame him. Nothing against you. He's been through a lot recently. He needs extra attention and love. I think he feels like he won't get that from me at home if we're together. Not that I'm a psychologist or anything."

Whatever, Peter. Danny is the last person I want to talk about tonight.

"What kind of wine did you say this is again?" I ask.

"You picked the Riesling."

"Riesling... I don't think I've ever had this before today."

"If you like it, I can buy another bottle for home."

"I might just take you up on that."

I look over at a few of the couples dancing. The band is playing "I'm With You" by Avril Lavigne.

"Oh, wow! I haven't heard this song in so long!" I yell.

"I don't think I've ever heard this song."

"It probably came out way before you even came to the United States. She's such a good singer!" I look over at the band again. "I wish I could sing."

"Can you dance?"

"Dance?"

"Yeah. Like them." He signals to the other couples who're slow dancing.

"I mean...can you?"

"Probably. Doesn't look too hard. Don't you Americans learn that in school or something?"

"No!" I laugh. "They taught us how to square dance in gym class, that's about it."

"Dancing in a square?"

I groan and put my head down on the table. When I rise, I prop my chin on my forearm.

"Are you asking me to dance, Peter?"

"Will you dance with me, Hayley?" He stands and puts his hand out.

I look down at his open hand, then up at his face. I think about it for a moment.

"Sure... Yeah, why not?"

We walk together, fingers interlocked, over to the dance floor. My heart flutters. Do I really feel this way about Peter? I mean, we aren't even a good match astrologically... Then again, neither are Tristian and I. Stars don't lie, right? Maybe I'm just confused. Maybe I only feel this way right now because he's really good at this...this...dating thing.

We face each other, and he gently grasps my other hand. Our foreheads touch since we're practically the same height and all. We start to dance, swaying slowly.

"You're pretty good at this." His breath smells like spearmint and wine, a big improvement compared to Tristian's Cheetos and weed.

"You're better than I thought you'd be too."

"Oh yeah?" he asks. "Did you think I was going to be a clodhopper?"

"I don't know. I never danced like this before."

"Me either. I'm glad I'm not as bad as you imagined."

"You're not bad. You're really not bad at all."

I look directly into his eyes. I feel safe and wanted. I feel important and first. His face looks different tonight, but why? What is it? Maybe it's the wine. Or not so much the wine itself, but the winery...the glass walls instead of chipped paint, the music instead of the TV. Maybe it's not who we are, but where we are.

"Oh!" He pulls his head away from mine. "I got you a birthday present."

"I thought this was the present."

He reaches into his pocket. "No. I got you a gift. I hope you like it."

He pulls a small box out of his pocket and flips it open. It's a necklace, a diamond-framed pendant with a red stone in the center.

"Is that a garnet?"

"It's your birthstone. I ordered it last week, and it just arrived this morning. I lucked out, I guess."

"That's— Wow! I don't have any jewelry."

"Do you not like jewelry? I can return it. The policy is—"

"No, no! I like jewelry. I just never... No one ever bought me jewelry before. Who would? I have no one, and Tristian... He—"

"Can I put it on you?"

"Yes." I turn around and lift my hair. He places the chain around my neck, fastens the clasp, and runs his hands onto my shoulders. I turn back to face him. He smiles and stares.

"What?" I ask.

"You're just... You're so beautiful, Hayley."

"Really?"

"Yes, really. You're going to ask me that? I've only been chasing you around for—"

I interrupt him by laughing.

"What's so funny?" he asks.

"You. You're really funny."

"I wasn't trying to be."

I take a deep breath. Am I really about to say this? I'm probably going to regret it later.

"I think... Maybe we should give this a try."

"Give what a try?" he asks, his eyes hopeful.

"Us. Give us a try. I don't know if it will work, but maybe it's actually worth a shot."

"Do you mean that? Do you mean that we can try to be more than friends?"

I don't think he's blinked yet. *Creepy.*

"That's exactly what I mean. I think you're...not like anyone I've ever been with before, and I'm starting to actually...like that? I don't know. I'm not sure. I'll try it, though."

"Even the man bun?"

"No, no. The man bun is still up for debate."

"What if I make it into a man ponytail?"

"Nope." I grab both of his hands, and we start to dance again.

"A man...braid?"

"Peter, you're really, really ruining this."

"Okay. I'll shut up now."

"Yup. That would be wonderful."

He's quiet. I rest my head on his shoulder. Do I really think this could work?

Danny

I'm sitting on the couch with the PlayStation controller in one hand and a can of Pepsi in the other. What a night. What do I want to play? My phone vibrates. I put down the controller and pick it up. It's Matt. All of us from the party are in a group chat now.

Who's down 2 play RL?

For real? I just left this guy's apartment. I've had enough of him for the day.

I know u online danny

What a freaking stalker!

I hear the key go into the door. *They're home.* I wonder how awful it was. Couldn't have been good.

Hayley walks up the stairs first, followed closely behind by Peter. He's holding a grocery bag. He puts it down on the dining room table.

"How was the party?" Peter asks.

"Fine," I say, putting the can of Pepsi to my mouth.

"That's good. Did you show the boys the new stuff we bought this morning? I know you were excited to do that."

"Yeah, I showed them."

"Did they like your cleats?"

"I guess."

Hayley sits next to me and unclips her shoes. She's wearing a big, shiny necklace.

"Where'd you get that necklace from?"

"I bought it for her. For her birthday," Peter says.

"Oh."

Hayley stands back up. She carries her shoes into her bedroom without saying anything. I hear her door shut quietly. Oh, sure, ignore me.

"So, did everyone at least eat what I bought?" Peter asks. "Or were they too disgusted?"

"Too disgusted. Matt's mom couldn't believe you would even have the nerve to buy such unhealthy things for us growing boys to eat."

"Oh yeah? Is she the one who gave you that soda too, or is that a different Matt's mum?"

I look down at the Pepsi in my hand.

"That's a different Matt's mom. There are two Matts. Actually, no... What I mean is Matt has two moms."

"You really are something else, Danny."

"Why? Can't a guy have two moms? This is the twenty-first century!"

"Danny." He sighs.

"What?"

He walks over to the couch and sits next to me. "I know this isn't about the spinach dip."

"I don't know what you're talking about."

"You didn't want me to go out with Hayley tonight, did you?"

"BECAUSE I FREAKING HATE HER!" I throw the empty Pepsi can onto the floor.

"Why, though? You two get along sometimes."

"Sometimes? Hardly! She's obnoxious and lazy. All she does is drugs all day and argues with you, and me...and everyone. You have to work two jobs because she won't even work one. I never get to see you. All you do is work. I just want her to leave!"

"She's not doing drugs."

"Are you serious? At Melissa's she got high EVERY DAY. Don't lie to me and tell me that she just stopped."

"Have you seen her take pills in the apartment?"

"No, but that doesn't mean anything. She hides in her room a lot, and then she's a zombie on the couch. I'm not freaking dumb. You think I'm the dumbest person alive, and I'm not!"

"Well, then, I'll tell you the truth. Can you handle the truth?"

"Of course I can. I am THIRTEEN years old! I want to start hearing the TRUTH!"

"Once again, I know how old you are, Danny. Take a deep breath in and out, please."

I breathe in and out. I kinda growl while I do it.

"Okay. I guess that's...good," Peter responds. "She's family. She's sincerely trying to quit right now. I'm not lying to you, and I would never let her stay here if I thought she was putting you in danger. You understand that you'll always come first, right?"

"She's not my family. I JUST TOLD YOU I HATE HER!" I stand and throw my arms in the air.

"Do you know that she can hear you? She's just down the hall." He places his hands on his knees.

"I hope she does hear me!"

He rubs his head and closes his eyes. "Go to your room. You need to calm down and change your tone before you speak to me."

"This is the only way I can get it through your BIG, THICK HEAD!"

"I'm not talking to you if you're going to carry on like this. When you calm down, we'll have a conversation, man to man." He leans back on the couch and crosses his legs. His chillness is making me even more angry.

"I don't want to have a conversation! You bought her jewelry? What is she, your girlfriend now?"

He doesn't answer me. He doesn't freaking answer me.

"ARE YOU SERIOUS, PETER?"

"I asked you to go to your room and calm down. Then we'll talk."

"I'm going to my room, but not because I want to calm down. Because I want to get away from you!"

"Okay. I love you."

"I DON'T LOVE YOU."

"That's fine."

I bust into my room and slam the door behind me. I lay down and close my eyes.

★★★

When I wake up, the room's dark. I must have fallen asleep. I smell something good.

I open my door and head to the kitchen. Peter's in there, sitting at the table. A tray's sitting on top of the stove.

"What is that?" I ask.

"I made you something."

"What'd you make me?" I rub my eyes, walk over to the tray, and take the foil off. Buffalo chicken dip...

"You want to eat some dip and watch a movie?" He smiles, holding a bag full of cut-up bread chunks. "Just you and me, bud?"

"Okay, but I get to choose the movie."

"That's fine."

"And it's going to be rated R."

"Okay."

"All right..." I grab the bag of bread from his hand.

"Do you love me again?"

"Huh?"

"I wanted to know if you loved me again. You said you didn't love me before you went to your room."

Oh my God, really? Who cares?

"I don't know. I'll see."

He laughs. "Well, I still love you, and I'll keep loving you. You won't ever escape it." He stands up and grabs me in a big hug. I'm too old for this. I'm thirteen freaking years old!

"Great." I wiggle like a slimy worm to get free from his grip. I grab the tray and head into the living room.

This Buffalo dip doesn't make the whole Hayley thing okay, but...maybe I was just a little too mean to him earlier. Why do I get so mean sometimes?

CHAPTER EIGHT

Nobody

Adair is playing tag with his friends on the hill in front of me. His bright red hair shimmers in the sunlight. It's always easy to spot him. He stands out from the other boys.

I'm tired. I throw down the hoe I'm holding. The sun is so strong today. It's usually cloudy or raining, but this is a nice change. I shield my eyes with my hand and watch Adair play with the other children. I smile.

He sees me watching from a distance and waves. He says something to the others and runs in my direction. When he finally makes it over to me, he's out of breath. He wraps his arms around me. He's sweaty but smells sweet like grass, not perspiration.

"What are you doing?" I ask. "You're so dirty. You're dirtier than me, and I'm working!"

He laughs. "Can you come play now?"

"I can't. I have to get this soil cleaned up."

"Clean enough."

"Nothing will grow here. If nothing grows here, we have no business left."

"Pop used to do it way quicker than you."

He frowns. I stop smiling too.

"Aye, but I'm not Pop. You see these muscles?" I lift my scrawny arms to make a joke. He laughs. I'm glad he's smiling again, even if it's at my expense.

"How about I try?"

"You're just a wee one. You're smaller than me."

"But I'm stronger."

"No you're not, Adair."

He gets down on his knees and digs into the soil with his bare hands.

"What are you doing? Stop! Stop it! You're making a mess!"

He pauses and looks up at me.

"You remember how dirty Pop was every single day after he was done working?"

"I do."

"Why do you look so clean, then? You have to get dirty. That's how it works, don't you know?"

I put my hands on my hips and look up at the sky.

"I'm trying my hardest, Adair. I really am—"

"Liar," he says with a chuckle. "You just don't like to do it because you're a pretty boy. Ma says you're pretty, and that's why you're bad at working!"

"Stop teasing me!" I pick him up and throw him over my shoulder. "See, I am stronger than you."

"Let me go!"

"Aye, I will, but you best go get cleaned up before Ma sees you."

"And you best go get dirty before she sees you!"

I roll my eyes and put him down. He's quiet again, just watching me.

"What's a passport?" *he asks suddenly.*

Huh?

"It's a thing that you need so you can travel out of Scotland. Why?"

"I saw papers in your bedroom that said 'passport' on them. I asked the other boys, even the ones that speak good English, but they didn't know either."

How did he find that? I tucked it under my bed.

"Why are you snooping around in my bedroom?"

"You want to leave here? You run away enough. You going to run away out of Scotland now, hmm?"

"No! I'm staying! I'm staying right here on our island. I'm not leaving. Besides, I can't get one, anyway."

He looks down and plays with the dirt. He cups it, and watches it fall through the cracks of his fingers like sand through an hourglass.

"If you don't want to leave, then why do you sneak around and lie all the time? You hate it here."

"I don't hate it here. I'm not leaving you."

"But you want to."

"Adair, I don't want to." *I pick the hoe back up.* "I'm staying. I was just curious, is all. It would be neat to visit New York City someday."

"Would you take a plane to New York, or a boat to New York, or a train to New York, or a car to New York?"

"I don't know. It doesn't matter. I can't get a passport."

"How would you even get money to take a plane, anyway? I heard they cost a million pounds."

"No, they don't cost a million pounds. I just told you I can't get a passport, anyway. I don't have a birth certificate."

"When you go on a plane to New York, I want to go, so get me one too, okay?"

"Are you listening to me?"

He stops playing with the soil and looks up at me blankly. He never listens to a single word.

"Okay, okay... You know what? I'll get you a passport. Sure thing. Now run along and get cleaned up like I said—and Adair?"

"Aye?"

"Don't tell anyone else about this passport stuff, including Ma. She, uh... She just lost Pop, and she'll think she's losing me too or something. But I'm staying right here, okay?"

"Sure."

"Thank you. I love you."

"I love you too."

He hugs me, covering my overalls with dirt in the process. I watch him run toward our house in the distance.

Hayley

It's six o' clock in the morning, and Peter's washing the dishes. I don't think he's gone to sleep yet. He's nuts. I head to the kitchen, sit at the table, and watch him. He looks over his shoulder and smiles.

"Good morning," he says and goes back to scrubbing.

"Morning. Did he like the dip?"

Peter turns the faucet off and grabs the hand towel hanging from the oven handle. "He said it tasted good, but he's still unsure if he loves me again yet."

"Yeah... I heard that whole conversation last night."

"I'm really sorry. Danny's been through a lot, and—"

"Oh yeah? Well, so have I."

"Okay, but you're twenty-one, and Danny is—"

"Whatever. Did his parents ever contact you?"

Wouldn't that be nice, if they came to take him away?

"Danny's parents?"

"Yeah."

"That wouldn't be possible."

"Yes, it would! They contacted Melissa once."

"Uhm...Are you sure?"

"Yeah, Melissa knew who they were."

"How would you know that? You were only at Melissa's for three years."

"Not true."

I want Peter to know my life was just as hard as Danny's. Harder, in fact.

"I don't understand." He turns around and leans on the cabinet.

"I was there as a child for a long time. Then I lived with my mom again as a teenager for a few awful years. After I turned eighteen, I had nowhere to go because she got arrested again. Melissa took me back. Why else would I move in there at eighteen? You don't re-enter foster care at eighteen. You go into a homeless shelter or a rooming house. Melissa saved me from that, from being all alone. Danny and I have known each other since he was a baby, since Melissa adopted him and not me."

He's quiet for a while, but he seems intent and concerned. I like that about him. I like the way he listens, sometimes. You can tell he's giving you his full attention, everything he has. I wish he could always be that way. I need that in a man, more than anything.

"Why wouldn't anyone ever tell me this?" he asks.

"You never tell us anything."

"All right, I don't care." He looks to his side and puts his hand up to his mouth. "But Danny's da, he contacted Melissa?"

Back to Danny? I lost him again. I always lose to Danny. Wait... How'd he know it was Danny's dad? Whatever.

"He came to the house once. He was a Black guy."

"Why do you even have to mention his skin color?"

"What? Black? Because he was Black."

"Okay, but does it matter? What does that detail add to this conversation?"

"I don't know...because Danny is Black? Or at least half Black? Haven't you talked to him about this?"

"No. It's just... I don't know the right way to talk about it, okay? Anyway, enough of this."

"He's starting to wonder, Peter."

"What are you talking about?"

"A couple of nights ago, he came out into the living room and asked me what nationality I was. I think it's because he's wondering about himself. So, yes, he's Black...and maybe you should talk to him about it. Tell him whatever you know."

"Maybe, but not now. I'll let him bring it up to me."

"I just think—"

"What did Danny's da say to Melissa? Was he interested in taking Danny back someday?"

God, I hope so.

"I don't know, Peter. I was like eight years old."

He stares at me intently but is silent for a couple of moments.

"Well, he can't, so it doesn't matter. I just thought I knew the whole story. I guess Melissa forgot to tell me that little detail," he says.

"Well, my dad... I don't even know who my dad is, so..."

"Mhmm..." Peter turns back around and starts putting dishes away.

"At least your parents died. It's not like they abandoned you."

"Yeah. Good thing they're dead, huh? My mum will never try to contact me, considering she's dead," he says, defeated.

Maybe I'm taking this too far? How do I get him back?

"Whoa, honey, I didn't—"

"Honey?" he asks as he stuffs a dish in a cabinet and turns around quickly. He suddenly doesn't seem so sad anymore. Got him.

"I thought we said yesterday—"

"We did."

"Can I call you that, then?"

"Absolutely," he responds eagerly. Then he looks down at the floor.

"What are you thinking about?" I ask.

"Nothing...Everything..." he laughs. "Life is so strange, you know? One minute you feel like you finally have everything under control, and then the next minute absolutely nothing is under control."

"I believe in fate."

"Fate? That's such horseshit."

"No, really, I do," I say. "Whatever is meant to happen, will happen. It makes me feel better. It makes me feel like all the fucked-up things that happened in my life aren't all my fault. Que sera, sera, you know?"

"I speak Gaelic, not Italian."

"I know you know what that means, Peter."

"I do know what that means," he says with a smile. "I've thought about that, as well. That maybe some higher force rolled the dice and decided what my life would be like before I even set out on it. Wouldn't that be nice? If I had no hand in contributing to half the mess I wound up in."

"Your life isn't that messy. Mine, on the other hand—"

"You don't know the half of my life." He turns around and continues putting the dishes away.

I want to ask him more, but I don't want to push—not yet. Maybe as this thing grows, this "relationship" thing, I can try to find out more. I pick up my phone and start playing "Que Sera, Sera" by Doris Day on YouTube. He puts the dishes down and laughs.

I stand. "Will you dance with me in the kitchen?"

"To this?"

"Yes!" I approach him. "Cheers to what was, what is, and what will be!"

We join hands and prance across the cold tile. I feel like I'm back at the winery again. I try to hold onto that image as long as I can, but then he steps on my toe accidently. The sun rises, illuminating the chipped paint on the walls of apartment 93A.

Danny

Knock, knock

Someone's at my bedroom door. I hide my head under the pillow, using it to cover my ears.

Knock, knock

"What do you want? I'm trying to sleep here."

"It's noon," Peter says.

"Yeah, so?"

"If you don't get up now, you won't be tired until very late at night. Tomorrow's Monday. That's no good."

"You're the one that kept me up all night with Buffalo dip and a terrible movie." I flip over and stare at the ceiling.

"You picked the movie, Danny."

"I can't help it if I have bad taste in movies! You should have steered me in another direction!"

He laughs. "You're right. My bad." He opens the door, walks over to my bed, and takes a seat next to me.

Really? Even I know I'm being ridiculous.

"Exactly... Are you working tonight?" I ask.

"Three o'clock to close."

"Which job?"

"The bar."

"And I have to stay here with Hayley?"

"You don't have to. You can make plans with your friends."

"Eh, I don't feel like it."

"Then you're staying here with your best friend, Hayley."

"Okay."

"You know... The one you've known for like...ever, apparently." He slaps his hands on his knees, giving me a weird look.

"So?"

"So, I thought we met Hayley together. I didn't know you knew her for years and years before I did."

"So what? Since you're a couple now, she just tells you random things?"

"I don't think that's random, Danny."

"It's not really even important. I hated her then, and I hate her now."

"Why'd you hate her then?"

"Same reason I hate her now. She's lazy, does nothing, gets away with everything. Blames everything bad she does on someone else. She always tried to get me or someone else in trouble to save herself. I thought I was going to finally get away from her the first time she left. Then she came back to Melissa's, and now she lives with me again. Yay!" I throw my hands up toward the ceiling.

"She doesn't do anything that bad."

"Oh yeah? How about the time she hid the crack pipe in your room after Melissa found out about it?"

"That was my... Look, it wasn't a crack pipe. It was a marijuana bowl."

"That was not your crack pipe, dumbass!" I yell at him.

"Whoa, don't call me a dumbass. People make mistakes. I've made mistakes, so I try to forgive—"

"My teacher told me it's not a mistake anymore if you keep doing it over, and over, and over, and over, and over—"

"That's enough 'overs.' Why did your teacher say that to you?"

"Because I cheated on my tests over, and over, and over, and over—"

"Danny, enough! When did you cheat on a test?"

"Eh, last year. Not your concern. You can save it. I had to hear it from Melissa."

"Jesus, Mary, and St. Joseph."

"Anyway, if you make the same mistake a lot of times, it's a decision. That's what my teacher said. I wish someone would tell Hayley that!"

Peter looks down at his hands, as if he's sad all of a sudden.

"You're right. I guess it is a decision at that point."

I sit up. "Why does that make you sad? You don't do that. Hayley does that!"

"Maybe she can start making good decisions now. It's not easy to do, but maybe she can."

"Yeah, well... I guess she made one good decision—you, instead of that guy that smells like ass."

He looks up at me quickly. "Wait. You met him? When?"

"Of course I met him!"

"Are we talking about the same person? What kind of tattoos did he have?"

"Nintendo! *Super Smash*! Horrible Nintendo tattoos. Looked like a baby did them."

"When did you meet him?" Now he looks angry.

"Uhm...all the time when you were at work?"

"He was here while I was at work?"

"A bunch of times, yeah."

"Nope. No. No." He stands up.

"What?"

"Oh, nothing, nothing. You keep on relaxing. That's what Sundays are for." He heads out of my room.

"But you said I should get up!" I yell.

"I changed my mind. Keep sleeping!" He shuts my door behind him.

Hmm... Maybe this will cause a fight. I smile big as I get comfortable in bed again. Good job, self.

Peter

I pull my apron out of the bottom drawer and tie it snugly around my waist. After checking the mirror, I adjust my collar and wrap the green bow tie around my neck.

"Why does he make you wear that stupid bow tie?" Hayley asks. She's lying on my bed, under the covers.

"It's part of the uniform. It adds to the aesthetic."

Like she'd know anything about aesthetic.

"What aesthetic? Dive bar for old men?"

"Excuse me, Irish dive bar for old men." I finish tying the bow and turn around to face her.

"Do Irish people wear ugly bow ties?"

"Maybe. How would I know? I'm not Irish. It's green though. Green...Ireland...? That's the thought process behind it. In Ireland—"

"It's stupid."

"That may be true, but there are a lot of stupid things that happen around me. This bow tie is the least of them."

She sighs very loudly and rolls over to face the ceiling. She covers her face with her hands and pulls them down slowly, dragging her cheeks with them.

"Are you trying to say something?" She rubs her neck and closes her eyes.

"Yes, actually. You know how I told you I never wanted Tristian at the apartment? And how I especially didn't think he was a good person to be around Danny?"

"Oh boy..."

"So, you brought him around Danny at night when I wasn't home? That was nice of you."

"Okay, so? I broke up with him. It was a mistake, God."

Mistake...

"How many times did you bring him here while I was at the bar? More than once?"

"Yeah, I guess."

"Not a mistake then." I sit on the bed and pull on my socks. My back faces her.

"It's over now. He won't be back here."

"You never told me what it was that made you break up with him, exactly. That frightens me a wee bit."

"It's my story, and I'll tell it the way I want to." She smirks and flips over completely so she doesn't have to look at me.

"Don't use that against me. You don't understand what I've—"

"Peter! It's over now. I'm not going to see him anymore. Just forget about it! When he came here, he didn't say one word to Danny. In fact, Danny was the one saying words to us, and we just ignored them."

"I would hope so. He's in middle school. You're an adult. Start acting like it!"

"How did I think this was ever going to work? It has been—" she picks up her phone. "Wow, not even twenty-four hours, and we're already fighting about something that happened WEEKS AGO!" She sits up.

"All I want is a simple apology. Just an 'I'm sorry that I didn't have any respect for you.' That's it! Could you say that for once in your life?"

"Sorry! Sorry, sorry, sorry! There. Are you happy, shit-for-brains?"

I'm quiet for a moment.

"I really did like honey better than shit-for-brains."

"Then stop lecturing me and be sweet like honey! I know you know how to do it. I saw you do it yesterday."

"I wasn't trying to be—" I sigh. "I just wanted you to... I just want to feel like I'm in control of the situation."

"Well, I'm not yours to control! You can't control everything and everyone!"

"I should be able to control what goes on in my apartment."

"*Your* apartment? Okay. It's all yours. We're in a relationship and you still. Can't. Share. ANYTHING!"

"We're hardly in a relationship. You just said it yourself. It hasn't even been twenty-four hours yet."

"It feels like it's been twenty-four years with you! You make every day seem like it's never going to end!" she yells.

"Yeah? Well, you're no better than I am. Yup! You just deflect everything on everyone else so that you don't have to feel guilty about anything! Me? I own my guilt. I swim—No, I drown in my own fucking guilt every day, and I don't blame anyone but me for the shit that I've done!"

Why did I just say that...?

"Like what shit? What shit have you done?"

"Plenty of shit." I stand.

"Like...?"

"It's my story—"

"Exactly. Why do I ever expect anything else from you?"

"I don't know. I could ask myself the same question. Why do I ever expect anything else from you?"

"Why do you love me, then?"

That was gallus. I stare at her.

"I never used that word."

"But I know you do. You let me live here, free of rent or any bills. You cook my meals. I had the best birthday I've ever had yesterday with you. You've gotten nothing in return from me. I don't really know what love is, but if I had to guess, I would say that's it."

I don't answer her. Instead, I walk out of the room and shut the door behind me. Maybe when I get back from work I'll have an answer to her question, but right now... I just don't.

CHAPTER NINE

Melissa

I sit up in bed. It's dark. I can hear the TV playing downstairs. I didn't know the volume went that high.

Hayley.

I grab my robe from my bedpost and enter the dark hallway. I'm so out of breath already... I can do this.

Danny's bedroom door is ajar. I stop and push it open the rest of the way. He's out cold. One of his arms is dangling off the bed. I don't know how he hasn't woken up from all the noise. I close his door, quietly but securely.

I continue making my way down the hall. Peter should be home from work by now. I wonder what he's doing? I peer into his room. His bed is neatly made. He's not in it.

I creep down the stairs slowly, gripping the banister. After a few short breaths, I start coughing, but it doesn't wake them. The TV illuminates their faces. Peter is lying across the couch. His eyes are closed. He's still in his work uniform. It's unlike him to fall asleep in "outside clothes," but I see why he did. His arms are wrapped around Hayley. Her head is snuggled into his chest. The quilt my mother knitted lays on top of them both.

I walk to the coffee table in front of them, pick up the remote, and turn off the TV. Somehow, this startles Peter. He sits up and turns on the light next to the couch. He's wide awake now. Hayley sits up next to him and slowly rubs her eyes.

"I was trying not to wake you," I say quietly.

"I was awake." He stands and fixes his shirt.

"Your eyes were closed."

He closes his eyes again. "Well, I was awake," he says with his eyes still shut. "You see how that's possible?" He opens them again.

He's so sarcastic. It's a defense mechanism, I think.

"It's not a problem, Peter."

"It is. You should be resting. It's very late. Please go back to bed, Melissa. You're sick."

"Hard to sleep with the TV that loud. I'm not sure how all three of you managed to do it."

Peter looks at Hayley who's still drowsy-eyed. She shrugs.

"You could have turned it lower too, Peter." I want him to know he's just as responsible for the noise as she is. I'm holding him to a higher standard now. He still has to prove himself if he wants my blessing to adopt Danny.

He looks back at me now with guilt and anxiety. "I know. I'm sorry. Please go back to bed."

When he walks toward the kitchen, I follow. Hayley stays on the couch.

Peter flicks on the light switch as he enters the room. There's a mess of flour, sugar, and eggshells on the table.

"What were you two doing in here?" I start to brush crumbs into the palm of my hand.

"She wanted cake, so, we baked one together. We saved some for you and Danny. I'm actually quite the baker. Anyway, I'll clean this up. Go back to bed, Melissa." He collects the vanilla extract and baking powder left on the counter.

I lean on the table and put one hand on my hip, watching him for a couple of minutes. He looks over at me.

"What?"

"You and Hayley."

"Yes? What about us?" He turns on the faucet.

"What are you two doing?"

"Doing? We aren't doing anything."

"You were snug on the couch."

He turns the faucet off and looks into the sink.

"We're friends..." He sighs.

"Only friends?"

"Yes. I told her about..."

"Danny?"

"Yes."

"And how'd she take it?"

"She needed cake to calm down."

"Ah..."

"I don't know. She said she thought it was going to be like two friends living together and having fun—no responsibilities—but it's not going to be that way now."

"Did you think she would react differently?"

"I was hoping she'd... Go to bed, Melissa."

He wets a sponge and scrubs the counter. I'm still watching him. He looks back at me. I know what he's thinking. He lets go of the sponge.

"Really, Melissa. Please, go to bed. I can do this."

I turn around and peer out of the kitchen and at the couch. Hayley's gone. I turn to face Peter again.

"This isn't going to be easy, Peter."

"I know that. Don't you think I know that?"

"Well, maybe this isn't a good idea. Maybe Danny—"

"No!" He yells, looking down at the countertop. "No, no, no, no!"

I sigh and rub my forehead with my fingers.

"You have to promise me something."

"What? What do I have to promise you?"

He looks up at me as if he's going to cry. Why is he so set on this? I know he loves Danny, but I still think there's much more to it. It's strange.

"Danny comes first," I say.

"Of course he does, Melissa! I know that. I'll do anything to make sure Danny has a happy—" He pauses. "No, the happiest, safest life possible!" Tears run down his face. The bags under his eyes make him look ten years older now.

"It's okay, Peter!" I wrap him in a hug, the kind a mother gives her child. He needs that. "I just want to make sure this is something you want to do...something you can handle. You understand?"

"I want to do it. I can do it." He holds onto me tighter. "And I'm not crying because I'm pretty and weak. I'm not! I'm crying because you're going to die, and I'm scared you won't let me take Danny. Don't take this as a sign of weakness!"

Pretty and weak? What does that mean?

"I don't think you're weak, Peter. I know you to be very strong, actually." He pulls away from my embrace, and I place my hands on his shoulders.

He sniffles and looks away from me. "I'm sorry about that outburst." He wipes his eyes. "Danny will come first. Believe me, he will. Always."

It's against my better judgment, but then again, I don't know what foster home Danny will land in...and Peter loves him dearly. That's more than can be said about a lot of foster parents. Maybe it will be a good thing for the three of them to stay together. I hope I'm making the right decision...

For them all.

Hayley

I'm sweating. Not that it's super-hot in here. It's okay, I just... I really need to take something, or drink something, or...something. It hasn't even been a week, pull yourself together! You can do this! I can do this, right? Yes, I can do this!

Maybe not.

I pick up my phone and scroll through my texts. I pull up the last conversation I had with Tristian. We don't have to be together for him to be my dealer, right? No, that's stupid. No!

I put my phone back in my pocket, stretch, and walk into the living room. Danny's on the couch playing car soccer again. I try to walk past him without saying a word.

"So, you and Peter break up yet? Lasted longer than I thought it would."

"We didn't break up." Brat.

Ignore him, Hayley.

I go into the kitchen and return with a bowl of ice cream. I sit next to Danny on the couch, watching as his car drives up the wall and toward the ceiling. Uh...I don't think that's how you play?

"So, how do you win this game?"

He looks at me a couple of times from the corner of his eyes, then back at the screen.

"You get the ball into the goal. Isn't it obvious?"

"That's not what you're doing."

He grunts.

"Well, what are *you* doing?" he asks.

"Uh, I'm watching you play this and eating?"

"Go eat somewhere else. Like the table. That's where you're supposed to eat." He jams the buttons on the controller.

"Fine. I'll go eat this somewhere else, I guess."

I leave and walk back down the hallway. I notice the door to the linen closet is open. It's overflowing. There are towels, papers, tools, and other junk all over the floor.

"Danny!" I yell.

"What?"

"What happened to this closet?" I walk back toward the living room.

"I needed to take a shower." He throws the controller down. "Great! Now I lost. Thanks."

"You made a huge mess!"

"I wanted a specific towel."

"All the towels are the same! Now you can pick all that up before Peter gets home. I don't want to listen to his mouth."

"Nah. I'll just leave it. I love hearing him bitch and yell at you. It's my favorite."

"Okay, but I'm not the one who did it! You did it. So, he'll bitch and yell at you, not me."

"I didn't do it," he says, smirking at me.

I stare back at him. We are in a full-on staring contest.

"You know what? I hear all the crap you have to say about me. You think I'm lazy? You're lazy. You're a big, lazy baby! Just to prove to you I'm not the lazy one, I'm going to go pick up the huge mess that you made. You can sit there and whine, and complain, and play car soccer all you want until Peter gets home."

"Awesome. Thanks, Hayley." He picks the controller back up.

"Fucking brat," I mumble under my breath.

Back at the closet, I start folding the towels and stacking them on top of each other. Hand towels, beach towels, shower towels... Hmm, maybe they aren't all the same.

After all the towels are picked up, I organize the other shit Danny ripped out of the closet. He did this on purpose! Okay. It's okay. Let's see... I'll put sheets to the left, pillowcases to the right, I'll put all of the tools back in the toolbox that they fell out of. The lightbulbs can go on the very top shelf, even though that giant baby will still be able to reach them from there.

I sigh.

Okay, random papers... I flip through some packets on the ground. Looks like our car and renter's insurance policy. I wonder how much that costs? I flop onto my butt and start reading.

Life insurance? A two hundred thousand dollar life insurance policy? I read the entire page. My name is on here. Danny's name is on here. We're...beneficiaries?

So, wait, if Peter dies we get one hundred thousand dollars each? That's insane! I've never even seen ten thousand dollars, let alone a hundred thousand dollars.

Why would he buy this? Just another fucking secret. This isn't even a good one. It's a boring one. Everything has to be a secret with him. Every little thing. It's really stupid.

I collect the papers, pull out my cell phone, and take a picture of each document—front and back—then I put them neatly away in the closet and close the door.

Peter

Hayley's in my room, sleeping in my bed. I guess she's moved in permanently now? We should move into her room instead. It's bigger! Oh well.

I change quickly into my pajamas and place my dirty work clothes into the laundry basket. I lift up the covers and get into bed, laying with my back toward her. I feel her turn over. She puts her arm around me.

"Hey," she says groggily.

"Are you staying in here now?"

"Do you have a problem with it?"

"No. Not at all. How was your night?" I turn slightly to face her.

"It was fine. Danny tore apart the linen closet looking for a specific towel."

"He only likes to use the gray ones, not the blue ones."

"That's stupid."

"I told you, a lot of things in my life are stupid. Did he pick everything up?"

"No. I did."

"You should have made him do it, but thank you."

"Yeah...and I found something I wanted to talk to you about."

Crap! What did she find? Fuck! I feel myself start to sweat.

"A life insurance policy," she continues.

Oh, that's all?

"Okay...?"

"Why didn't you tell me you're paying for that? That's stupid!"

"You think a lot of things are stupid lately, Hayley."

"Because they are stupid. You're not dying any time soon. It's a waste of money."

"I'm not paying for it."

"Oh, so it's free?"

"No. When it was decided that both of you two would be moving in with me, Melissa bought a life insurance policy. Then if anything happened to me, you guys would be okay. I told you I wasn't the favorite. She used all of her savings to protect you two. All of that money could have very well gone to her sister."

"Oh."

"Yeah." I turn over completely and caress her cheek gently. "Can I do this?"

"Yes."

I push her pretty red hair out of her face and look into her eyes.

"Peter," she says, "I'm having such a hard time."

"With?"

"Quitting. I don't know if I can do it. It's getting really difficult. I've been taking these stupid fucking pills since I was sixteen years old."

"It sounds hard," I respond, "but I'm here to help you however I can. Okay?"

"I know you are..."

"I know why I love you."

"What?"

I'd thought about it long and hard at work today, and she should hear it. She needs to hear it.

"You asked me why I love you before I left for work."

"So, you do love me?"

"I do. I love you very much. And it's okay if you don't love me yet, or ever, but I just want you to know that you are so deserving of love. All the love in the world, not just mine."

A tear falls from her cheek onto the pillowcase. I lift my hand, wiping away another one with the tip of my pointer finger.

"Don't worry. I washed my hands."

She laughs. "I wasn't worried about that, Peter."

"Do you remember the first time we saw each other?" I ask.

"Not really."

"I do. You walked by my room. I was sitting on the floor, facing the wall, talking to...myself."

"Oh, yeah. I do remember this now. You looked so sad, Peter."

"I was sad, and then I saw you staring at me and asked—"

"Who the hell are you?" We both say it at the same time and laugh.

She kisses me on the cheek.

"I told you my name, but you wouldn't tell me yours. You told me you were nobody," she responds.

"Sometimes I still feel like nobody. Do you remember what you did next?"

"I asked if there was anything I could do to help you, but you told me there was nothing I could do. I think you wanted me to leave."

"But you didn't."

"No. I came into your room, and I sat next to you. I know what it feels like to be nobody."

"You told me that you'd wait right there until I was ready to tell you my name. I thought, 'what a strange girl,' but then I turned and looked at you..."

"You thought I was pretty?"

"I thought you were the most beautiful girl I'd ever seen in my whole life, inside and out. You cared about me. You broke the silence in a moment when I needed it most. You have a way of doing that, actually..."

"Yeah, and then I offered you marijuana," she says and laughs.

"Yeah, and we smoked the shit out of it!"

"My first day back at Melissa's and I was already causing trouble. I really can't believe she took me back. No matter how strict she was, or how much I hated her sometimes, she was a great woman. I wish I was half the woman..."

"You are, though," I say. "You are a whole woman."

I kiss her on the forehead and gently cup her face. We gaze into each other's eyes for a long while. I think she likes what I said. She's waiting for me to say something else that she'll like, but I can't think of anything. Just like the first time we met, my mind is absolutely blank. She has that effect on me. She's a drug

all on her own, and I'll keep chasing her high as long as I live—
the empty, uncomplicated bliss of nothing but her. She's the
noise that creates the silence, the ringing in my ears, the
something that creates the nothing. *Nothing but her.* I don't
want anything else. She reminds me of what I've been missing,
waiting on, for all of the loveless years I can count. She fills that
void.

Her eyes open wider, and she smiles just a wee bit. She bites
her bottom lip. I look down at her chest and slowly back up at
her face. She puts her hands on my cheeks and yanks my face
toward her—violently, recklessly. We kiss. My heart beats faster
and faster. She pushes me flat on my back and climbs on top.
She leans over and kisses me again. I lean upward and pull her
down.

Knock, knock.

Fuck!

"Uh, just a moment," I whisper to Hayley.

Knock, knock.

"Are you serious, Peter?" she asks.

Knock, knock, knock, knock.

"HOLD ON, DANNY!" I yell. "Yes. Just a second," I say
to Hayley.

"Fine!" She gets off of me, lays down on her back, and looks
up at the ceiling. She exhales loudly and covers her face with
her hands.

I stand up and walk to the door. I open it just enough to
stick my face out. "What's wrong? I thought you were
sleeping?"

"I can't sleep. You wanna watch something on Netflix?"
Danny asks.

He tries to look past me to see what Hayley's doing. I close the door even more so that he can only see half of my face.

"Are you feeling all right? It's late."

"Sort of...My stomach hurts, and my head hurts, and also my throat kinda hurts too." He rubs his throat with his hand and coughs.

I stick my arm out of the door and put my hand on his forehead. "You don't feel warm."

"I didn't say I felt like I had a fever. I just wanted to know if you wanted to watch TV with me. God!"

"Okay, okay. Yes. Let's watch something. Just give me a minute. Go put something on."

"If I still feel sick tomorrow, can I stay home? We can hang out. Maybe you can take a day off?"

"Maybe. We'll see. Just go pick something to watch."

"Okay!" He turns around and heads toward the living room. I close the door and look at Hayley.

"I really can't believe you!" She turns away from me, covering her face with the blanket.

"I know, I'm sorry."

"Whatever, Peter. Good night."

"Later?"

"No, thanks. I'll be sleeping."

"I'm sorry!"

"I said good night!"

She reaches toward the nearby lamp and flicks it off. I'm standing in the dark now.

CHAPTER TEN

Peter

I park the car and pick up my phone to scroll through the list I made earlier today.

"Let me see that." Danny reaches over the center console and grabs my phone, scanning through the list. "Brussels sprouts? No!"

"You seem to be feeling much better. What a miraculous recovery."

"Yeah, it's weird. Guess it was just a twenty-four-hour thing."

"More like a two-hour thing."

"So about those Brussels sprouts..."

"Pick another vegetable in its place, then."

I unbuckle my seat belt and pat my pocket. It's empty. Where's my wallet? I open the center console and dig through a mess of pens, receipts, change, and other miscellaneous crap. I really have to organize this whenever I find the time. It's driving me wild. I'm never this disorganized!

"Okay, French fries—a good brand, though. Not the cheap store brand. Those never get crispy, especially when Hayley makes them. They're either soggy or they burn. Okay, Peter? Peter?"

"Yes. What?" I open the car door and step outside. I move the driver seat all the way back and squat, reaching around underneath it. I don't feel anything but dirt and trash. Why do I keep the apartment so clean, and the car so...not clean? I sigh. I'm aggravated with myself. I need to find some time to clean out this car!

"Good. You said yes, so it's yes." Danny opens his door and springs out. I hear the door slam.

What did I say yes to again? Oh yeah, French fries. Not the cheap kind.

"Fine, you can get French fries, but a vegetable too." I look up and out through the passenger side window. He's not within sight anymore.

"French fries are a vegetable. Do you know what they're made out of? Potatoes." I hear his voice coming from behind me. I jump. "What are you even doing, Peter? Why are you on the ground?"

I turn around, look up at him, and stand. He's holding my wallet.

"I was looking for my wallet! Why do you have it? Give it to me!"

I pull it out of his hand and shake my head, closing the car door.

"It was on the floor by my feet, so I picked it up. Oh, yeah, and your phone." He hands me that too. "Rest of the list looks okay, but I'm going to need to add some things."

"Some things? I'll see." We start walking. I grab a cart near the entrance.

"Yeah. Like pizza bagels."

"Fine."

"And gummy bears."

"Gummy bears? No."

The automatic doors open, and I push the cart inside. He follows close behind me.

"Why not? They're not that bad for you!"

"I don't have that much money." I check to see if anyone is within earshot. "We already used most of our food stamps for the month. I can't spend any more than I absolutely need to."

"Put it on a credit card," he says nonchalantly.

"Listen to me," I whisper sternly, and we stop walking. He looks me directly in the eyes. "I am not putting gummy bears on a credit card. This is why I never let you come with me to the store."

"They're literally like two dollars, Peter!" He whines, pouts, and throws his hands down to his sides.

"And French fries are four dollars, and pizza bagels are three dollars—"

"How would you know? We didn't even get to the frozen section yet!"

I don't respond to him. I just keep walking. He keeps going and going.

"Also, all together, four and three and two, that's what? Nine dollars? Wow! Nine whole dollars! Gee golly whiz, what are we going to do? How will we ever survive? We might have to boil water for our baths because we won't be able to afford electricity!"

What the hell is he talking about? I walk past the bakery. He trails close behind me, still rambling off nonsense.

"We'll have to knit our own clothing. I hope you know how to sew! All because of those nine dollars we spent on gummy bears, and French fries, and pizza bagels. We'll have to light candles, and catch squirrels, and cook them over the candles for food. That will take *so* long, cooking a squirrel over a candle. Hmm... It's too bad you spent nine dollars on groceries."

I stop and stare at the aisle in front of me. Wow...Look at all this bread. Just an aisle full of bread. An aisle dedicated solely to bread, all in colorful packaging. There's way more here than could ever be eaten, I think. I'd imagine a lot of it must go to waste. It's unfortunate, really.

What if the people back at home could see this? There are so many choices. It's overwhelming.

No matter how many times I see these stores, they still astound me. It's incredible. Something like this back at home would have changed all of our lives. Not that anyone there would have wanted that change. They would have forbid that change. That basturt, Glas—

"...and even Hayley said so too!"

"Excuse me, Hayley said what?" I pick up a loaf of bread, returning to the here and now.

"Oh, right. That's what you care about." He grabs the cart, pushes it quickly, and lifts himself onto it. He coasts down the aisle.

"Danny!" I chase after him.

He jumps off the cart and turns around to look at me with his hands raised in angry confusion.

"Don't do that." I grab the cart firmly. "Just... Go pick a dessert." I signal to the cakes and pastries up ahead. That will keep him busy for a few minutes, maybe.

"Fine!" He puts his hood up, shoves his hands in his pockets, and walks away from me.

Jesus Christ, Mary, and St. Joseph...

I watch as he picks up the first container he sees. He holds it up high in the air as he walks back toward me.

"Take your hood down, it's disrespectful."

He approaches and chucks the package into the cart. "To who? God?"

"Exactly, to God. Take it off because I said so."

I reach in the cart and pull the package out. Cream buns? *Of course...*

"Can we afford that? Or are we too poor?" he asks.

I look up at him.

"No, we can get this." I say quietly.

"Great. Wonderful. Terrific." He turns around and stomps down the next aisle. His hood is still covering his head. I sigh and follow. Around the corner, there's an abundance of rainbow-colored produce, delivered from all over the world; suddenly, I'm in awe all over again.

Nobody

It's a long walk to the nearest markets. There's also a few bed-and-breakfasts and some new tourist attractions. I actually enjoy when Ma sends me down here to fetch something. I get to see people—anyone other than the ones that live on or near our farm—and some come from all around the world. Mostly, I like going to the markets so that I can learn more English.

When I enter Glas' bakery, I see a family of three—a ma, a da, and a girl about my age. The girl is wearing ripped blue jeans and pink hiking boots. They're not ripped from hard work, though. Some tourists think ripped clothing is fashionable. I've learned that. She has on a matching pink, lacey blouse. Her rose-gold sunglasses are on top of her perfectly straight, glossy red hair.

God, she's beautiful. What would a girl like her want with a boy like me? I look down at my muddy boots and my worn-out blue jeans. I'll keep my distance and admire her from afar.

"This shop is just so charming!" she says to Mr. Glas in Gaelic.

Wow. A tourist who can speak Gaelic. Impressive.

Mr. Glas looks past her and straight at me. "Eh, how are you, lad? It's good to see you."

I approach the dusty, wooden counter. "I'm all right. I need a loaf of wheat bread, and whatever those pastries are that my brother likes. Three of them."

"The cream buns?"

"I don't know, he says they're different than normal cream buns."

"It's because I add maple. New recipe. You can tell him that."

I smile. "Yeah, yeah. I will. Thanks."

I start picking dirt out of my fingernails. I can tell the family's watching me. I don't look their way. I put my hands to my sides and clear my throat. I feel like an exhibit at one of those tourist attractions.

Why do outsiders find us so interesting? I get it, we live in a time-warp on a mostly uninhabited island. We're a bunch of rockets. How embarrassing.

I look over at them and grin. The ma smiles back.

"Do you live here?" she asks in Gaelic.

Is she talking to me? "Uhm... Yes, I do. On Catanach farms, just about a mile North East from here."

"It must be so peaceful. What a quaint little town!"

Quaint? How could anyone think that "quaint" is a nice way to describe someone's entire world? I stop smiling.

"Aye..."

I turn back around to face Mr. Glas. He's slicing my bread.

"We're 'glamping.' Trying to live like the locals!" the ma adds. Glamping is the only English word she uses in that sentence...At least I think it's English?

"Glamping?" I ask.

"We're staying in camping pods on the beach under the stars."

"Yeah. Sounds just like how us locals live." I'm being snide and rude. I don't care. I want to end this conversation.

"It's nothing like the cities," the girl adds.

I look over at her. She's talking to me. Maybe I don't want to end this conversation.

"Oh. I wouldn't know. I've never been to any of them."

"You've never been to Edinburgh?"

"I'm lucky I've been to Castlebay."

"Well, we're from Glasgow. Have you been there?"

"No, never. I've never been off the islands."

Mr. Glas walks back over to the counter and hands me my bag.

"Anything else, lad?"

"That'll do it."

I take my bread and pastries. I don't pay him. Our farm has some sort of weird deal with his bakery. I don't really know exactly what it is.

"Well, it was nice meeting you," I say to the family.

The girl watches as I walk toward the door. Before I exit, I turn around to look at her once more. She really is a sight....So very lovely. I wave. She waves back. I sigh. I'm heading toward our farm once again.

CHAPTER ELEVEN

Danny

One month. One whole month and they're still making it work. Valentine's Day was *disgusting*. I guess it hasn't been so bad. Of course they still fight, and every time I think "this could be it," it isn't it.

I look over at the stands and see Peter and Hayley squeeze by a bunch of other parents. The game is just about to start. They couldn't have gotten here any sooner?

"HEY, MARCELLO!" Reese shouts.

I roll my eyes and look toward him. He's always starting shit with me lately. Why? Is it because I'm different than everyone else on the team? I glance at the other players. I'm really starting to think it's because I'm the only brown kid here. He doesn't pick on anyone else. That's messed up.

"EYES ON THE FIELD. I'M NOT LETTING YOU SCREW THIS UP FOR US AGAIN!"

"WE DIDN'T EVEN START PLAYING YET!" I shout back at him.

"WHEN WE DO, DON'T SCREW IT UP!"

He thinks he is such a freaking tough guy. I throw my lacrosse stick on the ground and take off my helmet, walking toward him. He skips backwards away. HA! It's fun being the biggest on the team. This is the only way to shut him up sometimes.

"Whoa! Hey, man, the game is about to start," he says.

"Shut the hell up." I get closer and closer to him.

"Okay! Okay!"

I lean into his face. "If we screw this up, it's because you're the one who screwed it up for us. You, with your big freaking mouth. Not me."

"Break it up! Break it up, boys." Coach pushes my chest with his forearm. "Any fighting and you'll both be sitting out this game. Do you hear me, Marcello? No more fighting, with anyone!"

"I hear you," I mumble. I walk back to my spot and pick up my stick. I put my helmet back on and look forward. Reese is watching me. When I notice, he turns away real fast.

Coach walks to the stands where the parents are. Crap! Don't go to Peter, don't go to Peter, don't go to Peter... Go to Reese's mom! He's the bully, not me. Coach waves his hand. Peter looks over at Hayley and walks down the steps. Coach leans against the fence dividing them. Peter's listening. He looks over at me, squints, then shakes his head. I can just hear him saying, "What the hell, Danny?"

Crap. I face forward and bang my stick into the ground. Take your anger out on the game, take your anger out on the game...

★★★

The game's over. We lost. Reese screwed it up for all of us. I couldn't even concentrate because I kept thinking about him. What a shitshow.

Peter's driving, Hayley's in the passenger seat, and I'm in the back. The car ride home is quiet, probably because of the coach's conversation with Peter. I try to look in the rearview mirror to see his face, but it doesn't work. I think that only works the other way around, so that parents can keep their eyes on their kids.

Hayley rolls down her window. She plugs the USB cord into her phone and turns the volume up to twenty. Great. Time to listen to P!nk again.

Peter says something to her. I don't know what, though. I can't hear anything besides the music.

"WHAT?" she yells as she turns to him.

"CAN YOU TURN THAT DOWN?" he yells back.

She turns the music down.

"Why? So we can sit here in silence?"

"Yes. My head is throbbing. Can we just sit here in silence, please?"

"If you have something to say to Danny, just say it," she says. "You always do this. Just say whatever it is you have to say."

I lean forward in my seat.

"I'll talk to him when we get home. Not now," Peter says.

"What are we going to be talking about?" I ask.

"You know exactly what we're going to be talking about."

"Not really, but okay."

I sit back and pick up my phone. He looks in the rearview mirror.

"Who are you texting?" Peter asks.

"Eyes on the road," I respond.

He stops short, causing me to jerk forward. Good thing I'm wearing my seat belt.

He turns around. "You have to learn to watch your smart mouth! Maybe that's why you're always acting 'unsportsmanlike' and fighting with others at practice!"

"Oh yeah? I wonder where I picked that up from? What a mystery."

"That's it. The PlayStation is going in my room." He turns forward and starts driving again.

"Fine...I'll just watch cable."

I look back down at my phone.

"TV TOO!" he yells.

"Are you serious?! You aren't going to move the TV into your room!"

"Oh yeah? As soon as we get home you can watch me do it."

"I'll help," Hayley jumps on in. She turns to give me a mean Hayley smile.

"STOP LOOKING AT ME!" I reach forward to swat her away.

"Don't look at him," Peter says. "Just let him stew back there."

Hayley turns the music all the way up. It's even louder than before. She sings along to "Just Like a Pill," badly. Really badly. After all, she does suck at everything, even singing. Peter doesn't say anything to her. He puts his elbow up on the window ledge and rubs his head.

We get to the apartment, and I jump out of the back seat. Peter hasn't rolled up the window yet. He still has a cigarette in his mouth. It's getting pretty tiny now. How much smoke could he possibly suck out of that thing?

I lean into his window. "You know, I'm smarter than you. You think I'm dumb, but I'm so much smarter than you! Think you're taking the TV away from me? HA! I don't care! I have so much other better stuff to do."

I am smarter than him. When I grow up, I'm going to be way more than a bartender or waiter.

"Yup. You are smarter than me." He pulls the cigarette stub from his mouth and rolls up the window. He opens the car door. "Still punished, though. I'm sure even Einstein was punished at some point."

Hayley gets out of the car and walks around to Peter's side. "Can I have a cigarette?"

Peter reaches into his pocket and pulls out the box. I run up to the apartment door and start jiggling the knob angrily.

"Why don't you just use your key?" Peter asks me.

"Because I left it inside. Let me in!"

Peter throws his cigarette onto the ground. He walks over and unlocks the door. I push in front of him.

"Danny!" he calls as I reach the top of the steps.

"What?" I watch as he follows me upstairs.

"I'm sorry if I was too angry with you, but you cannot be fighting with your teammates. That's no good." He walks toward me.

"I won't fight with anyone anymore, okay? I'll let everyone say mean shit to me, and I just won't do anything about it. That's what everyone seems to want."

"If someone says something mean to you, tell the coach." He takes off his jacket.

"And be a snitch? No freaking way!"

"Who says mean things to you, anyway?"

"Everyone!"

"Even Matt?"

"Especially Matt! He thinks he's so smart, and so perfect, and so...better than everyone else."

"Try to talk to him about it. Tell him that what he says upsets you."

"No! I don't want to talk about my feelings. I want to yell at people and punch them in their heads."

"Whoa. I hope you've never 'punched anyone in the head' before."

"Not yet. I take all my anger out on the game, and then I feel a little bit better. Not all the way, but a little bit, at least."

Hayley joins us. "Who are we punching in the head?"

"No one," Peter answers. "We don't punch people." He leans down by the TV and starts unplugging it. Seriously? He doesn't understand, and he never will.

"What are you doing? I thought you said you were sorry for getting angry!" I yell.

"I am sorry for getting angry. I'm not sorry for punishing you." He lifts the TV and carries it into his room.

"ARE YOU KIDDING ME?"

"What? I thought you said you were smarter than me and have better stuff to do? Use your smart brain to find better stuff to do until your punishment is over." He takes the TV into his bedroom and puts it on the dresser. I follow him. I can't think of anything good to say...so...

"YOU SUCK!"

I hear Hayley laugh from the living room. I run back in there.

"STOP LAUGHING! YOU SUCK MORE THAN HE DOES!" I yell and point at her.

"Maybe when you feel like this, you should exercise," Peter says from behind me. "Maybe we should go for a walk. You said lacrosse helps you—"

I am so angry. I won't let him finish his sentence.

"I HATE YOU!"

"No, you don't."

I know I don't...but right now...

"YES, I DO! I HATE EVERYONE. MAYBE YOU TWO WERE MEANT FOR EACH OTHER! YOU'RE BOTH MORONS!"

Peter rubs his face with both of his hands. Hayley's staring at him.

"Yelling and throwing a fit doesn't make me want to give you the TV back. It actually has the opposite effect," he says.

I take a few deep, angry breaths. I clench my fists together. I say nothing.

"Good...We have to work on finding a way to calm down together," Peter says. "Let's take a walk now."

"Is *she* coming?" I jerk my head toward Hayley as I continue to breathe in and out loudly.

"Nope. Just us. Just a walk around the complex. We can talk it out. Maybe we can make a deal with the TV."

Get away from Hayley for a little while... Maybe I can get the TV back sooner?

"Okay. I'll walk with you."

"Cool." He looks over at Hayley. "We'll be right back."

"Fine. Enjoy your walk without me since I'm not invited."

"Don't be like that," Peter says.

"Yeah, don't be like that!" I run down the stairs and out the door. When I walk outside, I look up at the sky and smile.

Hayley

"Fifteen New Positions That Will Have You Both Craving More." Sounds promising enough. Page twenty-five. I flip to page twenty-five and read...What? Are they serious? I can't even do a cartwheel! Yeah...I don't think Peter can move that way either. This is so dumb. Who wrote this shit, an acrobat?

I mean, it's not like Peter and I have much sex, anyway. He's always too tired, and when we do have sex, Peter has to make sure Danny is definitely asleep—*twice*. It's so annoying, and then we have to be like really, really quiet. If I moan too loudly, he literally covers my mouth with his hand. I fucking hate that.

I should just stick to the fashion and astrology stuff. Maybe good sex just isn't my thing anymore.

I close the magazine and put it on Peter's side table. I wonder if I could figure out how to hook this TV up. Then I could watch something, anything to distract myself from the cravings. That could work, right? I think so.

"Hey." Peter walks in the room and closes the door behind himself.

"Has he calmed down?"

"Yeah. He's feeling much better," he says with a sigh.

"How are you feeling?"

"Me?" He clears his throat.

"I don't know. You look...stressed."

"I'm going to take a hot shower and go to bed." He digs through his dresser and pulls out plaid pajama pants and a white tee.

"I still don't understand why you got yourself into this."

"Into what? What are you talking about?"

"Parenthood, I guess. It's a lot. It's too much. I can hardly stand watching you do it. It could have been just us."

He walks over to his end table and pulls out a pair of underwear. As he closes it, he sees what's on the table.

"What is this shit? Why do you read this crap?" He picks up the magazine.

"I don't know. It's entertaining, I guess. Why do you care about a magazine? Don't change the subject."

"I wasn't changing the subject. I love Danny. That's why I did it. I already told you that." He rolls up the magazine like a tube and squeezes it. "But you're right. It is hard, and I'm clearly not very good at it either." He sits on the bed and hits the magazine against the end table.

"I think he's a lucky kid," I respond.

"Do you mean that?"

"I do. He has someone who loves him, and cares about him—a man, too. What are the odds!" I laugh.

He turns around quickly to look at me. He squeezes the rolled-up magazine tighter with both hands.

"What did you just call me?"

I just called him something... What did I call him?

"Uh...I didn't call you anything."

"What did you just say? Say it again."

"I said Danny has someone who loves him...and cares about him. Oh, yeah, and not like a mother, like a man. In my experience, men usually don't—"

"That!" He smiles very big, then slaps the top of his legs and crunches the magazine. "Thank you." He stops smiling and sighs, gazing down at the floor. "I don't think anything I'm doing is working with him."

Hmm...Okay, whatever.

"It didn't work for Melissa either. Don't feel too bad."

"Yeah, I know. She gave me a warning when we were working on transferring guardianship. I told her I can handle it...and I *can* handle it. I will do everything I can possibly do to handle it."

"A warning? That's so funny."

"Not that funny. She gave me a warning about you too, like I was about to become your guardian, as well, and not your boyfriend!"

"She was such a bitch sometimes, jeez."

"You were just singing her praise a few weeks ago."

"What are you saying? A woman can't be both a bitch and a hero at the same time? Those are the type of women who get shit done."

He laughs.

"Come here," I say and put my arms out.

"No, I really want to shower. I'm sore. I had a long day."

"I said come here!" I reach up and pull him backward by his bun. His head lands in my lap. "You don't need to shower. You smell good!" I rub his hair.

"It's the cologne that's masking the ripe scent of body odor," he says with a laugh.

"Close your eyes."

"Why?"

"Do you trust me, Peter?"

"I do."

"Then close your eyes and relax."

He closes his eyes.

"Now, flip over," I continue.

He smiles.

"What are you doing though, Hayley?"

"Can anyone ever be in control other than you? Flip over. Put your face into the pillow."

"With my eyes closed?"

"Yeah! Shouldn't be that hard."

He flips over. "Now what?"

"Now take your shirt off."

"It would have been much easier to take my shirt off before I closed my eyes and flipped over. These directions are way out of order. It should have been shirt, flip, eyes... Not eyes, flip, shirt. Very—"

"Stop talking. Just do it," I demand.

"Okay." He sits back up and pulls his shirt off. I stare at the tattoo on his right arm. He sees me.

"So should I close my eyes again and lay back down?"

"Duh." I point to the pillow.

"All right." He does just that.

I start rubbing his neck and shoulders.

"What... Are you—?"

"Just relax! I read how to do this in that magazine that you think is complete crap."

"I guess it's not so crappy, after all."

"Exactly. You have a lot of tension in your shoulders."

He laughs. "What, you're a professional now?"

"I am. I even watched a 'how to' video online. Am I any good?"

"Feels good to me. I never had one of these before. What's the English word?"

"Massage," I remind him.

"Right. Why couldn't I think of that? That's an easy one. Anyway, I think you're doing a great job."

"Maybe I should go to school to be a masseuse."

"I think you could do it. I think you could do anything you wanted to do."

I straddle his back, lean down, and kiss the bottom of his neck. I work my way up to his ear.

"That's definitely not something you would do to your clients if you were a professional masseuse, right?"

"I don't know. Depends on how much they pay me."

"That would make you a prostitute, and you don't have to go to school for that. But we could use the money..."

"Shut up!" I yell at him playfully. "Oh! Also, I read *your* horoscope today."

"Mine? You know I don't believe in all of that."

"Maybe this will change your mind. It said that Mercury has been in retrograde."

"How would that change my mind? I don't even know what the fuck that means." He moans with pleasure as I push my knuckles farther into his spine.

"It's not good. Retrograde can cause a lot of bad things to happen...and Mercury is your ruling planet, since you're a Virgo."

"Oh yeah? Tell me, how much longer will this horseshit go on then? I think Mercury has been in retrograde my entire life. It's stuck there."

"No, no. Only a little while longer."

"Sure, whatever you say. Can I turn around?"

"Why? You aren't enjoying this?"

"No, I am. I just want to look at you."

I stop rubbing his shoulders and get off of him so he can flip over. He pulls his hair out of the bun and lays on his back. I watch his chest move up and down slowly as he breathes.

"Thank you for that," he says. "It felt really good."

"You're welcome. You look so different with your hair down. I feel like it changes your whole face or something."

"Yeah? Well, it's a greasy mess right now. I really should take that shower."

"What does your tattoo mean?"

"Oh..." He looks down at the tattoo of a broken chain around his bicep. "I don't know. I just thought it was cool."

"There's no meaning behind it at all?"

"Uh...Not particularly. Do you like it? Makes me look tough, right?"

"Oh yeah. You look like a real tough guy. Who would mess with you?"

"Gee, thanks. That was convincing." He sits up.

Oops.

"Come on, Peter. You know you aren't threatening looking at all. You're just...so cute."

"I'm cute?"

Double oops.

"Yeah, like a cupcake. I mean, not like a cupcake. Like a full-sized cake. Like a manly cake. Cute, but manly."

"That's probably why Danny doesn't take me seriously either. You see him! He's my height, and he's not done growing."

"Maybe he is done growing, though."

"I hope not. Then he'll be stuck like me—a man cake, or whatever you just called me. No one wants to be a cake man."

"It's not just your height. It's your face too. Danny is more tough looking, like his bone structure and—" Triple oops. "Danny will be fine. That's all I meant. Stop worrying about him," I say quickly.

"Are you even attracted to me?"

"What?"

"I don't know. That was like...Damn." He reaches up and rubs the back of his neck.

"Of course I am! I just said I think you're cute."

"But do you think I'm handsome?"

"Uhm...Yeah. Yes."

"So the answer is no?"

"I said yes!"

"You said 'uhm' first." He stands up and stretches.

"No one is perfect."

"Oh, yeah? Great. Thank you."

"You're close to it, though."

"Stop lying. I know I'm not. I know what type of guys you like. I've seen them. I'm nothing like them. They're tall, and rugged...and very intimidating, quite frankly. I'm small, I have different looking facial features than a lot of people I've met here, I talk funny, I—"

I stand up and kiss him. To shut him up, maybe? Maybe because I honestly can't disagree with any of those things?

"Stop. Just stop." I pull away from the kiss. "You're spiraling out of control again."

"Yeah, and thinking never leads to anything good." He gathers his clothes once more. "I'm going to go shower now, clear my mind."

I appreciate him, and I care about him, but do I love him? It's not just because he's a typical Virgo...but, yeah, that's definitely a part of it.

Hayley Bayley

My head is leaning onto the back of my hand. My eyelids feel super heavy. They start to close, but the flashing light of the TV keeps me awake. Where is Mom?

I look behind the couch at the clock on the microwave. Eleven thirty already? She said she'd be home by ten o'clock. I can't sleep. What if a man at the restaurant tried to hurt her again, but this time...

I go to the phone hanging on the wall and dial her cell number. It rings and rings, but she doesn't pick up. Now her voicemail box is full. I guess I'd left her too many messages.

I sniffle and look at the little square table in the kitchen. There it is...the bottle of Mom's pills. She told me not to touch them, but I take a few every night, and somehow she doesn't notice.

I should try to clean up. I grab my bowl of cereal from the table. It's gone soggy. I carry it to the sink and pour the milk down the drain. I make sure the cereal doesn't fall too by using my spoon as kind of like a wall. I imagine the milk crying, asking the cereal for help as it falls, falls, falls.

I sigh and throw the cereal into the garbage can. I beat the bowl against its sides to get every last piece out. I rinse the bowl and put it in the dishwasher.

I wonder what Melissa's doing right now? I miss her and the other kids. I always wanted to live with Mom again, but now that I'm here, I'm lonely and scared all the time.

A key scrapes into the door. My ears perk up. I grab the bottle of pills off the table and dump a couple into my hand. I stuff them into my pocket quickly. Mom's home.

Two figures stand in the doorway. Mom turns on the light switch. A man in a suit is leaning his head on her shoulder. He looks like he's about to fall. His tie hangs limply around his neck, and his shoes are untied.

"Hey, Hayley Bayley," she says, throwing her purse onto the chair by the door.

"Hi..." I approach them slowly. I can't take my eyes off of the drunk man. "What's wrong?"

"Him? He's just sleepy. He had a long night," she says.

Okay...I know he's way more than tired. She treats me like I'm still a baby. We're picking up right where we left off, I guess. I look them both up and down.

"Does he work at the restaurant too?"

Mom laughs. I don't understand what's funny about that question.

"No, baby. I'm gonna go put him in bed."

"No..."

"Jack?" she asks as she pats his face.

"Hmph?" the man groans.

Mom looks back at me. "Go into your room for a sec."

"I don't want to."

"Hayley, go!" she demands and snaps her fingers.

I know how this works. I have to hide in my room so the men don't see me. Men don't like children, or even teenagers my age. That's why I never had a dad. I'm the reason he left. Men suck big time. I wish they didn't exist. I go into my bedroom and close the door, but I press my ear against it.

"You passed out, Jack." Mom laughs.

"I think I... I must have drank too much."

"You think? Whoa! Hold your horses! We aren't even in the bedroom yet!"

"I just—"

Mom's bedroom door closes. I know what comes next, and I don't want to hear it.

I pop the pills from my pocket into my mouth and chew, chew, chew. The more you chew, the faster they kick in. I dig through my end table, find my CD player, and stick my headphones into my ears, turning the music up as loudly as it can go.

CHAPTER TWELVE

Danny

I'm sitting at the kitchen table, playing with the cereal in my bowl. Red loops go on top, green to the right, then the yellow—

Peter sits across from me, still wearing his PJs and that weird grandma robe he puts on when he gets out of bed. He places a Christmas tree coffee mug on the table and cradles it with one hand. He leans back in the chair and looks at his phone.

"I've thought of so many things to do without the TV," I say.

"Like play with your breakfast?" he asks without looking away from his phone.

"I'm organizing them by color, like your sock drawer. I thought you'd be proud."

"That's funny. I only have white socks." He sips his coffee.

"How are you doing with the TV in your room anyway? Keeping you up at night? Giving you nightmares?"

He ignores me and sips his coffee again, really loud this time.

"It's not Christmas!" I yell.

"So what?"

"Your mug?"

He finally looks away from his phone and examines the mug. "My apologies." He takes another sip and looks back at his phone.

"Yeah. Your apologies."

"Are you going to get dressed for school soon?" Now he sounds kinda mad, tapping his fingers on the table.

"I am dressed! I'm wearing this."

He raises one eyebrow and looks me up and down. "No. You're not wearing that. Go get dressed."

"What's wrong with this?"

"I bought you a bunch of new clothes not too long ago. You're not going to school wearing an old, stained T-shirt. It's not even properly ironed."

"No one wears 'properly ironed' clothes to school." I mimic him in my worst Scottish accent. It's even worse than Hayley's.

"Okay. Wear that, then." He looks back at his phone.

Wow? Really?

"So, you want me to look bad?"

"Are you trying to fight with me right now, Daniel? You were mad when I told you not to wear it, and now that I say you can wear it, you think I want you to look bad?"

"It's not my fault that you don't understand how things work here in America."

He puts his mug down on the table and blinks at me very quickly.

"I don't understand? I think I understand quite well how things work here. You know what? You can have the TV back."

"I can?"

"Absolutely."

Uh oh. Uh oh. Uh oh. Uh oh.

"Peter, I'm—"

"Cable costs forty dollars per month, the PlayStation was three hundred, add in the ten dollars a month for Netflix... Okay. You can have the TV for three hundred and fifty dollars."

"I don't have three hundred and fifty dollars!"

"And you can carry it out of my room and hook it back up yourself."

"I just said I don't have three hundred and fifty dollars!"

"You can work for it. You can do the dishes, vacuum, the laundry. That's how you get money to pay for things. I thought you understood how things work here in this great country?"

"I do understand how things work!"

"Well, they don't work unless you do, right? Pull yourself up by the bootstraps."

"Peter, I'm sorry... I didn't mean—"

He picks up his wrist and looks at his watch. "Fifteen minutes until you have to leave. That's just enough time to get the dishwasher going. Oh! Don't forget this Christmas mug." He pushes it toward me.

"Are you serious?"

He doesn't answer me. He stands and walks out of the kitchen.

Peter

I've read so many parenting books that say work is good for teenagers, but then I think about myself as a teenager. Work did nothing for me. Perhaps it was the wrong type of work. All children are different. What if some responsibility will be good for Danny? Then I think about—

No! I close my eyes tightly. Not that type of work. Nothing dangerous!

"I'm leaving now." I open my eyes. Danny's got his backpack on, and he changed clothes. Now he's wearing clean jeans and a Nike sweatshirt.

"Have a good day at school," I respond from the couch.

"Peter?"

"Yeah, bud?"

"I'm not a good friend, and I'm sorry."

"Friend?"

"Yeah. I'm not a good friend."

"We aren't 'friends,' Danny."

"I know, but I shouldn't have said what I said." He sighs and kicks his left foot into the carpet multiple times.

"What's going on?"

He still hasn't looked up. "Nothing. I'm going to do the laundry when I get home."

"I'll be at work."

"I know."

"Danny, you don't know how to do the laundry."

"I'll vacuum then." He continues to kick his foot into the floor.

"Stop that. Take a deep breath."

"I'm trying."

"I want you to try to think of where this is all coming from, all the anger."

He's quiet. He rubs his lips together and makes a face. He's thinking.

"I don't know," he says.

"Put your backpack down."

"I'm going to miss the bus then!" He signals to the door.

"I'll drive you to school. You can be a little late."

"Really? I can?" He perks up. I knew that would make him happy.

"Yes. Put your backpack down."

He drops his backpack on the floor. "Can I miss all of first period? I hate that class."

"What time does first period end?"

"Eight thirty-five."

"We'll get you to school by nine o'clock."

"Okay." He sits next to me on the couch. We stare at the wall in front of us, since there's no TV.

"It's okay to feel angry. I feel angry, and sad, and scared quite often."

"When?"

"All the time. We're very similar, actually. We just have to figure out a way to deal with those emotions, other than yelling and fighting. That leads to nothing good."

"Lacrosse helps."

"That's a good start. Did walking help?"

"Yes."

"Great. So, we don't always know why you feel angry, but we do know how we can make you feel a little better. Maybe you should start a journal."

"That's for girls!"

"No, it's not. I write all the time. It makes me feel much better. It helps me understand why I feel the way that I do."

"I've never seen you write."

"I write when I'm alone. Only when I feel like I need to."

"What would I write in a journal?" He turns to look at me.

"Maybe write how you're feeling and what might have happened to cause that. Then, if I'm home from work, we can go on a walk, or a jog. I'm not that fast, though, and my legs are much shorter than yours." I make a joke at my own expense. That always seems to cheer people up.

He smiles. "Won't you be tired after work?"

"Nah. I'm never too tired for you."

"You always say you're tired."

"Then I'll push through it. Some exercise will be good for me."

"Can we go for a walk now?" he asks.

"Yes. Let me get dressed." I push up on my knees and stand, hearing my body crack. I feel so old for twenty-one. Danny doesn't notice.

"Can I miss first period every day so we can go on a walk?"

"Absolutely not."

"Was worth a shot."

I head toward my bedroom to get dressed for our walk. Maybe all those parenting books are paying off. That went quite well.

CHAPTER THIRTEEN

Hayley

Why am I doing this? Am I stupid? Desperate? I knock, then put my arms behind my back and clasp my hands tightly. Tristian answers the door.

"Hals? What the fuck are you doing here?!" He smiles and leans against the doorframe. The way he looks down at me makes me feel so small. I hate it, but...I kind of like it? No!

"Look, I need kickers." I don't meet his eyes.

"What happened to quitting?"

"I am quitting, but not cold turkey. Just like little by little."

"So, what you're saying is, you finally ran out of pills, and you've come crawling back to me?"

"I am not crawling!" I answer frustratedly. Is frustratedly a word? I unclasp my hands.

He steps outside and closes the door quietly behind him. "Jillian is sleeping."

"At one o'clock in the afternoon?"

"She works nights now. Makes more money."

"Good for her. So, how much will you charge me for just a couple of pills?"

"Just a couple? Free."

"Free? This is why you suck at what you do."

"It's not free for everyone. Just you."

"No way! I want to pay for them."

"How are you about to pay for them, Hals?"

"With cash!" I pull my wallet out of my purse and hold it up for him to see. He licks his lips a little, like he's tempted and wants to know more.

"Oh yeah? Where'd you get that?"

"From Peter."

"He didn't give you money to buy Oxys."

"No. He gave me money to buy groceries."

"You are such a piece of shit. Worse than I am." He laughs, looks up at the sky, and shakes his head back and forth slowly.

"I am not worse than you are! I have enough cash to buy both."

"I'm not taking his money. I'm better than that."

"You are? Because the exact reason why we broke up is I caught you taking his money."

"Well, I *grew*. You should try it. I'm a bigger man now, and I'm making mad money."

There's no way he "grew." He's a damn Taurus! Tauruses don't grow.

"Really? I don't believe you."

"Oh yeah," he says, so sure of himself.

"Then why are you still sleeping on Ryan's floor?"

"Haven't found the right place yet."

"Whatever. Here's twenty dollars. How many can that get me?" I pull the cash out of my wallet.

"I told you. It's free for you."

I don't have time for this. I turn my head and fold my arms, biting my bottom lip. How much could it possibly hurt to just take them? It's fine, right?

"Fine! Just give them to me. I still have to get to the store."

"Under one condition."

"Forget it. Fuck off." I put my cash back in my wallet and begin to walk away.

"You didn't even hear the condition!" he yells.

"I'm not that desperate," I call out without turning around.

"Yeah, you are."

I am.

"What's your fucking condition?" I turn around quickly and slap my sides.

"I'll give you the Oxys free of charge...but only if we can take them together and just chill."

"You know I'm with Peter now, right?"

He's quiet for a little while. "I didn't know that. That makes me want you even more."

"That's low. That's really fucked up."

I'm kind of into it. It sounds...exciting. I slowly approach him.

"What? He hates me. I hate him. Spending time with his girlfriend behind his back? Sounds very appealing to me." He licks his lips again like a hungry predator. "Tell me, what is it about him? Is it the big nose? Oh! Maybe the gigantic-ass forehead? Or the small man complex? I think it's the free room and board." He smiles maniacally.

"All of the above, jackass," I say, leaning closer.

"Hear me out. Just one night. Me and you. We're friends, Hals. You don't miss me at all?"

"I do miss you..."

Or maybe I just miss the Oxys? Or the thrill? The spontaneity? Or maybe all of it? I don't know any more.

"Good girl." He lifts my head up with his pointer finger, shows his teeth, and clicks his tongue. "I missed you too, Hals. It's been too long. You free tonight?"

"Yeah, I'm free tonight. Peter's working until around midnight."

"Cool. You wanna meet up in that park?"

"That's twenty minutes away from here."

"Okay, then we can Uber together. Like I said, I have money now."

"Fine. I'll come back at six o'clock."

I turn and walk away.

"Tell Peter I said hello!" He cackles.

I feel all of the blood in my body rush to my face. I feel so ashamed...and excited? Turned on just a little? Confused is probably the best word to describe me right now.

I get back into the car and take a few deep breaths.

Peter

A Father's Guide To The High School Transition. I still have quite a few months... Might as well be prepared ahead of time.

The door opens, and I look toward the stairs. Hayley comes in, carrying a single bag.

"Did they have milk?"

"Yes. Only a small one, though," she answers.

"Thank you. That's good enough until I can get to the supermarket this weekend." I close the book.

"How many of those books do you have?" she asks and unpacks the bag.

"Not too many. Most of them are from the library. I have to return them."

"That looks too nice to be from the library."

"No, no, not this one. They didn't have it there. I ordered it online." I walk over and hug her from behind. I press the side of my face to hers. She reaches up and touches my cheek.

"What are you cooking?"

"I'm roasting a chicken. It will be ready in forty-five minutes. There's a tray of asparagus in the fridge. They're all ready to stick right in the oven. They need about fifteen minutes. Take the chicken out of the oven, and put the asparagus straight in. The chicken needs to rest."

"I can do that."

"And do not forget to turn the oven off like last time. It was about one hundred degrees in here when I came home. Not to mention it's very dangerous."

"The cancel button turns it off, right?"

"Yes... I thought you knew that?"

"Just wanted to make sure."

That makes me a little nervous...

"I'm going to go out tonight after dinner," she continues.

"Really? Where?" I carry the milk toward the fridge, reading the bottle. Is this really the best date she could find? I bet she didn't even check it. I put it in the fridge, then peek inside of the oven.

"Well...I reconnected with Shaina. Remember her?"

"Shaina? No. I don't remember a Shaina..."

"We were friends in high school. We planned on seeing a movie."

"That's nice. Do you need money?"

"No. I still have your change from earlier today. Danny will be fine alone, right?"

"You know he'd prefer it." I laugh. "Have fun. Maybe you two can stop by the bar and have a drink on the house. I'd like to—"

"No! Shaina doesn't drink."

"I can make her a mocktail."

"No. She used to be an alcoholic, so even going near a bar would be—"

"Got it." I cut her off. I really don't care to hear more about Shaina's alcoholism, but it might be good for Hayley to connect with someone who's also trying to leave behind an addiction. I look down at my watch. "Time to get dressed for work." I kiss her on the cheek and walk past her down the hall.

"Peter?"

I stop in my tracks. Maybe this is it. Maybe she's finally going to say it! I take a deep breath and close my eyes.

"Yeah?"

"How long did you say the asparagus should be in the oven for?"

"Oh... Fifteen minutes."

"Thanks."

There's always tomorrow...

Hayley

I open my eyes slowly. My vision is blurry. All I see is a frizzy mess of blonde hair. Peter. He's rubbing my head. I'm lying on his chest. How'd I get into bed last night? I peel the crusty shit off my lashes. Think...Think...

Crap. I remember.

"Good morning," he says.

I feel an aching pain between my hips.

"Did we have sex last night? I don't remember."

"No! No way! Not in the condition you were in. I would never do that to you!"

Oh my God. I remember more now...

"Right. Must have been a dream."

He smiles. No, don't smile!

"Awesome," he says.

Not awesome!

"Hayley, you looked really bad last night," he continues. "I'm worried about you. Did you do anything with Shaina?"

Who the fuck is Shaina?

"Huh?"

"Maybe I'm remembering her name incorrectly... The friend you hung out with last night. Did you guys take anything?"

I sit up quickly. I'm breathing so fast. I remember...I remember...

"Oh yeah, her. Uh... I think we drank too much last night," I say. Good one, good one...

"I thought you said she was a recovered alcoholic who couldn't drink?"

MOTHERFUCKER!

"Right. She relapsed. It was so bad!"

"Hayley, that's horrible!"

"I'm sorry that I'm a bad influence on everyone." I stand up. "I'm just no good for anyone!"

"Whoa. I didn't say that." He sits up slowly "Maybe you should text her to see if she's all right."

"Yes, you're right. I should do that right now."

I rip the comforter off him and feel around the mattress.

"What are you doing?"

"Where is my phone?" I point at him with blame.

"You said it was dead last night. You asked me to charge it."

"WHERE?" I climb back onto the bed and crawl closer to him.

"It's on your nightstand. Right behind you."

"Oh." I turn around and see it. I pull it off the charger, jump from the bed, and run into the living room. I hear him get up and follow behind me. I sit down on the couch.

No, no, no, no.

"Hayley, did something else happen last night? I'm just very concerned—"

"Why do you need to know everything? It's not like you tell me everything. You tell me nothing. Nothing! I don't know what part of Scotland you're from, I don't know why you came here...or even how you got here! For all I know, you could be a murderer. A murderer who escaped from prison and swam across the border to freedom."

"Uh... I don't know how to swim."

"Oh, so the rest is true then?" I slam my phone down beside me on the couch, but I don't let go of it.

"I'm not talking about this right now. You're being too paranoid."

"Right now? You never talk about it!"

"It's my story—"

"Oh my fucking God! Just leave me alone, please! I just need a minute. Go back in the bedroom. Go back to sleep."

"I can't go back to sleep. Danny has to get up for school soon."

"Great. Go...pack his lunch or something!"

"That's what I was going to do." He walks toward the kitchen.

I pick my phone back up and look through it. Nothing here that looks suspicious... Still, I shouldn't let Peter anywhere near it. What if Tristian texts me? I push my phone into the pocket of my pajama pants and lay across the couch, shoving my face into the cushions.

CHAPTER FOURTEEN

Peter

"Peter, do me a favor and refill the freezer behind the bar," Sean says, peering out the back door of the building.

I wipe my head with a dish towel and lean against the cool bricks. "The ice machine stopped working."

"When?"

"When I came in this afternoon, it was completely empty."

"Great!" He shouts and throws his hands in the air. "Just fucking wonderful!"

He goes back inside, slamming the door. I'm just about to light a cigarette when he comes back out with a white bucket.

"Here. Walk down the street to that Japanese joint and ask them for some of their ice." He drops the bucket on the ground.

"I'm not going to walk to the sushi restaurant and beg them for ice. I'll look like a complete ass."

"You think I'm going to let you serve warm drinks at my bar?"

I laugh and roll my eyes toward the night sky, then back at him. He's serious. I put the cigarette back in the box and shove it into my apron before grabbing the bucket.

Bampot...Complete bampot... I don't even know how to approach this.

I follow the alley behind our building until I reach the rear of My Tokyo. I put the bucket down on the concrete and place my hands on my hips, puffing my cheeks out with air. Finally, I knock on the rusty metal door. A man in a white chef's coat pushes it open. He looks me up and down, then spits just past my shoe.

"Hi, uhm... I'm from McAlister's." I eye the little clump of phlegm near my foot. "You know, right down the street. Our ice machine broke, and—"

"And?" he asks.

"And my boss said I should ask you if we can have some ice."

"We don't sell our ice."

"Wow. Okay. I think it was supposed to be more like you do us a favor, and maybe someday...we can repay you."

"How can you repay me?"

"With alcohol," I answer without thinking.

"When?"

"Anytime."

"Your boss said that?"

"Yup."

I feel my phone vibrate in my apron.

"That's a pretty good deal. Frozen water for booze?"

"It's a one-time offer. Take it or leave it."

I feel my phone vibrate again. I hope it's not Danny. I hope everything's okay...

"Sure, I'll take it. How much ice do you need?"

"For now, can you fill up this bucket?" I say as I hand it over to him.

"No, but you can come inside and fill it up yourself."

"Okay, will do."

He holds the door open for me, and I walk inside.

"Where's the ice machine?"

"Basement." He signals toward some stairs.

"Cool. Thanks." I head down the stairs and feel my phone vibrate again. Three texts in a row? Now I'm really worried. I set the bucket down at the bottom of the steps and pull my phone out of my apron. It's a number I don't know.

```
I fucked ur girlfriend
last night.
I got ur # out her
phone.
This is Tristian
```

I put the phone down and pace around the basement. My left hand is on my cheek, and my right grips the phone tighter. I slap it against my leg, clenching and grinding my teeth. What the fuck? Maybe he's making this up to get a reaction out of me, but this would explain why Hayley got home so late and acted so strange...

My phone vibrates again.

```
I no u read my text. 2
pussy 2 answer?
```

I start typing, then stop. No, that's exactly what he wants.

"Are you getting ice or running laps around my basement?" the man asks from the top of the steps.

"Both." I pick the bucket back up and head to the ice machine. I don't want to argue with this guy now.

"Hurry up. My dinner service is about to start. There's too many people in the kitchen as it is."

I start furiously shoveling ice into the bucket. I'm really supposed to work a full shift thinking about this fucking— FUCK!

My phone vibrates again. This FUCKER! Oh... Never mind. It's Danny.

```
I need a shoe box 2
make some stupid
freaking diarrhea
Diorama**
LOL THAT'S SO FUNNY
```

Lord Jesus Christ, Mary, and St. Joseph.

"Are you taking ice or texting? I am not joking. You have to move!"

"All right! All done." I slam the machine door shut and shove my phone into my pocket. "Thanks."

I get out of there, hustling down the alleyway with my heavy bucket full of ice. When I get back to my bar, I hurry inside and dump the ice into the freezer. I pull my phone back out.

```
          You can check my
      closet, but I don't
   think I have any shoe
       boxes. Perhaps in
           Hayley's room?
        I hope this is not
           due tomorrow.
```

I put my phone back in my apron. I don't even release my grasp before it vibrates again. There's no way he looked in both closets that quickly.

I pull my phone out again and look down.

Yo what the fuck
u talking about man?

Fuck, I sent that to Tristian. Do I answer now?

That wasn't supposed
to go to you.

No fucking duh. Are u
gonna answer me bro?
Or na?

I said I fucked ur
girlfriend n ur talkin
bout shoes?

Ex-Girlfriend, I
suppose.

What would you like,
a round of applause?

Nah.

I wanna kick ur ass is
what I want.

I'm trying to work.

Also, your phone has
auto-correct, doesn't
it? Why is everything
spelled wrong?

STFU!

I will come 2 the bar
n kick ur ass.

I'm confused...
Shouldn't I be the
one who's angry?

Why are you kicking
my ass?

Another text...Danny

So I looked in ur
closet

no shoeboxes but I
found this like round
circle box thing and
it has a bunch of $ in
it

can I just dump the $
out and use it?

No!

No. Do not do that.

I won't lose any of
the money Peter!!!

I'll just put it
somewhere else for
safe keeping like one
of ur drawers?

No!

Do not open my
drawers. I'll find
you a shoe box
tomorrow.

It's do tomorrow.

Why do you do this to
me?

PETER WHAT AM I
SUPPOSED TO DO STOP
MAKING THIS ABOUT U

U ALWAYS DO THIS!!!!!
😠😠😠

Fine! Dump the cash
out! Put it in the
kitchen.

I want you to take
all of the cooking
utensils out of the
red jar on the
counter by the stove.
Put the cash in the
jar, then put the
utensils back on top.

Y?

```
That's soooooo much
work.
                              Just do it.
                    I have to get back to
                                    work.
Can I have 10$?
                    CASH. IN THE RED JAR.
                                     NOW.
Ok chill God 😑
```

I slam my phone down on the bar and rub my eyes. When I open them, there's Sean, leaning on the bar and staring at me.

"I don't pay you to text your friends."

"Neither one of the people I am texting is a friend."

"I don't pay you to text, period!"

"That sounds great to me. You want my phone? I don't want it right now."

"I don't want your fucking phone. I want you to get the bar set before we open. You haven't cut the lemons or limes yet, and I don't see any of the glasses taken out of the dishwasher."

"I'll do it now." I bend and open the mini fridge below the bar. I hear Sean mumble and walk away.

In the fridge, I find a bag of lemons. I also find a couple of bottles of Guinness...

Plenty of bartenders drink while they work. That might make this night a little better.

I feel my phone vibrate once more.

Okay, I definitely need this. I deserve this.

I sit on the floor and crack open the beer with my bottle opener. After a few swigs, I put it back in the fridge. I don't close the door, I just stare at the open bottle. I take it out once more and chug down the entire thing, then throw it into the garbage can.

I feel like a teenager again. Hey, at least Danny isn't doing this. That's a plus.

All right. Time to cut the lemons.

Danny

It's midnight, but I have my sneakers on. My diorama looks like complete freaking trash! I only have this round box, some construction paper, and some dried-up freaking markers. It's not my fault. What artist can work with these tools?

I'm on the floor, staring at this piece of crap, when Peter walks up the stairs. He's just standing there, watching me. I match his stare and kick the diorama for emphasis. He sighs, takes off his jacket, and heads toward the coat rack.

"Keep it on," I say. "We're going for a walk. Long day."

He stops. "You aren't kidding... Hey, I know I said I wouldn't be tired for you, but—"

"So you lied?"

"I was going to say..." He puts his jacket back on. "Let's go."

"Hey," Hayley says as she walks down the hallway past me. She kisses Peter. Oh, he looks *pissed!* "What's wrong?" she asks.

I kick my diorama again. We don't have time for this. PETER IS TALKING TO *ME!*

"Stop kicking that, Danny," Peter says.

"What's wrong is I made this shitty diorama! I didn't have the right supplies, and now I'm going to fail."

"I'll call your teacher tomorrow and ask him for an extension. I'll tell him it's my fault. But when you get to high school, you have to start owning your mistakes. It's time to start keeping an agenda book and starting your projects way before they're due."

"What, did you read that in one of those stupid books?" I kick the diorama again, harder. It flies into a dining room chair like a hockey puck. Peter looks down at it, and then back at me.

"Actually, I did...and I think it's a good idea." He puts his hand out to me. "Come on, stand up."

I don't reach for it. I fold my arms and glare.

"If you want to go for a walk, we're going now. It's already past midnight. You have school tomorrow, and I have work. You have ten seconds to stand up, or I'm going to bed."

"I'm so down to go to bed," Hayley says and grabs his arm.

I'm going to BARF UP MY GUTS.

"Yeah, not with you." Peter wiggles his arm free. Woah! What? HUH?

"Ten...Nine...Eight...Seven," Peter counts.

I jump up.

"Okay, I'm up. Let's go."

"What do you mean, not with me?" she asks.

"I want the bed to myself tonight. You can sleep in your own bed."

"Why?"

"Maybe he wants to stretch out...or maybe you fart in your sleep. Ever think of that?" I ask Hayley.

"Enough, Danny," Peter replies. "Let's go."

He walks down the stairs, opens the front door, and walks outside. Hayley and I both look at each other for a few seconds. I quickly follow behind Peter.

Peter

"I'M LEAVING!"

"You don't have to yell, Danny. I can hear you," I say as I walk into the living room.

"Okay, bye."

"Have a good day. I love you."

"Was it nice having your bed all to yourself again?" He holds tightly to the straps of his backpack and smiles. He's really enjoying this.

"Wonderful."

"Nice. Love you too. Bye!"

I watch him walk out the door, then I head back into my bedroom. I've collected all of Hayley's things neatly in a plastic tub. I pick it up and make my way into her old room. She doesn't have the door closed. I drop the tub on the floor. She's sitting up on her bed with her back against the headboard.

"I couldn't sleep," she says. "What's that?"

"It's all your shit."

"Why are you kicking me out of your room?"

"Because we're done. That's it."

"Why?"

Like she doesn't already know.

"Because! I was trying to work last night, and somehow Tristian managed to get my number out of your phone. He told me that he FUCKED YOU on Wednesday."

Her eyes grow wider, and she raises her eyebrows. She brings her knees up to her chest and wraps her arms around them. She takes a deep breath and starts to cry, shoving her face into her legs.

"I didn't mean to!" she says without removing her face from her thighs. "It was just supposed to be two friends getting high together...but it turned into—"

"What happened to quitting?"

"I can't do it. I tried! I keep going back."

"Just stay away from me for a little while, okay?" I turn around to walk away.

"It was a mistake!" she yells in between tears.

I face her again, and her mouth falls open. She whimpers and tries to catch her breath, choking on her own saliva.

Grow up.

"So, you regret it, and it will never happen again?"

She doesn't answer me, just looks down and sniffles loudly. She picks at a scab on her shin.

"Stop crying and answer the question," I add.

"I don't want to!" She squeezes her fingers together and pulls her legs in even closer. My heart falls.

"Answer it. Yes or no!" I demand and walk closer to her.

She snaps her head in my direction.

"No! I don't regret it. I don't! You want the truth? Unlike you, I can tell the whole fucking truth!" She lets go of her legs and roughly swipes her eyes with the back of her hand. When she stands, she points at me. I start to back away. "I'm only twenty-one years old. I need some fucking excitement, and you? You're fucking boring!"

"I—"

I'm still backing up, but she's coming closer and closer.

"Your personality is boring, and your sex is even...*boringer*. Everything about you is a total bore! You might have responsibilities, or whatever, but I *never* signed up to be Danny's mommy, and that's what I'm really starting to feel like. So yes, Peter, I was craving attention, and affection, and some fucking thrill, so I went to Tristian. Happy?"

My back hits the wall. Her finger is now digging into my chest, and her face is in mine. Tears race down her cheeks. Her teeth are chattering.

I press my lips together and move my jaw around in a circle, processing every word. I furrow my eyebrows and push her pointing finger off of me.

"Do you at least regret all the hurt that you caused me? You couldn't have just broken it off with me, then ran off with him? You had to lie to me? Cheat on me? And let him tell me?"

"It's not my fault! You—" She tries to point again, but I swat her hand away.

"Nothing is, is it? It's all 'Que, Sera, Sera', and fate, and fucking star signs, huh?"

"PETER!" I hear Danny yell and the front door slam. What the fuck? "I FORGOT MY DIORAMA."

I head toward the door.

"See what I mean? Do you see?" Her voice wobbles. "We can't even have this fucking conversation without—"

"Fuck off." I don't look at her. I just walk into the living room and pretend like she doesn't exist anymore. Danny is standing by the couch.

"I ripped the paper off and took my box back, Danny."

"You what? Why?"

"You said it was trash and it you were going to fail. Didn't I say I would call your teacher today? I'll stop at the store and get craft stuff for you. You're going to miss the bus. Get going!"

"Can I come with you to the craft store so I can pick my own supplies?"

"No. You're not missing first period again."

"How is an artist supposed to work when he can't even pick his own tools?"

"That's how all the best artists work." I don't even know what the fuck I'm talking about anymore.

"Like who?"

"Vincent..."

"Vincent?"

"The one with no ear. Okay, time for school."

Danny pulls his phone out of his pocket and taps the screen. "Look at the time... Darn! Looks like I already missed the bus. Aw shucks. Guess I'll just have to go to the store with you instead of math. I was really looking forward to numbers this morning too."

"Get in the car," I reply.

"Right now?"

"Yup. You might even be a little early. You can sit in the library and study."

"Uh...Maybe I can still catch the bus."

"Get in the car, Danny. Right now!"

He rolls his eyes at me, then walks down the stairs and out the door. I follow behind him. Now he's jiggling the handle of the car door. I press the unlock button on my key. He gets in the passenger side, sinking into the seat with his arms folded. I head to the driver's side.

"I need glue, glitter to make the sun, tissue paper, googly eyes, new markers, American flag stickers, scissors—"

"We have scissors." I buckle my seat belt and start the car.

"You didn't let me finish! I need those scissors that cut cool designs. You know, like wavy, to make the water look more realistic."

My phone vibrates in the cup holder. I must have left it in here overnight. Great. Just great.

"Who's texting you right now?" he asks.

"Santa. I'm actually an elf from the North Pole," I say while backing out.

"I'd believe it," Danny says.

I stop the car and look at him with my eyebrows raised.

"What?" He laughs. "I'm just joking!"

I finish pulling out, and he picks up my phone.

"Put it down."

"Who is this? Someone wants to fight you? I'll beat the shit out of this guy! Who is this? What's your passcode?"

"What'd he say?"

I pull out of the apartment complex. We're on the road.

"I showed up at McAlister's last night, and you weren't there," Danny reads. "Too afraid to fight me? I get it, I'd kill you."

"I was there! He never showed up."

Wow. That was fucking asinine... What kind of example am I creating?

"Who is this?"

"Tristian. Nintendo tattoos, smells like ass."

"Oh, I'd love to kick the shit out of that string bean," he replies.

"Didn't we talk about fighting? No fighting!"

"I thought you meant fighting with words?"

"You know I meant physically fighting too, Danny!"

"You were going to have a fight last night. I just read the texts!"

"No, I was not. I wouldn't have fought him. He's pathetic. I don't even understand why he wants to fight me. Because I'm much smaller than him? So that he can feel tough?"

"Is this why you told Hayley to sleep in the other room last night?"

"Yup."

"So, you're done with her?"

"Yup."

"So, she's going to move out?"

"No, Danny. She's not moving out."

"Why not? You want to live with your ex? That's weird."

"She has nowhere to go."

"She can move in with Tristian."

"He's sleeping on his friend's floor."

"What a loser." Danny laughs.

"Yes, because only losers get into physical altercations." I look over, and he rolls his eyes.

"Yeah, yeah. Did she cheat on you?"

"Why would you ask me that?"

"Seems like it. I mean everything was fine, and then it wasn't."

"Nope. No, that's not what happened." I cough a wee bit, gripping the steering wheel tighter—one finger at a time—and locking my elbows.

"She did, didn't she?"

"Is this diorama for history class? What is your teacher's name again?"

"Mr. Gates."

"Gates, like Bill... I'll remember that."

We pull up in front of the school.

"You said that the first time," Danny replies as he swings the door open.

"This time I mean it."

He gets out of the car and looks back at me. "She sucks, anyway."

"Yeah. Like you said when I took the TV... Way more than I do, right?"

"ONE THOUSAND TIMES MORE THAN YOU DO."

I laugh. "Have a good day, Danny."

"See you later."

He closes the car door and walks up to the building.

CHAPTER FIFTEEN

Hayley

"Why the fuck did you text him?" I ask Tristian as I approach Ryan's front door.

"Because I knew you wouldn't have the balls to do it."

"I was going to break up with him! You didn't need to hurt him like that. I still have to live with him!"

"Tell him to shut his mouth, or I'll wire his jaw closed for him." He puts a cigarette up to his lips. We start walking down the street.

"What is your obsession with fighting him? He doesn't want to fight you!"

"Tacos?" Tristian asks.

That was out of nowhere, but tacos do sound good right now.

"Sure... Okay." I dig around my purse.

"I have money," he says.

"I wasn't looking for money. I have this for you." I pull the spare key out of my purse. "You wanted it, right?"

He takes the cigarette out of his mouth, exhales, and smiles...like he's been waiting for this day forever.

"Thank you."

I place it in his hand, and he wraps his fingers slowly around it. He's completely still for a couple of seconds.

"Just do not cause any trouble with Peter, please."

"I'll try. You know how he is."

"Clean up after yourself if I'm not home. Don't leave any evidence that you were there."

"Yup."

"And don't steal anything, Tristian! I'm trusting you."

"Shut up, already! You changed since you got with him."

"No, I haven't. I'm just asking you to listen to me."

"Scared he'll kick you out?"

"Sometimes I don't know with him. He has like a switch in his brain or something. He can be the sweetest little thing, then the next minute it's like a bomb goes off in his head."

"I'm not afraid of a little fucking troll. I'll put him six feet under."

"Stop saying that."

"Why?"

"I don't like it. Is that a good enough reason? It makes me feel bad. Can you stop? Can't I tell you anything without you talking about murder?"

"Because he has little man complex and someone needs to put him in his place!"

"He doesn't want to fight you, Tristian! Will you listen to me?"

"Yeah, because he knows he'll die."

I start power walking away from him. I don't want to listen to this anymore. I don't want to hear another word about Peter.

"Where are you going?"

"I want to get away from you. I want to get away from everyone!"

"Hals!"

I stop walking and turn around.

"Don't 'Hals' me. I just want you to stop talking about Peter. Please! Oh...and if you want this to work, stop trying to fight my battles for me! You never should have texted him. Going through my phone for his number? That wasn't okay."

He digs around in his pocket with his tongue hanging out of his mouth. I fold my arms and stare at him.

"Well?" I ask.

"Sure thing, boss." He pulls out a small plastic bag filled with pills. "A deal's a deal, right? More Oxys for my very own key."

I snatch the bag out of his hand, inspect it, then shove it into my purse.

"I don't understand why you want a key so badly. It's not like I leave the apartment that much. I could just let you in,"

"It's the general principal. It's the idea of the key."

What the fuck does that mean? I side-eye him.

"What? Just feels good to hold it," he continues. "My dad always said a man feels differently when he's holding a key to his very own home."

"Yeah, except it's not yours, it's—"

"I don't want to hear it!"

"All right. Whatever... Did you listen to my rules?"

"Yeah. Don't fight your battles. Don't kill the troll. Got it."

"Right."

"Now tacos?"

"I want a quesadilla," I say and pout.

"Fine. They got those too."

We walk down the sidewalk hand in hand.

Peter

Hayley's watching TV, so I do what make sense. I turn on the vacuum, whistling as I push it around the coffee table.

"Fine. I guess I'm not watching anything, then." She presses on the power button of the remote.

I pretend not to hear her.

"I SAID I GUESS I'M NOT WATCHING ANYTHING. YOU MIGHT AS WELL JUST FORGET I'M EVEN HERE!" She yells.

I power off the vacuum and turn around quickly. Carpet's clean enough, anyway.

"Oh, I will. Didn't need the invitation. I'll forget you're here just like how you forgot about me."

"How could I forget about you when you're so fucking obnoxious?"

I laugh and turn the vacuum back on.

"There's nothing on the floor!" she yells.

"I like to clean!" I yell back.

"Yeah, when I'm trying to watch my shows."

I turn the vacuum off again. "You like to fuck other men when you're in relationships. Which one of those two things is worse?"

"I thought you were pretending I'm not here?"

"Oh, I absolutely am, but I won't pretend he's not here. I'm warning you. Do not bring him here!"

"You know what? I'm not going to sit around and be threatened." She stands, pulling a throw blanket off of the couch, and walks down the hallway.

I follow her.

"Don't think you can pull a fast one on me! If he comes here while I'm at work, I'll know it, and I'll make sure—"

She slams her bedroom door in my face. That won't stop me. That door isn't soundproof! I keep going, and going, and going.

"I'll make sure you're both out of here! He's been fucking with me long enough. I'll call the fucking police. I'll get an order of protection. I have proof that he threatened to show up at my job. It's all on my phone. That will keep him the fuck out of here!" I proclaim.

She opens the door. "Why? Because you know he'd kill you? If you two had a fight, you'd be fucking dead, and you're scared."

"I AM NOT SCARED OF HIM! I just want him to leave me ALONE. Do you think the way he's been antagonizing me is okay?"

"I already told him he's not going to fight you. That's fucking ridiculous! So, calm your tits, and get away from me."

"These tits will not be calmed! I'd fight that STUPID, GRIMY, FUCK any day of the week! I don't want him in MY house. I don't want him near DANNY. What don't you understand?"

"I don't understand why both of you are so obsessed with each other. That's what I don't understand, okay? I have to listen to him bitch about you when I'm not home, then when I come home, I listen to you bitch about him. Just shut the fuck up already! He's not going to hurt Danny or even say two words to Danny. No one gives a fuck about Danny besides you. Get over yourself!"

She slams the door in my face again. I want to say something else, but I have nothing else to say. I walk away from her room with my hands in the pockets of my jeans.

Yeah...I think I made myself crystal clear. Time for work.

Hayley

"What the fuck?" Tristian asks as he digs through our fridge. He moves meats and vegetables to the counter until he reaches the back.

"What's wrong?" I stand from the kitchen table.

"There's nothing to eat in here. Only stuff you have to cook."

"Yeah, Peter cooks it for us."

"What about microwaveable stuff?"

"Check the freezer."

He opens the freezer. "More vegetables? How many vegetables does this guy eat?"

"Honestly, I hardly ever see him eat anything. He usually cooks for me and Danny, and then goes to work. He basically lives off of granola bars and whatever Danny and I leave behind."

"That's probably why he looks like a fucking twig. Nah, this isn't working." He closes the freezer. "A man's gotta eat. We gotta get some food."

He's right. Peter is pretty skinny.

"Like what?"

"Microwavable pizzas, ramen, Jamaican beef patties."

"We could go to the store."

"Nah, let's just get fast food. More bang for your buck."

Fast food again? Can my digestive tract take any more punishment?

"Fine, but let's eat at the restaurant." I look at my phone. "Peter will be home soon."

"I don't give a fuck."

"Well, I do. Okay?"

"Why?"

"Because he said he would call the police if he saw you here. You really want to get the police involved? Let's just get dinner, eat there, and then I'll see you tomorrow or something."

"He's not going to call the police. He's full of shit. I don't know how much longer I can put up with this crap. Being told what to do. Being told I can't go to my own girlfriend's apartment. It's not working for me. I am straight up not this person. I'm gonna snap."

I know he's not that person. Tauruses hate being told what to do. It's not his fault.

I grab my purse off of the table and head toward the couch. I pull my sneakers on over my feet without untying the laces. For some reason, that always feels like a big accomplishment. I wonder what my horoscope says today? I'll check it out after lunch.

"Did you hear me?" Tristian calls from the kitchen.

"Yeah, I heard you. Instead of fast food, you wanna try something new?"

"Like what?"

"There's this new deli down the street. They make huge sandwiches. Peter and I split one once. It was pretty good. I think I have a picture of the menu in my phone."

"Fine. I'll take a look."

I sit back on the couch. I hope he doesn't choose something with roast beef. I'm not in the mood. Maybe I should get Peter something while we're there. When's the last time I saw him eat anything? But then Tristian might think—

Never mind. No way. Not putting myself through that.

I look around the room. Maybe I should do a quick sweep of the apartment now, just to make sure nothing is out of place or seems suspicious.

Nothing's out of the ordinary in the living room. I walk down the hall and look in the bathroom. Very clean. I inspect the dining room table last. I think I'm in the clear. I take a seat. Okay, what's taking him so long?

"Tristian?" I call.

"Yeah."

"Did you pick something?"

"What is this?" He walks into the living room, holding my phone.

"What is what? You're supposed to be looking at the menu, not going through my phone again."

"Well, I thought this was the menu, but it's not. It's...Is this a life insurance policy?"

What is he talking about?

"Give me it."

He hands me the phone, and I look at the screen.

"Oh. It's Peter's." I hand him back the phone. "Now, look at the menu. I'm hungry."

"And you're a beneficiary on Peter's life insurance policy?"

Why the fuck does he care? I feel my stomach rumble. I really want something with barbeque sauce.

"I'm just going to come out and say it... Can you choose something other than beef? I think I want chicken. Maybe barbeque sauce and onions?"

"Sure, whatever you want, Hals." He paces around the room staring at my phone.

"Can you call in the order?"

"So, if he dies, we'd get one hundred thousand dollars?"

"He's not dying. He's perfectly healthy."

"Young people die all the time."

I really don't like the direction this is going.

"I'm going to stop you right there, Tristian." I grab my phone from his hands.

"I'm just trying to understand how it works."

"I know what you're thinking, and I don't like it."

"What are you talking about?"

"Knock it off, Tristian!"

"I'm serious. What are you accusing me of?"

"Hurting Peter. I know you are."

"That's not what I was thinking at all," he says with a straight face.

"Oh, okay then. Sorry." Now I feel stupid.

"You'd have to do it."

What the fuck?

"I would never do anything like that!" I yell.

I am all shades of fucked up, but I would never kill anyone, especially not Peter.

"Why? You love him?"

"No, I don't love him. Because I'm not a fucking murderer, that's why!"

"This would hardly be a murder. You'd drop something in a beverage that may or may not be his. He'd pick up that beverage and drink it. He'd do it to himself without even realizing. So, kind of like an assisted suicide."

"Who do you think I am, my mother? I told you how I feel about all the shit she did. I can't believe you!"

"I can't believe you like being told what to do by some scrawny little fuck...and you don't even have the balls to stand up for yourself. It's self-defense."

"Stand up for myself? Killing someone is standing up for myself?"

"We'd have the money to get our own apartment. It wouldn't even be a bad death. You know what a bad trip feels like? That's basically what would happen to him, he just wouldn't wake up."

"SHUT UP, TRISTIAN! SHUT UP!" I hold back tears. Angry tears? Sad tears? Who is he? I know he always talks about fighting, but he's never planned a murder before—at least, I don't think he has? Maybe Peter was right about getting a restraining order.

I sit on the couch, cradling my head in my hands.

"Are you okay, Hayley?"

"Do I look okay? I am not fucking okay with what you're saying!"

"I'm sorry. It was just an idea. I thought I could share everything with you without any judgment."

"MURDER, TRISTIAN? MURDERING MY FRIEND? MY EX- BOYFRIEND? I don't love him, but I do care about him!"

"I just said it was only an idea. Are you listening to me? Nothing's going to happen to him, okay? As long as he doesn't do anything to hurt you, because if he does, then all bets are off."

Does he really care about me? What does he care about?

I look up at him. He kneels on the floor and grabs my hands. I take a couple of short, deep breaths.

"I want us to have our own place, I really do," I answer, my voice shaking, "but I won't hurt Peter to get it. Please, never say anything like that to me again."

"I won't, but someone has to put you first eventually, Hayley...and sometimes that person has to be you. Survival of the fittest, you know?"

Do I really care about me? What do I care about? I lean back, covering my face with my hands again.

"Let's go get you that barbecue sandwich."

I'm so upset about what just happened that I forgot I was hungry in the first place. I think if I eat now, I might vomit. I open up my purse and pull out a small plastic bag of pills. I place two on my tongue and pulverize them with my teeth.

"Fine. Let's go." I stand.

I feel so lost, trapped...like I've been stranded here for my whole life. My mother...Tristian...Peter...the pills... SOS.

Danny

I make my way up the stairs with my diorama of the battle of Gettysburg. President Lincoln flies over the top of the diorama in a superhero cape.

"TA-DAH!" I place it triumphantly on the dining room table. Peter walks over and inspects it.

"I thought this was for history class?"

"It is."

"What's Batman doing there?"

"That's Lincoln!"

"In a cape and face mask?"

"That's his hat!"

"Why is he beaming people with laser vision?"

"It's a modern take on the Battle of Gettysburg! Don't you have any imagination?"

"I guess not. Is your teacher going to be okay with this?"

"He appreciates true art."

"Okay. Sure."

"History is kinda cool. Lincoln was a bad ass."

"Well, I'm glad you're enjoying something at school."

Hayley walks down the hallway with headphones in her ears. She plops down on the couch, opens a magazine, and starts playing the drums on her lap. I wonder what song she's listening to. I can't tell by her drumming because she has crappy rhythm.

"Danny, go put your diorama in your room," Peter says.

"I want to show it to Hayley."

"What? Why? No. Go put it in your room."

"Because she said that my diorama was going to look like a big freaking turd no matter what crafting supplies I had. I want to show her how good it is." I pick it back up.

"It doesn't look like a turd. Let's go." He pushes me down the hall.

"What's the rush?"

We walk into my room together. I put the diorama on my bed. He closes the door behind us.

"If you see Tristian—you know, Nintendo tattoos? If you see him while I am at work *ever again*, you text me right away. No, you call me right away! As soon as you see him, you dial my number."

"Or I could just beat the crap out of him and call it a day."

"NO! DON'T EVEN JOKE ABOUT THAT! Do not go near him. Do not say *anything to him*. Go directly to your room. Lock the door. Call me ASAP. Do you hear me?"

"All right, all right! I'll go into my room and call you." I flop backward on my bed and put my diorama on my chest. I shake it and watch Lincoln fly around like a crazy guy.

"Good. I have to go to work, and I'm scared out of my mind."

"Why?" I look away from Lincoln.

"I need you to be safe. I need to know that he's not here, but if he does come, I need to know that you'll do exactly what I tell you. I don't know him very well, but I do know he's not a good person."

"Stop worrying. I'll do exactly what you said. Okay?" I go back to rocking Lincoln's world.

"Thank you." He takes a deep breath. "Have a good night. Do your homework. Dinner is in the fridge. Just stick the entire tray in the oven at three seventy-five for thirty-five minutes. No projects due tomorrow that I need to know about, right?"

"No, just some dumb essay on some dumb book that I'm almost done with."

"You actually started your essay ahead of time? That's great!"

"What? I meant I'm almost done with the book. I haven't started the essay yet."

He doesn't say anything to me. He just walks out of my room. I guess Hayley has to drive him to work now.

CHAPTER SIXTEEN

Nobody

It's two o'clock in the morning. I hear footsteps just outside my bedroom window. Is it Ma? Adair? They wouldn't be outside at this time. I peer out the window. A shadow of a person is walking toward our barn.

Fucking assholes trying to steal our chickens again! You'd think they'd be smart enough not to come by the fucking house.

I go into my hamper, pulling out a pair of jeans and a wool sweater. I slip on the moccasins by my end table. Not the best to wear outside, but I don't hear any rain, so...

Finally, I get on my hands and knees. I pull Pop's shotgun out from under my bed and hold it while leaving my room.

"Where are you going?"

It's Ma. She's standing in the hall, clutching the cross-pendant dangling from the chain around her neck.

"Going to see who's outside and what they want."

"You know how to shoot that?"

"Of course I do. I'm a man. Is Adair still sleeping?" I ask.

"Yes, he hasn't woken up."

"Just makes sure he stays inside. He thinks he's tough, but he's not."

I head out the door, pointing the shotgun in front of me with my finger on the trigger. I move slowly so as not to be heard. The chickens start going crazy in their coop. I run in that direction. Why can't these basturts get their own chickens? I know it's been hard around here lately, but come on.

I lean against the tool shed beside the chicken coop, taking a deep breath and closing my eyes to prepare myself. I've never done anything like this before. I turn the corner sharply, pointing the gun straight ahead.

"Get the hell away from my chickens!"

A lass screams. A girl? They sent a girl? I put my gun down. No... It's the beautiful tourist girl from the bakery this morning.

"What? What are you doing here?" I ask.

"I-I was just playing with the chickens!"

"You were playing with my chickens? Who plays with chickens? Chickens don't play!"

"Sure they do, see!" She points at them. They're running erratically in circles and screaming.

"They're terrified, for Christ's sake. That's fear! Also, it's the middle of the night. You woke us all up!"

"Sorry... I'm sorry. I wanted to see you! I left a note on the front door for you. Then I heard chickens and—"

"You left me a note?" I smile. "Better hope my mum doesn't see it. She doesn't want me near any girls."

"Why not?"

"She thinks I'm girl crazy. I should be focusing on my responsibilities and God." I laugh.

"Are you girl crazy?"

"Well..."

She laughs too.

"What's your name?" I ask.

"Teva."

"Teva from Glasgow... I like it."

"And you are?"

I tell her my name. She smiles back at me.

"Do your parents know you're here scaring my chickens and waking my family?" I ask.

"No. They're sleeping. I have my own glamping pod."

"Glamping..." I say again with a chuckle. "Is that an English word?"

"Yes. Why, you don't speak it?"

"We speak some. Just enough to get by and make sales. Our whole community is big on 'preserving the culture.' My ma is very strict about it too. We're not allowed to speak any English in our house."

"Wow. That's..."

"Crazy?" I say in English. "I know that word. Everyone here is a rocket. Isn't that why you tourists come here instead of the bigger islands? To see crazy people?"

"That is not why we came here! And I wasn't going to say crazy. I was going to say different. I speak English and Gaelic...Spanish...a little French."

"Wow!"

"My parents wanted me to learn as many languages as possible."

"That's so cool. I wish my mum wanted me to do something cool. No one here wants to do anything cool. They basically just started allowing tourists."

"Do you know that Glasgow is only a ferry ride away?"

"What?"

"You said you wanted to see a city?"

"My mum would absolutely disown me. We aren't even allowed to attend school. Not enough religion. All the kids get homeschooled."

"Then I guess I'll have to come visit you every once in a while."

I rub the back of my head and gaze down. "You'd come all the way here just to see me? What is that? Nine hours?"

"I would."

"Why? I hardly know you."

"I think you're handsome."

I can literally feel myself blushing. Good thing it's dark out. How embarrassing.

"Well...I think you're beautiful."

"How about tomorrow I meet you outside the bakery. Say...two o'clock?"

"Your parents will let you meet me?"

"Of course! My parents let me go to Japan by myself."

"Are you serious? Can we switch parents?"

"Well, not all by myself...but without them. They'll let me meet you, though. I can do whatever I want."

"Oh...okay."

"Do you have a phone number?" she asks.

"That's a good one..."

"Really? You don't even use phones here?"

"In my house? Not even phones."

"So how do you talk to people?"

"Write them letters, or just walk into town. It's a small community."

"I don't know how you stand it!"

"Me either. Now stop bothering my chickens, and go back to bed."

"But that one's cute!" She points to one in the coop.

I fling the shotgun over my shoulder.

"That one, right there?" I clarify as I kneel and gesture.

"Yes."

"Shame, really. That one's dinner tomorrow." I rub my chin.

"ARE YOU SERIOUS?"

I laugh. "No."

"Oh, thank God!"

"I mean...it's possible. We do eat them." I tilt my head and examine the selected chicken more closely.

"Haud yer wheesht!"

I laugh again and stand.

"Do you kill them yourself?" she asks.

"Me? Well, I..."

I don't know how to answer. I could tell her the truth. I'm a complete Jessie, and I won't slaughter any of the animals...but then maybe she'll feel the same way about me as my ma does.

"Seriously, I have to go back inside before my mum gets suspicious," I answer.

"Okay, okay..."

We start heading in opposite directions. Then I remember something. I should warn her about the hill in front of the road. I'm sure that's how she got here.

"Be careful walking down that fucking hill." *I turn around and point into the distance.* "I must've rolled down it a hundred times."

"I won't roll down it!"

"See you tomorrow."

I continue walking to my house, smiling the entire way. When I reach the door, I see the note. It reads:

```
Hey stranger,

It was nice meeting you today. You can
come visit me if you'd like. Our
camping site is called Samson's. I'm in
the second pod from the shore. I'll be
there until Monday.

I hope you come see me,

Teva (Girl from the bakery)
```

Samson's, eh? Haven't seen him or his kids in a long while. That's how he's making money these days? Tourists? "Glamping?" Farming really is a dying industry around here. Soil's been really bad. It's not all my fault, if even Goraidh Samson couldn't make it...

I rip the note off the door, shove it in my pocket, and walk inside. Ma is sitting on the couch directly in front of me. She stands.

"Well, who was it?"

I quietly shut the door, then turn to face her. "Just some of those daftys from the farm over. They wanted to borrow some eggs."

"Did you shoot them?" She steps closer.

"No, Ma."

"I knew you wouldn't. Did you give them eggs?"

"No, Ma."

"Okay, good. You must finish the fence. That will stop them from coming on our property."

I laugh. "Yeah, I'll build a great big fence, honey," I say in a deep voice, mimicking my dead father. "Fetch me a beer while I do it."

Ma slaps me behind my shoulder. "Don't do that!"

"I don't know how to build a fence, Ma."

"Adair said your father was teaching you two when he was working on it, before he got sick."

"Yeah, well, I didn't pay any attention."

"I wouldn't expect anything else from you, lazy boy. Ask Adair. He'll remember some things."

I roll my eyes and grab a cloth from the kitchen. I head to the couch, sit, and begin polishing the shotgun barrel.

"I'm not asking an eight-year-old how to build a fence. Stop making him feel like he can do everything better than I can."

"He can do a lot of things better than you can."

I snort and shake my head. "Okay. It's decided then. Adair is building the fence."

"He is not building the fence! He'll tell you what he remembers about building the fence, and you will build it."

"Fine, fine!" I put the gun down. "But not tomorrow. I already have so much to do."

"Like?"

"First of all, the chicken coop needs to be cleaned. Also, I have to...tend to the corce beag for the sheep."

"Fine. Saturday, then."

"Yes, of course." I lean back on the couch. "On Saturday, I will build the fence while my supervisor Adair hollers instructions."

"Get your arse back in bed. I'm finished with you."

"I thought you'd never ask."

I pick up the gun and rag, then go to my room. Once inside, I put everything I'm holding under my bed.

As I'm about to get undressed, I remember the note. I pull it out from my pocket before changing back into my pajamas. When I lay down in bed, I shove it under my pillow.

I'm so tired.

CHAPTER SEVENTEEN

Peter

I turn off the car and stare at our apartment for a few minutes. My feet are throbbing. I close my eyes just for a moment. The thought of going inside and taking a hot shower excites me. I have three hours before I have to be at the bar. I fling the driver door open, and head inside. When I unlock the door, I smell something weird...but not like pot or cigarette smoke.

Did Hayley try to cook something?

I walk up the stairs and drop my keys on the coffee table. The apartment looks very clean, just the way I left it, but what's that scent? It's spicy, almost. I can't identify it. I've definitely never smelled it in here before...or anywhere, as a matter of fact.

The kitchen also looks suspiciously tidy. Hayley would never normally leave the apartment this clean. Then, I look in the sink. One dirty plate. I have to admit, I'm glad it's not two dirty plates.

I wash the dish and put it back in the cabinet. A few crumbs are on the floor, but other than that, it's spotless. I grab the broom and begin sweeping the kitchen. Strange.

I bend by the table to reach any hidden dirt. Something's down there. I lean the broom against the wall and get on my hands and knees. It's a man's wallet, and it's not mine. Tristian's ID is inside.

This basturt was in my apartment again!? I knew it! What the fuck did he cook in here? I can hardly stand the smell!

I crawl out from under the table with the wallet, grabbing my cell phone from my pocket. I dial Hayley's number. It rings as I walk into the living room.

"Hello?"

"Where are you?" I ask and take a seat on the couch.

"I went to get lunch."

"Were you home?"

"When?"

"While I was at work."

"Yes."

"By yourself?"

"Mhm."

I recline and lean back. I put my phone on speaker and stretch my arms above my head.

"Oh. That's weird because I have Tristian's wallet here in my hand. It was under the table in the kitchen."

"Oh. That's...weird"

"I told you I don't want him here. How many times do I have to tell you the same thing? You don't listen!"

I lay my phone on the couch arm and dig through his wallet. A gift card to Wendy's...two dollars wrapped around a condom—how pathetic—a key... Wait, a key? To where? I get a strange feeling.

"I know you said that, but I feel like it's my apartment too, and you're being a control freak again," she retorts.

"Well, don't feel that way until you start paying half the rent."

I'm a basturt. I know it.

"You could be a little fucking nicer. As if living with you wasn't bad enough."

"When you actually get sober, maybe we can talk about how mean I am."

I grab my keys off of the coffee table, comparing my key to the one from Tristian's wallet.

This is definitely a copy of the key to our apartment. I set my keys down, go out the front door, and shut it behind me. If I'm wrong, then I just locked myself out of the apartment, but I'm that confident.

"Whatever, Peter."

"I don't want Danny around him. I don't want him in my apartment. I've made myself clear multiple times. I don't care if you love him and hate me, you still have to listen to me while you live under my roof."

"You keep saying it's your apartment like you're the only one that lives there."

"I'm the only one who pays the bills around here, so yes, it's my apartment. How many times should I explain that to you?"

I insert the key into the knob and twist. It turns. I'm not locked out. I walk back inside and lock the door behind me. No one's getting in here without my say-so.

"We have to talk when you get home."

"Why?

"We just have to talk."

"Are you gonna fucking lose it and yell at me again? I'll be home in like an hour."

"Don't bring him here. He is not allowed inside of this apartment. Do you hear me?"

"What am I, your child?"

"Stop acting like it, and I won't have to talk to you this way."

"I know, I heard you. I'll tell him," she says...but not to me. She's not alone.

"Who are you talking to right now?"

"Tristian. He needs his wallet back."

"Oh, perfect. You're with him now? Great. Don't worry, he'll get it back."

I hear a click. She hung up on me. Fuck her, I don't care. I tuck the key into my pocket and walk back up the stairs. Now I have two.

Hayley

Tristian and I are walking back from McDonald's. We're almost at the apartment. He seems frustrated. I'm actually very scared for Peter. I can't forget what Tristian said, even if it was "just an idea."

"That motherfucker better not have taken any money out of my wallet," he grumbles and kicks a pebble on the sidewalk.

How can I calm him down? How do I convince him that Peter won't act like an asshole? Hell, how do I convince myself that Peter won't act like an asshole? He's definitely going to act like an asshole.

"You didn't have any money in your wallet."

"I had a few bucks. He better not have taken my condom. That's the last one!"

"He didn't take your condom. Trust me."

Really, Tristian? We can get free condoms at the clinic. Plus, Peter's allergic to latex, but I'm definitely not going to tell Tristian that.

"Yeah, because they wouldn't fit him. I'm way bigger...right?"

"Whatever you say, Tristian."

"Wait. Oh, fuck... Hayley, my key was in there!"

"You put it back in your wallet?"

"Yes."

Fuck... Peter's definitely going to act like an asshole.

"Why? I gave you a key ring."

"Does it matter why? Fuck!" He puts his hands on his head.

"He didn't look through your wallet. Even if he did, he won't know it's a key to our apartment."

There is a one hundred percent chance Peter looked through Tristian's wallet, found the key, and knows it's a key to our apartment, but I need to calm Tristian down right now.

"He's a smart fuck. He definitely knows it's a key to the apartment!"

Maybe Tristian knows Peter too well to try to calm him down now.

"I guess we'll just see then."

He's quiet. I study him. He notices and turns my way.

"What?"

"I just think you're handsome."

"Thanks," he mutters. He pulls a box of cigarettes out of his pocket.

"You're welcome."

"Fuck, I hate walking! You should start driving him to his first job so you have the car in the morning."

I laugh. "No way in hell is he going to let me have the car during the day. I already get to use it at night most of the time."

"Why, so it can just sit in the parking lot of his job? He's such a selfish prick."

How does Peter help Danny cool down? It usually works. Maybe I should try it on Tristian.

"Can we stop talking about Peter for one minute and talk about us? Let's enjoy the rest of our walk, just relaxing... Not talking about anything or anyone who makes us angry."

"It's hard not to talk about him when he's such an ugly little weasel."

We're quiet for the remainder of the walk, but I can tell Tristian's thinking about something—and not something pleasant, either. He keeps shaking his head and mumbling. We finally reach the door of the apartment. I knock.

"You didn't bring your key?" Tristian asks.

"I thought you had yours, Tristian."

"Hey, fuck face!" Peter yells from above us.

Shit. No. I look up. He's leaning out of the window.

"Peter, let's not do this. This is not a good time," I call up to him.

"You forgot your wallet."

Peter chucks the wallet as hard as he can at Tristian. It bounces off of his head and lands on the grass.

"Oh my God, are you okay?"

Tristian doesn't respond. He leans down, picks up his wallet, and starts searching through it.

"My key is not fucking in here. It's not fucking in here! I told you!"

I hear Peter laugh and the window slam shut.

"Peter, unlock the door! I don't have my key."

He opens the window again. "I'll let you in, but not your stupid fucking boyfriend."

Good thinking, Peter...an excuse to tell Tristian to go home.

"Sounds like a plan!" I say.

Peter looks at me, suspiciously.

"Don't worry," Tristian calls out, pointing up at him. "I'll just come over when you leave for work and take my key back, you little pussy."

"Pussy? Me? Want me to come down there? I'll fight you. That's what you really seem to want."

No. No. No. No.

"Yeah, I'll fight you right now. Not like last time when you hid behind the fucking bar at McAlister's!"

"Tha thu breugach!"

"What the fuck did he just say to me?" Tristian turns frantically toward me.

"I have no idea. All right, time to go. Let's all just calm down—"

"I said, YOU'RE A FUCKING LIAR. YOU DIDN'T COME TO THE BAR!"

"YOU TWO ARE NOT GOING TO FIGHT," I interject. "Peter, stop it!"

I step forward, scowling up at him. Tristian grabs my arm.

"Why? Let him keep going. You know I'll beat the shit out of that twerp." He rolls up his sleeves. "You can watch me do it."

"First, you have to get rid of the knife in your pocket. And I'm the pussy? You're going to fight me with a knife? What kind of horseshit is that?" Peter asks.

How the fuck does he know Tristian has a knife?

"Anyway," Peter continues. "Get the fuck out of here before I call the police. Hayley, I'll let you inside when I see his sorry ass start walking away from our door. He's not coming anywhere near me. I'll be waiting." He slams the window shut again.

Thank God...

"Tristian, just leave. I'll see you later."

His face is very red. He doesn't answer me. I know he's trying not to say something I wouldn't like. I'm kind of proud of him?

"Calm down. We'll get our own place one day...right?" I continue.

"Yeah, sure." He says quietly.

"We'll figure it out. Just leave. I'll text you later."

I kiss his cheek. He starts walking away. As he goes, he punches the air and curses. I hear laughter and look up.

"What a fucking rocket," Peter calls down. "I'll let you in."

I wait at the door with my arms folded. I hear Peter run down the stairs. He opens the door.

"We have to talk about this whole key thing," he says.

Here we go...

CHAPTER EIGHTEEN

Peter

I'm singing "She's Always a Woman." I love Billy Joel, but my voice is loud and off-key. I know I'm off-key. I'm sober enough to know, but I'm drunk enough not to care. I slide my back down the brick building. The wall scrapes my skin as my shirt rides up. Sean follows. He slams the metal door behind us.

"Get off the ground."

"You're ruining a good time."

"GET OFF THE GROUND!" he demands.

I stand.

"What is this?" he asks.

"What is what?"

"You can't drink the alcohol you serve. You're working."

"I'm not that drunk. Plenty of bartenders do it. I'm proving the product is effective."

"Yeah, everyone can fucking see it's effective. You're spilling drinks all over the bar. You're costing me money."

"I think everyone is having a good time, and you're being a killjoy!" I shout. "Ask any of the regulars inside. They ask me to drink with them every night, and every night I have to say, 'Sorry, my boss is being a crìochnaich fhaighean!'"

"What the fuck did you just call me? In English, scumbag."

"Forget about it."

"You know how easy it is to replace you? I know you need this job, and I've been kind, but my kindness meter is running really low. One more chance. That's it. Go the fuck home. Come back tomorrow ready to work."

"No. I want to finish the night."

I walk toward the door, but he blocks me.

"I said you're done for the night. Go home. Call your girlfriend to pick you up."

"Are you serious?"

He goes back into the bar, closing the metal door behind him. I hear it lock.

Fuck.

Danny

I run up the stairs and hang my backpack on the wall. Hayley's sitting on the couch watching *Long Island Medium* all by herself. I ignore her and go into the kitchen. Peter isn't there. I check the bathroom. The lights are off, and the door is open. I go down the small hallway to Peter's bedroom, but he's not there, either.

I return to the living room. "Hayley, where's Peter?"

"I don't know. He didn't come home." She stares at the TV.

"I thought I saw the car in the lot."

"Was he in there?"

"I didn't look."

"That's weird, then. I don't know," she says monotone. Her pupils are so tiny that it looks like she has none. Just big blue blobs. She looks possessed.

"I'm going to go look," I say.

"Okay." She picks up the remote and makes the medium lady with the big hair even louder. *Useless.*

I walk back down the stairs and out the door. I jog to the back left of the parking lot where Peter normally parks. I see the car and head over to the passenger side window. He's in the driver seat with his eyes closed, but he's talking...to no one...in another language? Is that Scottish? I've never really heard Scottish before. Maybe that's it.

The car is full of smoke. All of the windows are up. He's holding a cigarette. I knock on the glass. He stops talking, opens his eyes, and clicks the button to make the window go down.

"What are you doing?" I ask.

"Just...relaxing." He sniffles and looks the other way. His eyelids are really red and puffy.

"Okay...Were you on the phone?"

"Huh?"

"Seemed like you were talking to someone."

"Oh." He looks at the empty passenger seat. "Yeah. Just to myself, I guess. No one's here, right?" He pats the empty seat.

What the hell?

"Peter, were you crying? Are you okay?"

"No, I wasn't crying."

"Why are you out here talking to yourself and smoking with the windows closed?"

"Well, when you put it that way... I don't know. I like the smell of smoke."

"Hayley didn't know you were home."

He takes another drag of his cigarette and sniffles again.

"Because I didn't go inside yet." He coughs.

"Peter, what's wrong? Is this because Hayley cheated on you? Screw her."

"No, this really isn't about Hayley. Go back inside."

"Did I do something?"

"No, this has nothing to do with you either."

"Peter, I really want to know what's going on."

"Nothing that can be undone or fixed. Why bother talking about it, right?"

"You should still tell me about it. Is it something that happened at the restaurant this morning? Or the bar last night?"

"No."

"Something that happened a long time ago? Like in Scotland?"

He sighs and sniffles, looking away from me.

"So, Scotland?" I ask again.

"Danny, really, I'm okay. I'm coming inside now."

He puts the window back up and gets out of the car. The cigarette dangles from his lip. He grips it, throws it on the ground, and stomps it into the concrete.

"I don't think it's good to smoke with the windows closed. You could get sick."

He stares deep into my eyes, puts both his hands on my shoulders, and squeezes them a bit—almost like he's making sure I'm really here.

"I'm sorry about that."

Sorry? Why sorry? He's being very weird.

"It's okay..."

"I love you."

"I love you too. What's going on? You aren't acting normal."

"I just want to make sure I do everything right when it comes to you. I want you to be happy and safe."

I hug him. I think he needs a hug. I don't know what else I can do. I don't even know what's wrong. We hug for a few moments, then he pulls away.

"Let's go inside. I have to get ready for McAlister's," he says.

"Okay."

We walk back together, silently. That was different. I've never seen him cry before. I don't like it.

Kara

"We should pre-game before this party."

"Jess, you're driving." I put my knees against the dashboard and cross my legs at my ankles while playing *Candy Crush* on my phone. It helps to distract me way more than drinking does. It's like she doesn't even know me at all.

"*You* should pre-game. I'll only have one drink."

She pulls to the side of the road and tries to parallel park. She must have put the car in reverse at least four times...and the front of her car is still sticking out onto the road! People are honking. I sink lower in my seat.

"It's just... Kara, come on." She squeezes my cheeks and pushes my face toward hers. "You just aren't very social when you're sober."

"Where are we?"

"I don't know. McAlister's? See it?" She points. "Next to that restaurant."

I see it. I also see that she could have just parked in the lot. Why the hell are we here, anyway?

"Okay..."

"I don't know. It's the first bar I saw. Let's get your drink on."

"I don't really want to."

"Kara, forget about work for one day—"

I laugh and look out the window. "Yeah, forget that I'm losing all of my income. Okay. Let me forget that."

"You would have had today off, anyway, bitch." She punches my arm playfully, and I glance over.

Does she really think this is helping? It's not. Great, now I'm thinking about work again. I tried so, so hard. I did everything right! I was the model employee, actually. Why should Lisa get to keep her job? Do they even know she sneaks out the side door fifteen minutes early every day?

"I thought I was doing such good work."

"You were. They just hired too many people, and you were the newest, right?"

"I had so much hope for this one, Jess." I'm starting to get emotional. She notices.

"All right, that's it. Get out of the car." She opens her door and walks around to the passenger side. She looks in the window and sticks her tongue out.

I laugh but try to hide it. I don't want to laugh. I want to be miserable. I don't want to be here, and Jess should know it. I look back at the bar's entrance.

"This place looks like a dump!" I yell through the closed window.

"What?" She smiles. I know this biatch heard me.

"I said this place looks like a—"

"OKAY, I'M GOING IN NOW. BYE."

I crack my neck. It helps relieve my anxiety. I decide to get out of the car. When I stand, I pull my mini skirt down. I haven't even taken one step and these heels hurt my feet already. How did I let her do this to me? I need to learn the word "no." It's healthy to say "no."

I walk as quickly as I can in these shoes, but Jess is already inside. She's always so fast to get to the liquor. I enter and hear Irish music. This place is full of smoke and gross old men. It's dimly lit so you can't see just how gross the old men are, but I can still tell they're fat, ugly, and bald.

Where the fuck is Jess? I hobble toward the bar.

"What's a pretty thing like you doing here?" some goblin asks.

EW! I don't answer or acknowledge him at all. I continue to scan the place.

There's Jess. She's talking to the bartender. He's the only guy our age. He's small...pretty thin, and rather short. His long hair is combed back into a bun, but a few curls have fallen out. He's got perfectly white teeth and a very nice smile.

I approach and the guy looks at me. His brown eyes are huge. They're almost too big for his face, and those are some of the longest eyelashes I've ever seen. Why can't my eyelashes be that long? He has a familiar, welcoming air about him, but doesn't any salesman?

Jess is smiling and laughing. She's completely fallen for him, bending over the bar. I can totally see her panty lines through her leggings.

"Jess, there you are!"

"Kara, this is Peter!"

I look at him again. He's nice to look at.

"Cool. Can we go? This place is—"

"A shithole?" The bartender smiles. I wasn't expecting that. Such a nice, innocent face, and one of the first words I hear out of his mouth are "shithole."

"Uhm, well... I wasn't—"

"No, come on, it's a shithole. I've been getting my ice from the sushi restaurant for the past week and a half."

He has a beautiful Irish accent. I won't tell him that. I'm in no mood to be nice.

"So, is that a fake accent? Is that part of the vibe in here? You an actor?"

"I'm a bartender. It's a real accent."

"Oh, yeah? Then what's it like in Ireland, smartass?"

"Kara, stop—" Jess adds.

We both ignore her. It's just him and me now.

"I wouldn't know, Miss Thing. I'm from Scotland."

"Oh..."

"That's okay. What can I get for you?"

"Sour apple martini." I pull up a wooden barstool. The legs wobble, and it's covered in scratches. Probably covered in piss too. I'd hate to put a blacklight up to anything in this dump. He looks directly at me and laughs. "What's so funny to you?"

"Okay, sure. Let me pull out our martini kit. Look: we have beer, whisky... I do have vodka, but I don't have any sour apple mix. This isn't that kind of place. I can mix it with soda. Warm soda."

"Oh, so you're judging me. Cool."

"Kara, why are you so defensive?" Jess asks.

She knows what kind of week I've had! She doesn't understand why I'm in a bad mood? As if! She's a terrible friend. I turn to the bartender.

"Give me one whiskey."

"One whiskey?" he asks.

"Exactly."

"All right... Which one?"

"Any."

He laughs again. The bastard.

"How?"

"With your hands. What do you mean how?"

"Straight or neat?"

"Oh. Yeah, uhm...neat? Neat. Yes."

He rolls his eyes at me like I'm just another dumb bimbo and walks over to the wall of bottles behind him.

I look at Jess, and she hisses, "He's totally cute! Why are you acting like such a bitch?"

"He just wants a big tip."

"So? I'll give him a tip. Kara, you're going to hate what you just ordered."

"I'm going to drink it anyway...to prove a point."

"You're crazy."

"You wanted me to drink tonight, I'm drinking. Okay?"

"Fine. Okay." She picks up her phone and uses its camera as a mirror.

The bartender comes back with my drink. He places it in front of me, glances at the glass, then smirks. Okay, weird. I pick it up and sniff. I don't break eye contact with him. This is just alcohol. There is no mixer. Literally nothing. My face must grimace.

"Problem?" He leans over the bar, giving me a sort of half smile. What an asshole. Why do I always meet douchebags?

"No, actually, this is just the way I like my whiskey." I start to sip.

"Oh, good. Because I gave you top-shelf Scotch. Wouldn't want to waste Johnny Walker Blue."

"How much does this shit cost?" I want to lean over this bar and smack him. Maybe I'd feel better then.

"On the house. For you only."

"Free?"

"Did I stutter?"

"I don't know. I can't understand you because of your fake accent."

He laughs. Jess is just watching us. I feel challenged, so I raise the glass and chug my drink. I think I'm going to lose my lunch.

"Okay, okay. I'm impressed, little lady," he says.

"Don't call me that."

"Should I call you a big lady?"

"You... You're a smartass."

"Listen. You want anything else? All these men are paying...but not you."

"All women drink free?"

"Uh, no. You do, and your friend."

I look over at Jess. She looks super excited, like she might have just pissed herself. She smiles at me knowingly with her chin up, like she just did something great, like this was all her doing.

"How many women do you say that to?"

"Honestly? I need the money. I can't lose this job. So, one. I'm taking one risk. Is that okay with you?"

This guy is so damn smooth. Eh, it's probably just the alcohol hitting me already.

"Okay. Peter, was it? Peter?"

"Yep."

"Give me something to write on."

He reaches down behind the bar and hands me a small square napkin. I pull a pen out of my purse and write my phone number down. He smiles.

"How many men do you give your phone number to?"

"Honestly? I don't need the attention. I'm not a whore. So, one. I'm taking one risk. Is that okay with you?"

I can tell he's surprised by my comeback. Surprised and impressed.

"I like it." He folds the napkin up and sticks it into his apron pocket. "I'll text you, Kara."

He says my name with that accent, and I almost melt into my chair. But I can't let him know that.

"YES!" Jess says as she claps her hands.

★★★

It's one o'clock in the morning now, and this party sucks. I didn't go to college, so why am I at a frat party?

I'm on the patio in the backyard. Lord only knows where Jess is. I check my phone, again. He still didn't text me. I'm starting to feel stupid. Maybe he just collects phone numbers. Maybe that's his kink. Maybe he has no real interest in me. I should have demanded he write his number down too. After all, it would only be fair. Damn, I should have done that. I could go back to that bar... No, I'll look desperate. I'll—

My phone vibrates. I can't unlock it fast enough. Since when did I become this girl? Ew. This must be rock bottom. I've seen girls like me before. I hate them. I look at my phone screen. It's a number, not a contact. Yes!

```
Hey, Kara. 😊
It was a pleasure.
Text me anytime.
- Peter
```

Where the fuck is Jess? I need to know exactly how long I should wait before I respond. Wait. Since when is she any good at this? I'm just as good, AND I am a grown woman, so I can answer anytime I want to.

```
                              Hi.
                  Yes, it was nice
                    meeting you. I
                thought you weren't
                    going to text me.
```

Smiley face or no smiley face?

No smiley face. I click send.

My phone vibrates. *Wow, he's fast.*

```
Why would you think
that?
```

Because it's 1am.

Well, I just closed
the bar.

Oh...

Can I make it up to
you?

Make what up to me?

The apple martini.

I smile. I'm here smiling at my phone. Disgusting... I look
around to see if anyone is nearby.

Sure. When?

When are you
available?

Right now.

Oh my God... Why did I just write that?

LOL 😊

You laugh a lot.
Don't you?

Because you're a funny
girl.

Okay, right now. I'll
see what I can do.

Where are we meeting?

You can come to my
place.

Hopefully this guy doesn't murder me.

All right. Give me a
wee bit.

What's your address?

65 Jayne ave,

```
                                   East Islip.

Eh, a little way from
us. We are in Medford.


Us? US!?


                                          Us?

Well, me.
I live with a roommate
and my brother.

                                     Oh, OK.
                               So... what time?

I just walked in the
door.
Maybe 2am?

                               OK. I'll see you
                                          soon.
```

I stuff my phone in my purse and walk back into the house. I don't see Jess anywhere.

"Jess?" I call as I push through a crowd of drunk people.

Where is she? She's nowhere in the living room. I should check the bedrooms. Or, no... Maybe I shouldn't. Who knows what I'll see in there? I'll just text her.

```
                               Hey. I'm tired. I'm
                               calling an Uber.
                               Thanks for a great
                               night. I had fun.
```

Kissy or no Kissy?

Peter

"What are you doing?" Hayley asks as I pull apart the kitchen.

"I'm looking for the jigger."

"Why are you looking for the jigger?"

"So I can make drinks. Why else would I want the jigger?"

"You usually don't want to make drinks when you get home."

"Because I do it all night long." I continue looking through the cabinets, shuffling other kitchen gadgets aside, but I don't see it. "Where the fuck could I have—"

"I guess I just don't understand what you're doing," she interrupts me.

I stop digging and look at her. "I'm going out. Just like how you go out. With Tristian? Like that."

I go back to searching, opening the drawer under the sink. There it is! In the way, way back. I grab it and hold it up for her to see. I twirl it around in my fingers and stare at it.

"Wait. With a woman?"

I throw the jigger up in the air and try to catch it. I nearly drop it, but I make a smooth recovery. I raise my eyebrows and look back and forth between her and the jigger.

"Uh, yeah. With a woman."

She rolls her eyes. "So, you met someone? Did you show her that little trick?"

"Yeah, in fact, I did. Wasn't it incredible?"

"Sure. So, you're leaving now. What time will you be home?"

"I might sleep there, if I can."

"And leave me here to take care of Danny? I told you—"

"He's thirteen. You don't need to take care of him. He's sleeping right now, anyway. Since when does that bother you?"

"Where'd you meet this hoe?"

Maybe she's jealous? Jackpot.

"I met her at work. I don't know why you care. You cheated on me, said everything about me is boring, and now you're mad? Grow up." I drop the jigger in a black plastic bag along with a bottle of vodka, lemons, and schnapps.

"I'm mad because you're leaving me here with Danny. I'm not mad that you somehow found a dumb bitch to have bland-ass sex with."

"Leave me alone!" I snap back at her.

"Fine. Goodbye."

Thank God she walked away. I take a deep breath, walk into the living room, and eye the key hook on the wall. I don't see my car keys.

"Wait. Hayley, wait. I, uh... I need the car." I rub my forehead as she laughs from the other room. "I pay for the car. It's my car. Give me the keys."

"Come find them."

Fuck. I look at my phone. Shit, it's late. I guess I better start looking.

CHAPTER NINETEEN

Nobody

I open my eyes slowly and look up at the ceiling. I'm starting to devise a plan.

How can I sneak away from my work and not get caught? Maybe I can head toward the coop and begin to clean it. Ma usually doesn't come outside unless she's hanging out the laundry, which I think she just did a couple of days ago. Even if she does come outside, I doubt she'll check on me or notice I'm gone. I'll be fine. No one will—

"Get up time! It's get up time!"

Adair flings open my door and jumps onto the bed with me.

"I'm awake. Can't you see I'm awake?"

"You overslept. Why were you outside last night?"

"Huh?"

"I saw you from my window walking out toward the chicken coop with the gun."

"You were awake?"

"Yes."

"Someone was out there bothering the chickens—"

"A girl?"

"No. No, not a girl."

"She looked like a girl to me."

"It was the people from the farm over."

"Oh. Why were they bothering our chickens?"

"You know what, Adair? I really don't know." I sit up and rub my eyes.

"Did you shoot them?"

"No. I didn't shoot anybody."

"I would have shot them!"

"That's why you're the man of the house, right?"

He laughs. "Ma's making breakfast."

"Yeah, but she's not going to have me sit down and eat. It's already past eight o'clock." I stand. Adair sits comfortably on my bed.

"You got work to do?"

"Yup."

"Are you going to do it?"

I take a deep breath. "Yes. Stop asking me questions, okay?"

"You're cranky today." He throws himself backwards, laying across my bed.

"Sure." I dress in my cleanest jeans and my nicest button-up flannel.

"ADAIR! BREAKFAST IS READY!" Ma calls from the kitchen.

"Okay!" he shouts back, then springs up. "I'm going to go eat now."

"Yes. Great." I tie up my work boots and look at myself in the mirror hanging on my closet door. I let my hair out of the messy bun, pulling it tighter to redo it.

"Why are you looking so nice to clean the chicken coop? You look like you're ready for church!"

"I'm not looking so nice."

"You look nicer than normal."

"Are you saying I normally look bad?" I stare at him.

"No!" He laughs.

"Okay, good. Are you going to go eat breakfast, or do you have more questions?"

"I'll go eat." He leaves my room.

I sigh, go to my dresser, and open the second drawer. Underneath my clothing, I find my roll of duct tape and stick it in my pocket. I walk into the bathroom and brush my teeth. My homemade deodorant is in the cabinet along with Pop's one-and-only bottle of cologne. He never wore this crap. I sniff it. It smells better than the chicken coop. I spray some on my wrists and rub it in.

I head down the hall to the kitchen. Adair is at the table, but Ma is nowhere to be seen. Adair has a glass of milk and a plate with eggs, tomatoes, beans, and toast. He also has a smaller dish with one of the pastries I got from Mr. Glas. A meal fit for a prince. I grab a slice of toast off of his plate.

"I know why you think they're so good." I point to the cream buns.

He looks up at me with his big blue eyes. Everyone in our family has blue eyes and red hair, except for me.

"Why?"

"Mr. Glas says he puts maple in them." I take a bite of his toast.

"I KNEW IT! I knew there was maple in here. Ma! Ma!"

Ma comes stomping down the hallway from her bedroom. She wants me to know she's coming...and she's angry.

"What are you doing?!" she shouts as she eyes me standing by the table.

"There's maple in here! Remember, I told you I thought that? I was right!" Adair exclaims.

"I'm not talking to you, Adair. I'm talking to your lazy brother!"

"I'm heading out there now," I reply.

"Not before you eat your brother's breakfast, though?"

"I'm eating a piece of toast."

"You should have been out there an hour ago! Your father would be out there at six in the morning during this time of the season."

"Fine." I take one last bite and put the toast down.

"Ma! Did you hear what I said about the pastries?"

"I did, mo laochain," she says calmly as she walks over to the sink.

"It'd be nice if you made me breakfast too," I add.

"You're a grown man. You can make your own breakfast."

"You always made Pop breakfast. I'm pretty sure he was a grown man."

"You're right. He was a man. That's why he didn't do women's work like preparing breakfast." She starts scrubbing the pan in the sink. "Men who work need energy."

"I do work too, Ma! I do work!"

"You hardly do anything except run around town chasing after tourist girls. Leave the girls alone! Maybe I'll make you breakfast when I see the fence completed."

"I told you, I don't know how to—"

"I remember how!" Adair calls out, mouth full of eggs.

"Not now, Adair..." I whisper and look at him.

"I remember how Pop was doing it, though!" he answers me.

"I knew he'd remember," Ma says.

I look down at the floor. "Yeah...I'm going outside now. I have work to do."

"That's right. You do." She doesn't turn from the sink.

I walk out the door silently.

I don't give a fuck what she thinks. Soon, I'll be seeing Teva—someone who actually likes me and wants to be around me.

Kara

I'm half asleep on the couch when the doorbell rings. I sit up. Oh my God, it's him! Why did I tell him to come over tonight? I fix my hair while walking to the door.

"I'm sorry I'm late," he says.

"I don't even know what time it is, to be honest..."

He looks at his iPhone.

"Two thirty. Can I come in?" He smiles that little half smile.

I open the door all the way and smile back, curtsying as I do it. YUP, I just did that. I'm *that* tired. He looks at me strangely, then he bows and laughs.

"Sorry," I say. "Just come in."

"Okay, m'lady."

Oh God, what have I done?

"Yeah, well... Welcome to la casa de Kara."

"It's nice." He walks past me and into the apartment. I close the door and turn around. He's already gone. What?

I walk into the kitchen, and he's standing at the island. He pulls two martini glasses and a few bottles of liquor out of his bag.

"What are you doing?" I ask.

"Making martinis."

"For real?"

"Kara, I told you I would make it up to you. I'm not a liar."

I smile. Okay. That's nice.

"So, Peter..." I sit on a bar stool at the island, swiveling back and forth. "You're here in my apartment, and I don't really know you..."

He smirks as he shakes the martinis.

"So, Kara... I'm here in your apartment, and I don't really know you..."

"Well, that's true." Shoot. What can we talk about? "Tell me about Scotland. I've always wanted to travel—I mean, not to Scotland, but somewhere. I don't go anywhere."

"Scotland? Oh, It's boring."

"Is that why you're here now?"

"You could say that."

He pours the drinks from the shaker. I'm amazed by the pretty color.

"How could it be boring?" I ask and stare into the glasses.

"Trust me. Where I'm from, it is. I'm not from the big cities you have in mind." He pushes a martini toward me and raises his own in the air. "Sláinte."

"Sláinte?"

"It means cheers," he says.

I raise my glass to his and they clink. A little bit of my drink spills out onto the countertop. Crap. What were we talking about again? Oh yeah, cheers.

"In what language?"

"In Gaelic," he answers. He's fixated on the spill.

"I'll clean it up later. I didn't even know that was a language. Do you speak it?"

He looks back up at me. "Yes, it is. Scots Gaelic. I don't speak it anymore. I could if I had to, but I haven't in a very long time."

"Oh, so in Scotland you spoke Gaelic, and it was so boring that you came here?"

"Uh... Yup." He starts to drink. He doesn't smile at all.

"Okay." I sip my drink. It's too quiet now. "Wow, this is really good!"

"I can make drinks, that's about it." He smiles. "They say everyone is good at one thing. Lucky me, huh?"

"I bet you're good at other things."

He puts his glass down and leans over the island. He raises his eyebrows and smirks.

"Oh my God. I wasn't suggesting that."

He laughs. "Well, I told you about myself."

"Not really."

"I told you enough. Tell me about you. I want to know more about Kara."

I don't want to talk about it, but here it comes.

"I just got let go from my job."

"Ouch. Why?"

"I'm a clerk typist. The department hired too many people. They had to let someone go. Guess who? They said they'd call me next time there was an opening."

"Don't worry. I'm not far behind."

"How the hell do you get let go from a bar?"

"Keep drinking on the job, that's how," he says with a wink of his eye and a snap of his finger.

"Why do you drink on the job?"

"I don't know. I like to drink."

"You know, you're not impressing me."

"I was trying to impress you with my honesty, not my alcoholism. Oh! And comfort you, since you're newly unemployed."

"It just sucks. You know?"

"I do... Well, I don't, but I do. I've never been unemployed, but I definitely know 'sucks,' if that makes any sense?" He takes another sip. "God, this is so sweet."

"I like it like that." I smile.

"I figured you would."

"What is that supposed to mean?"

"I watched you drink that whiskey earlier today and..."

"Right. So, you live with your brother. Older or younger?"

He gulps down the rest of his drink. He grabs the bottle of vodka and fills his glass nearly to the top with just that. Ew? Maybe he really is an alcoholic.

"Younger. I'm his legal guardian."

"Did he hate Scotland as much as you did?"

"Look, I don't hate it there...and no, he's not from Scotland."

He sips the pure vodka like it's water.

"What?"

"His adopted mum fostered me, but then she died. So, I adopted him. Kind of confusing."

"Oh, wow. Okay. I mean...not wow, just...cool. That's cool."

Oh my God. Cool? I am such an idiot.

He laughs. "Sure...cool. You live here by yourself?"

"Me, myself, and I."

"Is it one bedroom or two?"

"One. I could never afford two, are you kidding me?"

"Ours has three. One for each of us."

"Jesus, how much do you pay?"

"About twenty-five hundred a month."

"Holy shit!" I slap the island.

"I told you I need my job, did I not?"

"Well, your roommate... I'm assuming he contributes, right?"

He laughs again. "She does nothing."

"She?"

"Yes, she. She does nothing but look pretty."

"So, you think she's pretty?"

"That's not what I meant. That's an expression."

"How did you meet her?"

"Uh, well... She's also... We had the same foster mum."

"So, she's your sister?"

"Nope. No."

"Got it. Okay."

"It's just... Danny and I, my brother, were together in that house for so long. Since I moved in, what, five years ago? Hayley was relatively new. Would you consider someone you've only known a little while a sibling?"

"I guess not."

"Exactly."

His eyes wander away from me.

"So...five years?"

His eyes dart right back over to me. He taps the island with his fingertips impatiently. "What is this, an interview?"

"I mean, kind of. You're in my apartment. I'd like to get to know you."

"I came to the United States five years ago."

"And your parents didn't come?"

"Nope."

"You came alone?"

"Yup."

"How old were you?"

"Sixteen."

"And they let you do that?"

He sighs. "Yup."

"That's...interesting."

He puts his palms to his face and rubs up and down. Then, he drags them all the way down past his chin. He blows out through his mouth so that his lips vibrate and make that motor sound...like he's frustrated with all of my questions. He takes a big gulp of his vodka.

"They're dead. Dead people can't make rules."

"Oh... I'm sorry."

"Yeah. It's okay. They both died a long time ago. Dead." He takes another sip. We're both quiet for a while. Finally, he breaks the silence. "You have a TV?"

"Of course I do."

"Let's watch something."

"Like what?"

"I don't care."

"Okay."

We walk into the living room and take a seat on the couch together. He's so close to me. I like it.

"This might be weird, but...can I lay on your chest?" I'm so lonely. I don't know this guy, but I need this.

"Not weird at all. Sure, you can."

He puts his arm around me, and I lay my head on his chest.

"You smell nice," I say.

"Thanks. I bathe regularly."

"You're such a smartass."

"I've heard that before."

I put something on Netflix, anything at all. I just click whatever comes up first. I'm too tired to think about it, and I'm so comfortable. I close my eyes.

CHAPTER TWENTY

Peter

At eleven o'clock, I show up at home. Hayley's peeking through the blinds as I get out of the car. I laugh to myself and head to the door. She opens it before I can even touch the knob.

"Really? It's noon!"

I look at my phone. "It's eleven twenty-four."

"Close enough. You can't be spending all night and morning out of the apartment with some bitch!"

"Wrong. I can do whatever I want." I walk past her and up the stairs.

"If you can tell me what to do, I can tell you what to do," she yells and follows me.

"Whoa. That's totally different. I told you I don't want your dirty, idiot boyfriend in my apartment around Danny. That makes sense. That's logical. You can't tell me where I can and can't go. Understand?"

"Don't talk to me like that!" She pushes my chest.

It takes me a while to process what just happened. I stare at her, perplexed. "Did you just push me? Don't touch me. I would never touch you."

Danny walks out of his room with a bowl of cereal in hand, chewing. I look away from her.

"Hey, good morning," I say.

"Where were you all night, Peter?"

"I...I stayed at a friend's house. Weren't you sleeping, anyway?"

"I woke up at nine. Hayley said you left last night."

"Oh, sorry. I overslept. I won't do that again."

"So when he asks you not to do that, it's different," Hayley retorts with her arms folded.

Danny walks away from us and into the kitchen.

"If you're allowed to go out with your boyfriend, I'm allowed to go out with my girlfriend."

"Girlfriend? You just met the hoe!"

"Why do you care? I'm asking sincerely. Why do you care, Hayley?" I grab her gently by the arms. "Say the word, and I fucking swear to you, I'm yours. Say you want me back," I whisper desperately.

"I..."

I look longingly into her eyes. I don't understand her. What can I do to make this right again? To call her mine again? Kara's pretty. Too pretty, almost. She's just not Hayley.

"Danny's a pain in the ass. I don't want to be responsible for him. That's all. I don't care if you have a girlfriend. I've told you over and over how I feel."

I drop my hands. "But him? Why?"

"I don't have to explain that to you. You already know."

"Well, I don't have to explain Kara to you either because *you* already know!"

She smiles. "Oh yeah, I think I do." She starts to laugh.

Fuck! I turn around and head to my bedroom.

Kara

So...
You just left me last
night?

Crap! It's Jess. I guess that was kind of messed up.

I was so tired, and I
drank too much.
Sorry.

K

Shit. She's pissed. Change the subject

Peter texted me last
night.

Who?

The guy from the bar

Is that why you left
me alone? 🐚🐚

No! No! We just
texted

K. What did he say?

Nothing really. We
just chatted, but
Jess... he lives with
a girl

Like a gf?

According to him, no.
But who knows?

Are you going to keep
talking to him?

Yeah, I think so. I
need this

You do you

> How long do you think
> I should wait before
> I text him again?

You should let him
text you first

I hate that answer

> Yeah, you're probably
> right

I put down my phone and look around my apartment. Better start cleaning now. Maybe I'll start in the kitchen, get it out of the way. I stand up and twist side to side, cracking my back.

When I walk into the kitchen, I see the sink. Where are the dishes? Did I put them in the dishwasher? I take one step to the right and prop it open. It's completely empty. What? How?

Okay... Where's my phone?

I find it on the couch in the living room. Peter...Peter... There he is. I click on his last text.

> Hey, this is weird
> but... Did you wash
> the dishes in my sink
> last night?

Yes. And I think I put
everything away in the
right place too.

> What? Why?

You looked tired, and
I like to clean.

> You like to clean?

Cleaning clears my
mind. I like that.
It gives me something
to focus on.

Okay. Thanks

Sure.

Did you get to watch any of that movie you put on last night?

Uhmmmm, no. I fell right asleep. IDR it at all.

Be glad. It was horrible.

Your head was on my chest. I was trapped.

You pick worse movies than my brother.

LOL.

Well, you got up somehow to clean the dishes

Yeah. Halfway through you flipped over.

Thankfully.

Next time you pick the movie then

Next time?

I like the sound of that.

Oh, really? When will next time be?

Whenever you'll have me. Maybe you'll let me take you out to dinner?

Yay!!!

That sounds really nice

Are you free this Friday? I actually have the night off.

Friday night works
for me

Great. That's perfect.

Can we meet at your
place?

Three dots appear on the screen. He's typing. They suddenly vanish. They reappear. They vanish again...He's thinking of how to respond.

Why? What's wrong with his place?

Sure. Yeah.

Cool.

Great. ??

Awesome.
Can't wait to meet
your brother and
roommate.

You won't meet my
brother. He won't be
home. He's going to
dinner with some kids
from school.

Your roommate then.

The dots again...

Yeah. Can't wait.

CHAPTER TWENTY-ONE

Peter

I lie on my back, staring straight up toward the ceiling. I might as well try to sleep. My hands fold together like I'm about to pray, but I wouldn't do that anymore. There is no God. It's all horseshit. I shove my hands under my head. My cold palms are warmer now. I try to close my eyes, but I open them again.

Hayley doesn't love me.

I sigh. It's what I think of when I wake up, and it's what I think of before I go to sleep. It wasn't always this way. I used to think about—

Never mind! I'll let Hayley continue to take up that space in my head.

But now I can't stop thinking... She reminds me of you, Ma. Maybe that's why—

THAT'S HORRIBLY DISGUSTING.

I sit up and violently shake my head to erase the thought from my mind, like an Etch-A-Sketch, until I can't see either of your faces. I hold my head steady on my palms now.

I wonder if they're still looking for me?

A sudden sense of dread fills me. Why haven't *you* looked for me, Ma? It's been five years. I bet you're glad I'm gone. You meant it. You really, really meant what you said...

Maybe you didn't. Maybe you're trying to protect me, or...maybe you're not. Maybe you hope they find me, but they just can't. Maybe I'm as good at hiding as I am at running.

They say everyone's good at one thing. Lucky me, I'm good at more than that.

Danny

"It's dark. Too dark..." I whisper to myself in a deep voice. I laugh. I mean, of course it's dark. It's nighttime. I just wanted to say that out loud, for some reason. It's badass. Do I even know what movie that's from? I guess I don't.

Anyway... I feel around for my cell phone and find it underneath my pillow. I switch on the flashlight and get up. I'm thirsty. If I'm really quiet, I won't wake anyone—and I can steal that Cherry Pepsi Hayley left in the fridge. HA!

I creak my door open and peek outside. CRAP! A light's coming from Peter's room. Why's he still awake? I turn off the flashlight and tread lightly. His door is cracked open, so I push it open just a little more. The door didn't even make a sound!

Peter's sitting off the side of his bed with a box of envelopes beside him. One envelope is out of the box, all ready to go. It's face down. He's hunched over a piece of paper on his lap, tapping a pen against his leg. Looks like he's writing something important, thinking hard about it too. He stops tapping and starts writing. He seems angry, writing so hard that his pen rips through his paper.

He mumbles something, then he slams the pen down and takes a breath. He looks up and sees me. Shit. He says something angrily in Scottish. I push the door open wider.

"Huh?"

"Sorry... I meant, what are you doing?"

"I was getting water, but I saw you were awake. What are *you* doing?"

"Me? I'm just..." He looks down at his lap and lifts his hands up. "I guess I'm just writing."

"Writing?"

"I told you I do that when I...feel like I need to."

"Yeah, but I never actually seen you do it." I step into his room.

"Because it's just for me."

I lean forward, trying to get a look at the paper.

"What are you writing about?" I ask.

He raises an eyebrow and opens his mouth a little, moving his jaw to one side. He puts the paper on the bed, face down like the envelope.

"It's just for me," he says again, but slower.

"Yeah, I heard you the first time."

"You heard me, but did you listen to me?"

What is this, philosophy class?

"All right, whatever. What, is it like a journal?"

"Yeah, sure. It's a journal."

Liar.

"Then why isn't it in a diary book?"

"Because I don't have a book."

"What is that?" I point to the box of envelopes next to him.

"These are called envelopes, Daniel. You use them when you want to send letters to people." He smirks.

Oh my God, I know what they are!

"What I really wanted to say is, I know you're writing a letter and not a journal! Who's it to?"

I lunge forward and grab the paper. He's fast, though. He grabs it at the same time, and it rips right in half. He stares down at the ripped paper in his hand and then up at me. He sighs. I look down at my half. The writing is all in cursive. I don't know how to read cursive!

"Why do you write in cursive all the time?" I ask.

"That's what you have to say for yourself?"

He stands and holds out his open hand. I peek once more at my half, then hand it to him. He stares at both halves for a little while. After a while, he tears the paper until it's only little pieces and dumps them into the garbage basket.

"Why can't you just tell me what you were writing?"

"Because it doesn't matter. It really doesn't!" he yells.

"If it doesn't matter, why would you write it?"

He looks down into the garbage. "I don't know, Danny. Please, go back to bed. I'm going to sleep now."

"No, you're not—"

"Yes, I am!" He puts one hand up to shush me and walks back to bed, lifting up the covers.

I look down at my feet and see the envelope he was going to use. It must have fallen. YES! I step on it and pull it closer to me with my foot.

"Oh, okay. Well, goodnight then!"

He turns around and gives me a weird look. I begin to back up, sliding my left foot and dragging the envelope out the door. I guess he doesn't see me do it because he just gets into bed like he really doesn't give a shit. HA!

"Good night, Danny. Try to get some sleep, please." He reaches for the lamp on his bedside table and turns it off.

I keep sliding, and finally make it out of the doorway. I bend down and pick up the envelope, running into my room with it against my chest. It's freaking dark! I stub my toe on the door frame.

OW! CRAP, CRAP, CRAP, CRAP!

I flick on my light switch and hop to my bed on one foot. I pull the envelope away from my chest...

BLANK? IT'S BLANK!

All that work, and there's not even a name or address on here!

CHAPTER TWENTY-TWO

Peter

Blue checkered? Black? Which brings out my eyes more? I hold the shirts against my chest as I stand in front of the mirror in my room. Black. Definitely black. Hair down? Or up? I don't think she's seen me with my hair down yet. Hayley did say it "changes my face." That's a compliment, coming from her.

"PETER, THERE'S A SPIDER!" Hayley yells from the living room.

"Are you fucking kidding me?" I call back from the bedroom.

"I wouldn't kid about something like that!"

"Jesus, Mary and St. Joseph," I mumble, pulling on the black shirt and buttoning it.

I go to the living room dressed in only my boxers and shirt. Hayley's pointing above the TV. A small spider's right where the wall meets the ceiling.

"It's there!"

"How am I supposed to reach that? I'm just as short as you are."

"Stand on something! Hurry, before it runs!"

I grab a chair and a napkin from the dining room and climb beside the TV. Even with the chair, I'm a shrimp. I'm on my tiptoes and still can't reach the spider.

"It's going to fall! It's going to fall!" she yells.

"Then it will fall on me, not you. Gòrach píos de cac!" I yell, stretching as far as I can. Finally, I crouch and spring up, smacking the wall. Got it! I land back on my feet and stabilize myself.

"EW! THERE'S A BIG SMOOSH ON THE WALL!"

"Well, that was my best effort." I climb down off of the chair. "Now it won't bother you anymore. It's dead."

"Thanks." She breathes in and out like she's having a panic attack.

The doorbell rings. FUCK!

"Who's here?" Hayley quickly lifts a couch cushion and pulls out a small plastic bag. She presses it to her chest.

"I have to put on pants. Do NOT answer the door!"

"Why?"

"Just don't. Go in your room and calm down." I run back into my bedroom, putting on the pants I'd laid on my bed. Why is Kara so early?

Kara

I'm pretty sure this is it. I ring the bell, but no one answers. Maybe the doorbell isn't working? I knock instead. I'm about to knock again when the door opens.

A girl about my age stands in front of me. She has shoulder-length red hair, almost the same hue as mine—except mine's dyed. I think hers is natural. Lucky bitch. Any-who, she has droopy blue eyes and a tiny nose. It looks like she tried to pluck her own eyebrows but failed miserably. There's like hardly any eyebrows left. She's medium build...not fat, not skinny. She definitely doesn't do Pilates. Her red bra straps stick out from under a black tank top that reads "mornings suck." She's wearing a tiny pair of pajama shorts...too tiny. Her thick white thighs stick together.

"Hi. I might have the wrong apartment. I'm looking for Peter."

Her nose twitches and she moves her lips all the way to the right side of her face. She bites her bottom lip.

"No. You have the right apartment. Who are you?"

"Oh, hi!" I release a quick giggle. "My name's Kara."

"Yeah. It's just that he didn't tell me you were coming, so...uhm...okay." She looks me up and down.

"Well, surprise!"

She jumps backward. I didn't think I was that loud.

"Come in, I guess." She holds the door open for me and jogs up the stairs. I follow her.

She stops abruptly about halfway up, and I almost collide with her back. She breathes in and out three times. As she inhales, she lifts her arms above her head. She lowers them as she exhales.

Uh, okay? Good time for some yoga, I guess? Maybe she does do Pilates?

She walks the rest of the way up. Fucking weird, but I follow her.

"So...Where is he?"

She answers with a groan.

Rude. Okay. She sits on a couch in front of a TV, picks up the remote, and presses play. She stares at it wide-eyed, almost like she's in a trance. Some trashy, annoying reality TV show begins.

"You're Peter's..."

"Friend," she answers without looking at me...or blinking.

"Friend. Got it. And your name is...?"

"Hayley."

"Nice to meet you, Hayley."

"I'm trying to watch this."

"Oh... Well, it's just that you didn't tell me your name when you opened the door, so—" She turns the TV louder. "Okay, cool," I respond.

Peter walks out from a hallway in front of me. Thank God...

The girl—I already forgot her name—shoots him a look. Not a nice one, either.

"Hi, Kara." He walks over and gives me a hug.

"Hey! You look nice."

"Really? Thanks. So do you."

"You could have told me someone was coming," the girl says.

Peter looks at her. "Sorry, next time I will."

She scoffs. "No, you won't."

"Okay..." Peter turns toward me. "Are you ready?"

"I guess I'm home alone tonight?" she adds.

"Guess so."

"And if there's another spider?"

"I don't know, Hayley. Throw a shoe or something."

Right, that's it. Hayley.

"Nah, I'll just have Tristian get it." She smirks and scratches her head roughly without looking away from the TV. OMG, does she have lice? I look at Peter. His face turns bright red very quickly. Wow.

"No. That's not happening. I'm leaving. Let's go, Kara." He grabs my hand and leads me down the stairs. We walk out the door, and he locks it.

"So, who's Tristian?"

"Her boyfriend." He doesn't look up from the doorknob.

"So, why would you care if he got a spider?"

"Because she knows I don't want him in my apartment. He's a drug addict. So is she, can't you tell? She's high off her ass right now."

"Oh. No, I mean... I don't know."

We start walking toward his car.

"I really wouldn't care, but my little brother will be home, and I won't be."

"I get it. Sorry if I sounded like I was accusing you."

"It's fine."

He clicks the unlock button on his car keys and opens the passenger side door for me. I get in. He walks around to the driver's side and joins me.

"Just a second," he says as he looks at his phone. He starts typing away.

"Who are you texting?"

"Calling, actually. My brother, Danny. He's at Friendly's with some kids from school, but now I don't want him coming home if I'm not home. I want to see if he can go to a friend's house afterward."

He puts his phone up to his ear. "Hello? Yeah, hey. Are you having fun?... Good. Sorry I'm bothering you. Is there any way you can go to Matt's place after Friendly's?... No, everything's fine. I just won't be home... I know, I know... Just ask his mum when she picks you up. If she says no, call me right away. Got it?... Okay, I love you. I'll see you later... Okay, bye." He clicks the end call button. He turns to look at me and puts on his seat belt. "Sorry about that. I'm just worried, you know?"

"I don't have kids, but...yeah."

"She's just trying to ruin this for me."

"Why?"

"Because she's out of her mind when she's high, and he's...*Tristian*, her *boyfriend*...I think he's dangerous. He's always trying to fight me for some reason."

"Why don't you tell them to leave? Kick her out?"

"It's not that easy. I think she has rights. Tenant's rights. Secondly, I just can't do that to her. I do care about her, she's like—"

"A sister?"

"No! Not at all. A best friend, maybe."

"Well, it doesn't seem like she cares about you...or anybody."

"She's just not in the right headspace. If you got to know her—"

"You make a lot of excuses for her."

His phone rings.

"Oh! Hold on. Just a second!" He picks it up.

"Mrs. Rogers? Yes! Hi...Would that be okay? I won't be home for a little while." He leans back and smiles. "Thank you. You don't know how much it means to me. Can I drop a bag off for him at your apartment?... Great. I'll pick him up at around eleven o'clock tomorrow... Thank you so much!"

He hangs up and smiles.

"I have to go back in the house and pack an overnight bag for Danny."

"His friend's mom said he can sleep over?" I ask.

"Yes. Woo!" He smiles. "Fuck this, I'm not driving. We're calling an Uber. I need a drink...or five. Yeah, five." He flings his door open. "Wait here. I'll go pack a bag and put in the request for an Uber. Be right back."

"Uh...okay. Sounds good."

I don't mind waiting in the car, as long as I don't have to see Hayley again.

Peter

I whistle as I unlock the apartment door and jog up the stairs.

"Back so soon?" Hayley asks as I strut past her on the couch.

"Oh, don't you worry. I'm leaving again. Don't know when I'll be home."

"Then why are you back in here?"

"None of your business." I walk down the hallway and into Danny's room. I continue whistling as I open his closet doors. I pick up a drawstring bag and begin packing. Hayley appears in the doorway.

"I asked what you were doing," she says with her arms folded.

"Yeah, and I said, 'none of your business,'" I remind her. I stand up with the bag and walk into the bathroom. I pull Danny's toothbrush from the holder.

"Is Danny staying out tonight?"

"Yes, but good try at ruining my date. Almost succeeded." I push past her and into the kitchen. She follows me.

"So, you think I was trying to ruin your date?"

"Absolutely." I open a cabinet.

"Hate to break it to you, the world doesn't revolve around you."

I laugh. That's a good one. I pull an unopened package of cookies out of the cabinet and stuff it into the bag.

"Oh, the world doesn't revolve around me? Says the person who thinks I should stay at home just in case there's another spider? I suppose my life's purpose is to sit around the apartment waiting for spiders to crawl out of the cracks of the walls since you're too high to handle it?"

"I thought we were spending the night together."

I stare at her and squint my eyes just a wee bit. I sigh and turn away. "Don't play this fucking game with me. I'm done with it."

"Well, you—"

"Done!" I cut her off and sling Danny's bag around my arm. I walk out of the kitchen. "And don't think that because Danny won't be home you can have your slobby boyfriend in my apartment. He is not to come in here. *Ever.* Got it?"

"Don't talk to me like that. Major turn-off."

"Turn-off? What kind of game are you trying to play? This is my apartment. Mine. My name is on the lease agreement. I won't be threatened by you or him in any capacity."

"I didn't threaten you."

"You did. You fucking did. Right when you said you were having him come here. I don't feel safe around him and neither should you. He's threatened me with bodily harm multiple times. If you want to make bad choices, *make them somewhere else.* Danny and I will not be dragged down with you."

She looks away from me. Maybe she heard me. Maybe she finally fucking heard me.

I start whistling again as I head down the stairs. She doesn't say another word. I slam the door behind myself.

Kara

"Have you ever thought about this, though," he says and pounds his empty glass onto the table. He looks to his right side, licks his lips, rubs his chin, and turns back to me. "They're listening to us through our phones." The waiter walks by our table. "Yeah, can I get another round?" Peter asks, and the waiter nods.

"I've thought about it." I sip my wine.

"These ads on Facebook cannot be a coincidence! You can be talking about something, not even typing it into Google, but still, all of a sudden, ads! It's ridiculous." He scrolls through his phone. "Ads about bug spray... I just squashed a spider in my apartment!" He looks up at me. "I'm going to prove it." He holds his phone close to his mouth. "I'm pregnant. I'm pregnant. I'm pregnant. I'm pregnant," he repeats into the phone. The waiter drops his drink off, appearing confused. "I'm not actually pregnant," Peter says to him. "In case you were wondering." The waiter walks away.

"I'm sure he knew you aren't actually pregnant," I say.

He laughs. "All I'm saying is if I get baby ads tomorrow, point proven." He picks up his drink and takes a big sip.

Okay. If I want to enjoy tonight at all, I have to catch up with this guy. I chug down the rest of my Moscato like a lady.

"Nice," he says.

"Just trying to keep up with you, but you're not making it very easy."

"You would pass out on the table before you kept up with me. I'd have to carry you home, lass."

"Lass?"

"When I'm drunk I become more Scottish. It's a thing." He swirls his drink around in his glass. "Be honest with me," He leans forward, "is this the worst date you've ever been on?"

"Actually, far from it."

"What's the worst date you've ever been on then?" He laughs. "Worse than sitting here with a drunk Scotsman?"

"One guy took me to Burger King, which is cool. I'm not a gold digger. Then he suggested we go back to his place. Well, I didn't know he lived with his elderly mother, who he argued with about purchasing the wrong size adult diapers. Then, once he was done fighting with her, he tried to take me into the basement and have sex."

Peter's expression goes blank, and his mouth opens a little. I think I broke him.

"Wow, that is much worse than this. I'm so sorry you have such bad taste in men." He smirks and gulps the rest of his drink.

"Another round?" The waiter asks.

"Yeah. Her too! She needs it. Jesus, Mary, and St. Joseph."

"It was not that bad."

"Keep telling yourself that, hon. I hope you didn't get something off the dollar menu."

"Nope. I got a combo meal."

"That'a girl!"

"Still didn't have sex with him, though."

"I'm astounded. Not even for a combo meal? Those have to be what? Five dollars?"

"Closer to eight dollars, but yeah...not even for that."

"Were the diapers too big or too small? That matters. If he bought them too big, his mother could have been insulted, but I think they're still usable. On the contrary, if he bought them too small, it's very flattering, but they have to be returned."

"I feel like you're thinking about this way too critically." I laugh.

The waiter puts down our drinks.

"Do you really want to catch up with me?" he asks.

"Yes."

"Okay." He swaps our drinks with one swift motion.

"I cannot drink whiskey."

"Why not?"

"I just... I don't know!"

"You did it at McAlister's the other night."

"And I never want to do it again."

"It's a small glass. You can do it."

I pick up the glass and hold my nose. I shoot it down the back of my throat, making as little contact with my tongue as possible.

"Now it's a party," he says. "Another?"

"I haven't even finished swallowing this one yet, and you're asking me if I'm ready for another?" I cough and shake my head slowly.

"Is there something wrong with your throat? How long does it take you to swallow?" He picks up my wine and takes a leisurely sip. He crosses his legs and flips his hair behind his shoulder without smiling.

"Are you mocking me?"

"No, why? Do you do what I just did?" He teases, leaning in closer.

"Not as well as you do it."

"Thank you."

"Hey, I told you about my worst date. Your turn to tell me about yours," I insist.

"I don't have bad dates."

"Oh, yeah? I wonder if the women feel the same way."

"Judging by how the night usually ends, I'd say they do."

"You think this date will end the same way?" I ask, raising one brow and slouching over the table. I'm surprised at how brazen I've become. Then again, I am really starting to feel the alcohol.

"That's entirely up to you," he answers. "But I'm open to it, just so you know."

I pick up my phone. "I'm getting an Uber now."

"Hopefully to your place because mine—"

"Yeah, I know," I interrupt him.

"Check, please," Peter says with a big smile as the waiter approaches our table.

Tristian

Hals fell asleep on the couch, and she has her head dug deep into my fucking rib cage. She's dead asleep and drooling all over my fucking shirt. I lift her head a little and try to slide out from underneath her.

"Where are you going?" she asks groggily without opening her eyes.

"Bathroom."

"Ugh. All right."

"I'll be right back."

I lay her head back down on the couch. She immediately starts snoring. Awesome.

Now, if I were an ugly little weasel, twerp, rat, troll...where would I hide a key?

CHAPTER TWENTY-THREE

Danny

"Why do the weekends go by so fast! It would be okay if the school days went by fast too, but they don't!" I yell as I pick up my toothbrush.

"I don't hear any brushing!" Peter yells back.

"BECAUSE I'M BRUSHING QUIETLY!"

"If you were brushing, your mouth wouldn't be able to complain."

I grunt as I turn on the sink. I carefully squeeze the paste until I have a perfect amount. I start with my two front teeth slowly and gently. Peter appears in the doorway. His hair is down. He's still in his pajamas and old lady robe.

"Do I have to teach you how to brush your teeth? You have to do them all."

"I TOLD YOU I'M BRUSHING QUIETLY."

"Yeah. That's important. Wouldn't want to wake the neighbors."

I spit. "They're the ones that wake me up with their loud music and fighting!"

"I was kidding. They don't care about anything. Everyone minds their own business around here. Just finish brushing, please? Let's get going."

"Well, someone should file a noise complaint!"

"Are you joking? No one around here wants to see the police. That's a big no-no. Also, do you hear how loud Hayley has the TV sometimes? We'd get one too! Now, let's go. Finish up."

"Stop interrupting me, then!"

"Where is your game today?"

"Bellport."

"What time will you be home?"

"When the game is over, duh."

"All right. Just text me. Keep me updated."

I rinse off my brush and push past him. I walk straight into my room.

"PETER, WHERE ARE MY GLOVES?" I shout.

He sighs and approaches me. "They're in your closet, top shelf. Did you even look?"

"No, but I never know where you put things. You just put things everywhere sometimes." I slide my closet door open and pull out my gym bag.

"Yup, that's me. Putting things everywhere."

"I'm not going to answer you when you're sarcastic to me."

"That statement didn't require an answer. Do me a favor and get your laundry together quickly. That way I can do a wash this afternoon."

"Fine." I look around my room and spot a pair of gym shorts on the ground. I pick them up, shove them against my face, and sniff. "Yup. These need a good washing!" I hold them up with pride.

"Cool. Put them in the basket. In fact, put every item of clothing that's on the floor in your basket."

"But they're not all dirty."

"Did you wear them?"

"Yes."

"Then they're dirty. Basket. Now."

"Fine." I get on my knees and gather everything on the floor in my arms like a big loader truck.

"Beep. Beep. Beep." I dump the clothes into the basket. "Okay. All done."

"Thank you." I pick up my gym bag and head toward the door.

"Have a good day. Don't forget to text me when the game is over," Peter adds.

"Okay, bye."

"Love you."

I walk down the stairs and go to the bus stop.

Kara

"Come in," Peter says. He winks and holds the door open. He's holding an open beer bottle. His hair is messier than I've ever seen it before. He turns around and stumbles up the stairs.

"Whoa... Don't fall."

"Wouldn't that be really funny?"

"Why is it that every time I see you, you're drinking something?"

"You haven't met my brother yet, so that's probably why." He takes a seat on the couch.

"You're saying a thirteen-year-old boy is driving you to drink?"

He looks at me, completely baffled. "No. That's not what I meant at all. What I meant is I would never get drunk in front of him. Every time I see you, he's at school, or his friend's place. It's the perfect opportunity to get wasted!"

"Maybe we can see each other without getting drunk?" I walk over to the couch and put my purse down next to him. He watches.

"Why? Drunk is fun."

"You have an alcohol problem, Peter. Don't you have work tonight? Where's your roommate?"

"Yes, and I don't know. Not here. She doesn't have to tell me where she goes. I'm not her keeper. Want a beer?"

"No. I hate beer."

"Wine, then?" He tries to stand but falls back down on the couch. He laughs and laughs.

"All right. Just stay there. I'll get you water."

Am I really about to babysit him? That's not why I came over here. The last thing I need in my life is a man-child.

"I don't want any water. I am not an alcoholic! Alcoholics drink all the time. I only drink when I see you, apparently."

"Great," I respond. "Maybe that's why you come off as an alcoholic to me. Ever think about that?"

"If you had to live with your ex, I'm sure you'd be drinking too. She's driving me crazy!"

EX?

"Hayley is your ex-girlfriend?"

"Oh, uhm... No."

"Yes, she is. You just said so."

"It was a short go. Hardly a relationship."

"I guess that explains why she's not your sister. Because you fuck her?"

"No, not anymore. Only a couple of times. I could count them on my hands—on one hand, actually! Wasn't even good sex. Let me tell you, it was *so* boring. She's *so* boring at sex. I didn't enjoy it at all. That's why I had to break up with her."

"Oh my God!" I fold my arms. "I don't want to hear this. And also, I don't care if it was the worst sex in the world. You told me you were just friends!"

"We are friends...now."

"You left out the 'now' part!"

"It's not like you and I are in a serious relationship, Kara. Calm down."

"Hold on. We're not in a serious relationship? I'm very confused right now."

"You are? I mean...are we an item? We can be."

"I am not going any farther with this until you prove to me that you can stop all the drinking and start telling me the full truth about everything!"

"Good luck with that. Anyway, do you want Greek food? I'm really craving spinach pie. You came over here to eat lunch, right?"

"Can I ask you something?"

"Sure."

"What's wrong with you?"

He cracks up and throws his head back. "I don't understand the question."

"After we left the restaurant last week, you were adamant that we were a couple, and we were going to be together forever. It was very sweet, actually. I thought you really meant it, but I guess I was wrong. Maybe you just wanted to get into bed with me, and you were just really, really, *really* drunk—as usual. *Sloshed.* Now, I'm here, I'm trying to talk to you about this, and you're talking about food."

"Huh. I said all that? I'm sorry, I don't remember it at all."

"You're unbelievable!" I grab my purse and head to the door.

"Kara!" He runs after me.

"What? What do you want? I never should have hooked up with some random bartender. That was just me asking for trouble!"

"I really like you. I'll be better. I'm sorry. Look, I won't drink anything else the rest of the day, and I'll mean everything I say. Will you please stay?"

I take a long hard look at him. Why does he have to be so adorable? His smile. His eyes...

"I'll stay, but I want Italian food, not Greek." I put my purse back down on the couch.

"Done," he says. "Anything for my...girlfriend." He does a sarcastic little half smile and bites his lip.

"Nope. Not girlfriend."

"Girl...pal?"

"Pour the beer down the drain, and I'll consider 'girl pal.'"

"Okay. I'll grab the menu for Bianca's while I'm at it." He walks away.

I shake my head and cradle it in my hands.

Peter

There's nothing good on the radio. I click the power off button as I pull into the complex. Now I'm alone with my thoughts again, great...or am I? I check the rearview mirror but no one's in the back seat. Okay... What can I think about other than...

Kara! I'll think about Kara. Wow. It's already been two weeks since Kara, and I've become...what's the term they use? "Official?" I think I've been doing a better job with my drinking habit. It's probably for the best. I didn't have one drink on our date tonight. I hope she's proud of me—at least, I feel proud of myself. It was somewhat enjoyable without beer or whiskey.

I park in front of Danny's friend's apartment. I get out of the car and knock on the door. Danny answers it.

"You're answering their door now?"

"I knew it was you. You know, I could have just walked home. I do it every day from the bus stop."

"I was passing by, anyway." I look past Danny and see Matt's mum.

"Thank you!" I say to her and wave.

Danny turns around halfway and gives a small wave to Matt, who's standing next to his mother. He steps outside and closes the door behind himself.

"How was your night?" I ask.

"It was good."

"What did you do?"

"Played video games."

"That sounds like fun."

"How was your night?"

"Mine?"

"You weren't home. Where were you?"

"I went to dinner with a friend."

"Like a date?"

"Yes."

"Not with Hayley, right?" He smiles.

"Not with Hayley."

"Nice."

I unlock the car door and he throws his bag inside. It hits the windshield.

"Hey, don't do that," I reprimand him.

"Sorry. What's her name?"

I shake my head, and we both get into the car.

"Kara."

"Am I going to meet her?"

"I don't know."

"What did Hayley do tonight, then?"

"I guess you can ask her when we get home."

I back out of the parking lot and drive toward our building. I park in my normal spot. Danny opens the car door and runs up to the apartment. I get out of the car much more slowly and follow him.

"Whoa, what's the rush?"

"I want to download a new game."

"You can't just use my card to buy games whenever you please. How much does it cost?"

"It just came out today, but I *need* to have it. Everyone's getting it. If I don't have it, I'll be the only one without it."

"That's not what I asked. I asked how much it costs."

"It's the low, low price of sixty-nine ninety-nine," he responds and turns back toward the door.

"Sixty-nine ninety-nine? Are you out of your mind? No, rent is due this week. I can't pay sixty-nine ninety-nine."

"Come on, Peter. It's a credit card. You can just pay it off later. Please, please, please."

"I said no, Danny. Maybe when it goes on sale."

He lets go of the doorknob.

"What if I don't get the deluxe edition, and I only get the regular edition for fifty-nine ninety-nine?"

"Oh, okay. So you were going to use my card to buy the deluxe edition?"

"Yeah, but you know deluxe is much better. It has all the added content."

"I'll tell you what... Your math quiz is on Tuesday. If you get an eighty or better, I'll buy you the deluxe edition."

"But I need to get the game tonight!"

"Nope, you're not getting it tonight. Sorry."

"But, Peter, that's four days! Everyone is going to be so far ahead of me by then!"

"Yeah? Oh my God." I put my hands on my cheeks as in realization and shock. "Imagine how far ahead they'll be if you don't get an eighty on Tuesday? I don't think you'll ever catch up!"

"Ugh!" He rolls his eyes and stomps his feet, wiggling the doorknob again. "Unlock the door!"

"So unfair, I know." I twist my key in the knob and swing the door open. We walk upstairs.

"Matt's going to have the game, and that's all he's going to talk about on Monday. I'm going to lose my mind!"

We reach the top of the steps. From there, I can see her. Two bare feet are sticking out from behind the couch. Hayley's lying on the floor, covered in her own vomit.

"Is she okay?" Danny asks.

I don't have the chance to answer. Tristian sits up on the couch, clearly startled. His hair is standing straight up.

"Danny...I want you to go back downstairs and sit in the car." I hand him my keys.

"What? No! Hayley?" he calls out.

"I'm going to take care of it. Just please, go sit in the car."

He takes the keys from my hand. I think he's about to argue further, but then Tristian stands and walks toward us. I shoot Danny a look that tells him I'm not kidding around, and he runs down the stairs. I hear the front door close.

"She's good, man. I swear." Tristian stumbles over and pats my back. "Happens all the time."

I kneel beside Hayley and pull my cell phone out of my pocket. My beautiful Hayley... What have you done to yourself? What have you let him do to you?

"What are you doing, man?" he asks.

"Stop calling me 'man,'" I snap. "I'm not your man."

"Are you calling nine-one-one? You can't call nine-one-one. We'll all be fucked!"

"Oh yeah? Watch me!" I dial and put my phone to my ear.

As the phone rings, I grab Hayley's wrist. I feel a pulse. Thank God. I can breathe again. I carefully roll Hayley over on her side, just in case she vomits again. I rub her back as the phone rings.

"What's the location of your emergency?"

"I'm not playing! Put down the fucking phone, you leprechaun!" Tristian demands.

I laugh. Leprechaun? That's actually a good one.

"Hi. I live at ninety-three A, Oak Commons, in Medford. I came home, and my roommate is unconscious on the floor. It looks like she overdosed on something. There's some empty bottles here, but all of the labels are ripped off, so I couldn't even tell you what she took." I examine an empty pill bottle on the coffee table. "Probably Oxycodone. Maybe something else too."

"Looks like we already have a report."

"You do?" I ask.

Danny must have called. Damn, he's fast.

"I'm not fucking kidding with you!" Tristian kicks the coffee table, then sits on the couch and rubs his foot in pain. He just gets more and more pathetic.

"So, someone should be here soon?" I ask the dispatcher.

"Yes."

"Thank you." I end the call.

"Why the fuck did you call them?!" Tristian yells.

"Because your girlfriend is unconscious on the floor, and you don't even give a fuck so long as you save your own ass!" I stand and walk toward him.

"What, do you wanna fight me?"

"Hell, no!" I respond. "I don't want to fight you. That's the last thing on my mind, you crazy basturt! Besides, you're so fucked up right now it'd be too unfair."

"I'd still kick your scrawny little ass!" He stands and stumbles again.

"Last chance. The police are on their way. You could leave, or you can stay here and wait for them. That's your choice." I walk back to Hayley. "If they show up here and you're 'kicking my scrawny little ass,' I think it might turn out pretty bad for you."

I kneel down, pulling the hair tie out of my own hair. I put Hayley's hair back into a ponytail, tying it nice and tight. I look down at her and caress her face.

"Keep your hands off my girl!"

"I'm trying to help my friend. What are you doing?" I ask. "Nothing...and I'm 'the little man'?"

Red and blue lights beam through the window and reflect off the wall. I smile and look directly into his eyes. It's his turn to run... Run away from this. It feels good to be only a spectator.

"Run. Run away," I whisper. "Go!"

He backs up from me slowly, then faster, until he bangs into the sliding glass door. He turns around and opens it, sprinting down the balcony stairs. I shouldn't be smiling, but I still am.

Hayley

I wake up in a white room to the sound of beeping machines. I know where I am. Fuck. I close my eyes again.

"Hayley?"

I look to my right, and see Peter sitting in a chair across from my bed. He's dressed nicely but looks...messy. That's unusual. What happened?

"Yeah," I respond quietly.

"You scared the shit out of me."

"What did I do? Where's Tristian?"

"He ran off when I called the police."

"You called the police?" I open my eyes wider.

"I had to. You were on the floor. I didn't know what you'd taken. This is no good, Hayley."

Oh yeah. Now I remember.

"I don't want to be lectured right now." I try to turn over, but the wire in my arm gets caught on the bed rail. "Crap." I try to unhook it.

"I'm not lecturing you." He stands and untangles the wire from the railing.

"Good because you were out with Kara all night again."

"What does that have to do with this?"

What does he mean? That has everything to do with this! If he were home, Tristian wouldn't have come over. If Tristian wouldn't have come over, I wouldn't have taken any pills.

"You left me home all alone."

"To be an adult and make your own choices? Should I babysit you now?"

"You knew this was going to happen eventually!"

"Sure, blame me for it. Wouldn't be the first time I get blamed for something totally fucked up."

I manage to turn around and face the opposite direction. I can't listen to him. Like he's so perfect? Classic Virgo behavior.

"Now they're going to keep me here for God knows how long—and probably in the psych ward, too!"

"Can you be quiet? I'm trying to sleep!" someone calls from the curtain past Peter.

"Great, I have a roommate?" I ask.

"Yep. Why would you get a private room?" Peter asks.

"Just leave me alone, Peter. I can't deal with you right now. My head hurts too much. You're really fucking pissing me off."

"Same," he says.

"What's that supposed to mean?" I shout, still looking away from him.

"You're really pissing me off too."

"Me three!" the dumbass calls from behind the curtain. I hear Peter's stupid fucking raspy-ass laugh. Now my head is pounding.

"If LUCKY THE LEPRECHAUN would leave the room, then I'd shut the fuck up—ASSHOLE!" I yell at my roommate. We're off to a great start.

"Oh, yeah. I forgot I'm the cereal leprechaun now. That's a new one. I like it. Was it Tristian or you who decided that?"

"Both," I respond quietly.

"Great. Thanks. Well, Danny is in the waiting room because, you know, he had to suffer through this too."

"I don't care."

"I know you don't. That's the problem."

I flip him the bird without turning around.

"You're welcome," he says.

"For what?"

"Eh, for saving your life, and for being here. Funny... I don't see Tristian anywhere."

I flip him the bird again, closing my eyes. I listen as his footsteps grow farther and farther away.

CHAPTER TWENTY-FOUR

Somebody

I'm waiting in front of Glas' bakery. According to my watch, I'm a wee bit early. I have my back against the storefront. It feels as if someone's watching me.

When I turn toward the shop, I catch Mr. Glas staring straight at me. I can see his bald head and big bloodshot brown eyes from here, but I pretend I can't. I face front again and close my eyes. The bell rings as the door opens.

"What are you doing out here?" he asks.

"Me?"

"Is there anyone else out here, lad?"

"I'm waiting for someone."

"Who?"

"A friend."

"Shouldn't you be home? Your mother will be cross."

"Then let her be!" I pull a cigarette and a matchbook from my pocket, lighting up.

"If she comes around here, I'm going to have to tell her I seen you."

"Go ahead. I'll be long gone."

"Is this new attitude because your father died?"

I laugh and take a drag of my cigarette. "First of all, it's not new. You don't know me. Also, it's quite the opposite. I wish my father had died. He's still alive, apparently. He's me, I'm him, and...and I wish I were dead."

"Don't say that!"

"I'll say what I want. I can't compare to my father. I can't even compare to Adair. I can't do anything right."

"Your ma tell you that?"

"What? I don't know. Why would you even ask me that?"

He folds his arms and raises one eyebrow. He's looking at me—no, through me. What the fuck?

"Guid gear comes in sma' bulk," he finally says. I don't answer him. I take a long drag and blow out a big cloud of smoke. "It's an English phrase," he continues.

"I know, Mr. Glas. I've heard it before. It doesn't make me feel better."

"I'm a small guy, too. I'm pretty successful and happy. Just because you aren't a farmer doesn't mean you can't be something else. You ever thought about being a baker?"

I laugh again. My mum would never want me to be a baker. She scoffs at Mr. Glas any turn she gets. She says he does "women's work," and that he's a "feeble man." Actually, she's speaks very unkindly about him for no real reason. Then again, she does the same to me...except to my face.

"Mr. Glas? Please leave me alone."

"I just thought maybe you'd like to be my new apprentice. I could use some help around here, and it would keep you out of trouble. Get your mind off of things. We could spend some time together. That would be very nice, I think. We could—"

"I'm not in any trouble. Thanks for worrying about me. I appreciate it very much, but I don't want to be your apprentice.

I don't want to live anywhere on Na h-Eileanan Siar, and I especially don't want to live here. Look, just, please... Go back inside. I'm fine, really."

I take one last drag of my cigarette and crush it into the cobblestone.

He sighs. "Well, if you change your mind..."

"Trust me, I won't."

He goes back inside of the bakery. Jesus, Mary, and St. Joseph...

I stare straight ahead. Maybe she's not coming. Maybe she couldn't get here after all. Maybe her parents said, "No, you can't see that farm boy you just met yesterday." It would make sense. I wouldn't let my daughter hang out with me.

I wait another five minutes. I contemplate going home, but then I see her turn the corner. I smile.

She runs towards me. "Hallo!"

She gives me a hug. I'm so stunned that I don't even hug her back. I just stand there, paralyzed. She releases her embrace.

"Do you have another cigarette?"

"What?" I laugh.

"You smell like smoke. Share?"

"Sure. I rolled them myself."

I reach into my pocket, pull one out, and hand it over. She sticks it in her mouth. I light the cigarette for her with my matchbook.

"Thanks!" She takes a drag. "Any good bars around here?"

I feel my face drain of all color.

"Uhm, Teva... I'm only fifteen."

"So? Me too."

I feel relieved.

"*Oh... You have to be eighteen on the islands. Is that different in Glasgow?*"

"*You don't have a fake?*"

"*A fake what?*"

"*A fake ID?*"

"*I don't even have a real ID.*"

"*What?*"

"*I have nothing, not even a birth certificate. I told you we're crazy here.*"

"*I'll get you a fake.*" *She takes a drag of her cigarette.*

"*You can do that?*"

"*Uh, yeah. My friend Harris can get them.*"

"*Will the picture look like me?*"

"*Close enough.*"

"*All right, cool! I mean... There's a tiny distillery in town, and he'll sell to anyone. I usually just buy my whiskey there. But once you leave our town everyone is much more strict, and there's sheriffs, and—*"

"*What do you want your name to be?*"

"*Huh?*"

"*On the ID.*"

"*Can't I just keep it the same?*"

"*Uhm, no. Sorry.*"

"*Oh, okay. Well, then... I don't know.*"

"*You look like a Peter to me.*" *She throws her cigarette onto the cobblestone.*

"Peter?"

"Yes. Actually... YES! I think it's perfect. It just rolls off the tongue."

"Okay." I smile. "Peter... I really like that, Teva. It suits me, I think."

"I think so too. I'll have Harris order it when I get home."

I stare at her for a moment. She's the coolest girl I've ever met. Actually, she's the coolest person I've ever met, man or woman.

"What?" she asks.

"When your trip is over, and you're all done 'glamping,' will you really come back here to see me?"

"Of course I will, Peter."

She says my name... Well, it's not my name, but it feels like it should have been my name all along—and it'll actually be on an ID! A real ID! Well, not a real, real ID...but a real fake ID! I'll feel like a person! A person that actually exists in this world! I'll feel warm and happy...

I'll feel like somebody for the very first time!

Peter

Danny and I walk upstairs. I put my keys down on the coffee table.

"Is she home?" he asks.

"I don't know. Can you do me a favor? I saw you didn't put your laundry away this morning. Can you do that please?"

Hayley's only been home from the hospital for a couple of days. She's caused me so much grief since her incident.

"Yeah, okay." He heads toward his room, and I follow. He dumps the contents of his laundry basket onto his bed.

"That was all folded nicely in there, you know."

"It's okay," he says.

I shake my head and rub my eyes. "I'm going to close your door."

"Why?"

"I have to talk with Hayley. Nothing you need to be involved in."

"About the—"

"Yeah. If you need me, I'll be in the kitchen."

"Okay."

I close the door slowly and walk to the kitchen. I open the fridge, looking inside, but I don't reach for anything.

How am I going to do this? Maybe I can find a place for Hayley to go, like a rehab or something? No, I don't have enough money. I could try calling around, see if anyone will let her stay with them? We don't have any family though. Who would I call? DSS might know if there's anyone that can help her, someone who isn't me, or...maybe I should just let her figure it out on her own.

What's done is done. I made a new start for myself. It all worked out. If I can do it, she can too. I suddenly notice that I'm letting a lot of cold air out of the refrigerator. I close it quickly.

I stretch, feeling myself getting emotional. STOP. I can't show her that I feel this way, that I'm pretty and weak. She'll never take me seriously when I tell her to leave, and she has to leave. There are no more options left. The caseworker said it's her or Danny, and I choose Danny.

I clear my throat. This is going to be messy, but if anyone's going to be an emotional wreck, it has to be her and not me. I have to be in control of the situation. I'm not a "little man." It's time for me to prove that.

I sit down at the kitchen table and begin to go through the paperwork the caseworker gave me.

Hayley

Wednesday, April 13th

It's time to make that big leap, Aquarius! It may seem like things haven't been going your way.

Now it's your turn to change that. If you're looking for a sign to make that big decision, this is it.

Don't be afraid. Go out and make it happen!

I put my phone down. What should I wear? I go into my closet and pull out one of Peter's old sweatshirts I've been hiding. This is nice and baggy... Now that I *know,* I feel like everyone can tell.

I pull the sweatshirt on over my tee, and I walk past Danny's room. His door is closed. I know he's in there. He just doesn't want to see me.

When do I tell Peter? Is he going to believe that it's his? It has to be. Tristian and I use condoms. How is he going to take it?

I take my time going to the kitchen, picking at the cuticles of my hands. Peter's sitting at the small table, looking over some papers. Maybe something with Danny's school?

I walk by and open the fridge. I haven't said much to him since I've been home. He's said nothing to me. I don't know how to tell him the news. He hasn't been in a good mood lately. I'm starting to think he won't be very happy about it at all. I grab a string cheese from the fridge door. Maybe I should start the conversation lightly...

"Did you have a good day at work?"

"Excuse me?" He sounds very impatient.

"Uh...work, this morning. Was it—"

"I didn't go to work."

"Oh. Where were you?"

"Try court."

"Court? Why?"

He picks up the papers in front of him. "I guess, according to New York State—and, I'm sure, every other fucking state in this country—it's not considered 'safe' to have a minor in a home where there's the presence of drug abuse. Makes a lot of sense, huh?"

Yeah, I know. I heard all that at the hospital after they told me... Yikes. Double yikes. I didn't even think about Danny.

"Oh." I try to walk out of the kitchen. This is not a good time.

"You realize I'm going to lose custody of Danny."

I stop walking. "Sorry. I hope not—"

He stands. "Do you think 'sorry' is a magic fucking word? That 'sorry' takes away all of the bad you've caused in the world? I wish! I wish 'sorry' could change a lot of fucking things, but that's not how it works."

"I guess Danny—"

"Don't talk about Danny. He's not going anywhere. It's been settled."

"The court ruled in our favor?"

What a relief. Maybe this won't be so bad. We can work on it together before the baby's born.

He laughs. "'Our?' The court said either you go, or he goes. Guess who's going?"

I stare blankly, feeling myself start to sweat.

"When I'm at work, he's staying at Matt's. That's happening until you're gone. You have seven days." He stands and approaches me. "Get gone," he whispers in my ear.

"Peter... I have nowhere to go!"

"That sucks." He walks past me. "Go to DSS. They'll put you somewhere."

"You can't make me leave!" Tears rush to my eyes.

I'm getting kicked out again, but this time there's no Melissa. There's no back-up plan, and...I'm pregnant. I look at him. I really, really look at him. I can't read his face. He loves me, doesn't he? He wouldn't abandon me, would he?

"You're right," he says. "Come here."

He opens his arms. I run into him and sob against his shoulder.

"I don't know where I'd go! I have no one! I don't want to go to a shelter!"

"You're not going anywhere. Not with my sweatshirt."

"What?"

"Take off my fucking sweatshirt and start packing your shit."

"No. I'm not packing! You can't kick me out, Peter!"

"Oh, honey, I can, and I am. I've already spoke with the sheriff's office about evicting you if you don't leave on your own. Either you pack your shit, or I throw it out the fucking window and change the locks."

"Peter! Please... Please listen to me! Danny can go to a foster home like Melissa's just for a little while until I can prove I'm getting sober. He'll be fine! Then you can take him back, like my mom took me back."

"That is not happening. That's never happening. I warned you months ago. I'll choose him every single time."

I fall on the floor and curl up into a ball, wrapping my arms around my legs.

"Cut it the fuck out," he says.

"I... I can't. I don't..." I say as I try to catch my breath. "Tristian told you not to call the police that night, but you did! You motherfucker, you did!"

I jump to my feet and shove him into the wall. He looks surprised. I hold him there. He doesn't struggle.

"I saved your life. You should be grateful," Peter says. "Tristian wanted to let you die on the floor, covered in your own vomit. I've done all I can do for you, you fucking leech bitch."

"Maybe I didn't want you to save my life! For fucking what?" I grab his shirt by the collar, pounding my fists against him, but he doesn't try to stop me or hit me back. He keeps his hands at his sides and lets me beat on him. He's being extra careful.

"Are you done punching me? Or should I call the police again and have you removed right now? You'll definitely have some place to go then. Maybe being locked away would help you straighten your fucking life out. You might find a roommate who's nicer than me. Actually...I'm sure of it." He smirks deviously.

"Tristian was right about you! I wish I could bash your fucking face in right now." I try to catch my breath. I release my grip of his shirt.

"That would be bad for you. Worse than it would be for me." He starts walking toward my bedroom.

"WHAT ARE YOU DOING?" I dive toward him.

He opens my door and goes right inside.

"Peter!"

He pulls all of my clothes out of the closet and throws them onto the floor.

"Stop! Calm down!" I yell. "Please, stop it!"

He doesn't stop. He grabs a plastic tub from under my bed.

"Go ahead, start putting your shit in there. Go on."

He rips out the drawer of my bedside table, dumping the contents into the tub, then he throws it onto the floor.

"Why are you doing this? You don't understand!" I yell and I wipe my eyes.

"I understand perfectly well." He kicks the empty drawer. "Seven fucking days."

He storms out, slamming the door harder than I ever have.

I collapse onto the floor and wail into the carpet. The one person who I thought would always be there for me...and I'm having his baby. I should have known this would happen. He told me. He fucking said it himself. *Danny comes first.* Why didn't I listen to him the first time?

Still sobbing, I pick up my phone. My tears left wet marks on the carpet. What am I going to do? Homeless and pregnant. Another one of those fucking statistics...

I pull up Tristian's text box.

```
Hes kicking me out of
  the apartment!! I'm
going 2 be homeless!!
        IDK what 2 do!!
```

The three dots appear on my screen. He's typing.

```
I had a idea but u
said...
```

He's right. Even my horoscope said it was time to make a change...to make that *big decision*.

```
OK let's do it.
```

Peter's choosing Danny over me, just like he said he would. It's time for me to choose myself and my baby. Someone has to choose us. Tristian was right. Survival of the fittest.

CHAPTER TWENTY-FIVE

Danny

"Do I have to go to Matt's today?" I ask as I stuff a binder into my backpack. Peter's standing over me, watching.

"Every day after school until Wednesday, just for now. On Wednesday you'll come home. We'll order pizza or something."

"Are you sure?"

Peter looks at me confused. "Yes, I'm sure. Why would you ask me that?"

"I...I don't know."

"What's wrong with going to Matt's?"

"Nothing, I guess. I don't know. I like hanging out with him, but sometimes I'm tired after school and practice, and I just want to lay down in bed."

"You'll get to do that soon."

"A hundred percent positive?"

"A hundred and ten. Danny, what's up? Talk to me."

"I heard you and Hayley yesterday. I mean, you were really loud."

"I'm sorry. It had to be done."

"Well, what if she doesn't leave?"

"Then I ask the landlord to change the locks. Or better yet, we move into a different apartment. Nothing else will happen, but she's going to leave. She has no choice."

"You swear?"

"Danny. I am going to be here for you until I take my last breath. I swear. No one is taking you anywhere."

That's a relief. I don't want to be put into foster care. I won't know anyone. Home won't feel like home. It's scary.

"What do you want for breakfast?" he asks.

"I'll just take a granola bar with me on the bus."

"Okay. They're in the cabinet. Your lunch is in the fridge."

"Got it." I head into the kitchen.

"Don't forget your cleats today. I'm not going to have any time to drop them off at school."

"I left them in my gym locker."

"All right. Good. You should only bring your uniform home on Friday so we can wash it. Other than that, keep it at school, please."

Yeah, yeah, yeah... I'm much more concerned about what's happening with Hayley than with laundry.

I grab the brown bag out of the fridge and throw in a granola bar. When I get back to the living room, Peter's got his coat on, all ready to go.

"You don't have to walk me to the bus stop."

"Yes, I do. Just for this week. I have to."

"Ugh," I moan.

"How about I stay at the end of the block? No one will even know I'm there. I'm not that embarrassing anyway, am I? I never thought I'd be an embarrassment. It's kind of funny, actually."

"No. You're not embarrassing. It's just that I feel like everyone knows something's wrong."

He puts his hand on my back. "Nothing will be wrong. Not on Wednesday. Everything will be normal, for once. I promise you."

"Okay." I pick up my backpack.

It's going to be such a long day, such a long week...

Peter

                    Drinks tonight?

Are you serious?

                      Kind of

What about work?

            You can come to the
         bar, and we can drink
                    there

You really think it's
a good idea to get
drunk at work again,
Peter?

               No. I think that's a
                 horrible idea.

            I think getting tipsy
             at work is a good
                    idea.

You are not funny.
This has to stop.

            You are being so
        lame, Kara. I haven't
        had a drink in a long
            time. I need one
              right now.

No. You're being lame.
You're the one that

always says you're
going to get fired.

> I know, but I'm so
> stressed out lately.
> Even more so than
> usual.

What's going on?

> Can we talk about it
> over drinks?

No. We're not
drinking.

You told me you
would stop drinking.

Why do I ever believe
anything that you say?

> OK. OK. Sorry.
>
> I'll stop.

Will I see you this
weekend?

> The only way you're
> going to see me is if
> you come to
> McAlister's.
>
> I have to be home
> every day.

Why?

> Something with my
> brother.

Oh...

Can I come to your
place then? Still
never met him.

> Now is really not a
> good time to come to
> my place or to meet
> him. Like I said, we
> can talk about it
> over drinks 😊

No, sir, we cannot.
Don't try me.

> OK.

I bought beer with no
alcohol. Tastes like
sadness.

All for you.

Thank you

I wouldn't drink
sadness for any other
woman.

K

Really? K? If she only knew what I was going through right now...

All right. I'll talk
to you later then.

She doesn't answer. I'm fully prepared for her next text to be "This isn't working out." It's okay. If it is, it is. I don't need the added heartache. Maybe women aren't even in the realm of things I should be thinking about right now—or ever, any of them. They just cause me problems. Not that it's their fault. It's usually mine.

"It's always yours!" a small, familiar voice says.

I snap my head quickly to the left, but he's not there.

I set my phone on the side table, rubbing my eyes with my palms. I turn over in bed. I don't have to be at my first job for another two hours. I can fit in some rest. It's hard to sleep at night knowing both Danny and Hayley are in the apartment. When Danny's at school, right before I have to go to work, that's the perfect time.

I set an alarm and close my eyes.

Hayley

I hear the coffee machine brewing in the kitchen and peek around the corner. Peter's facing the wall. He picks up the cream and pours a tiny amount into his mug. He turns around, and I hide, tip-toeing back to the couch. When he leaves the kitchen, he walks right by. He doesn't even acknowledge me. Fuck you...

He goes into the bathroom. When the shower starts, I get on the floor and reach under the couch. I pull out the water bottle filled with the "solution." Tristian hasn't told me what it is exactly, but he says you can't taste it or smell it. I twist off the cap and take a sniff. Smells like water.

I go into the kitchen and stare into Peter's coffee cup. He likes to let it cool down before he drinks it. I have to do this. I have no choice. I rub my stomach and look down at my hands. My eyes well with tears. We can't be out on the street with nothing...we just can't.

I take a deep breath and pick up the mug, pouring some coffee down the drain. I empty just enough solution into the mug so that it doesn't look like anything's missing. After a quick wipe with a napkin, it's impossible to tell that anything was poured out.

I give the sink a quick rinse, then I open the fridge to see if I can find anything else that he might drink. There's a big bottle of red Gatorade, missing only a few sips. It's zero sugar, so it's definitely not Danny's. I take it out of the fridge and pour a bunch of it down the drain. I empty the rest of the contents of the water bottle into it and shake.

The shower turns off.

I throw the empty water bottle into the garbage and run back into the living room. I sit back down on the couch.

```
                         I did it ur sure he
                            wont taste it?
```

```
Yup. I saw this on one
of those tru crime
shows
```

```
                                     OMFG!

                         If you saw it on TV
                        the person must have
                               got caught!!!
```

```
Yea he did But im
smarter.
```

I throw the phone down and stand. Maybe I should just pour everything down the sink. This is never going to—

Peter walks out of the bathroom. His wet hair's in a bun, and he's dressed for work. He looks directly at me.

"Good morning," he says. "I hope you've been looking for places to stay."

"I have something planned."

He walks into the kitchen and comes back with his cup of coffee. "Oh? What's that?"

"Uh...I don't need to discuss my plans with you."

"That's true." He puts the mug up to his lips and takes a sip. He pulls it away and frowns at the cup.

Fuck...Fuck...Fuck...

"W–What? What are you looking at?" I ask.

"Uh...The mug."

"Why?"

"It looks like it must have chipped in the dishwasher."

"Oh."

He takes another sip. "Time to get ready for work."

He walks back into the kitchen, and I close my eyes. *True crime shows?* Really? Even my mother was smarter than that, and she still got caught!

Peter pokes his head back out of the kitchen. "Did you want coffee?"

"Why? Do you suddenly care about me again? Fuck off."

"All right. I'll go fuck right off, then."

A few minutes later, he leaves the kitchen while holding the Gatorade from the fridge. "I'm leaving."

Can he tell I'm nervous?

"Bye," I say as calmly as possible.

He puts the Gatorade on the coffee table and goes into the bathroom once more. I stare at the bottle.

"I thought you were leaving?" I yell from the living room.

"Yeah, I am. I just... I'll be right out. Coffee always makes me feel sick. I don't know why I drink it. Should switch to tea!"

I run into the kitchen and check the sink. There it is. The empty coffee mug.

Peter

I pull into the parking lot of the apartment complex. It's only one o'clock, but I feel terrible. Once I park, I rest my head on the steering wheel for a few minutes. Maybe this is a really bad migraine? A stomach virus? I'm sweating profusely. I reach into the cup holder and pick up my Gatorade, taking a sip. They usually suggest electrolytes for a hangover, so maybe they'll help now too?

I get out of the car and walk into the apartment. There she is, still on the couch. I have nothing to say to her.

"You're home?" she asks.

"Yeah. I really don't feel well. I just couldn't make it through the day. I'm going to lay down before I go to McAlister's tonight."

"If you don't feel well, maybe you shouldn't go."

"I can't lose that job." I gulp down some more of my Gatorade. Hayley's staring at me. It's a wee bit uncomfortable. "What?"

"I just don't think you should be serving drinks sick...getting everyone else sick."

"Maybe I'll just see how I feel later."

"What do you feel like?"

"My head is hurting, and I've been vomiting and shitting all morning. Would you like to know more?"

"Nope. That's enough."

"Thought so."

In my room, I fall onto the bed. There are cramps in my chest and abdomen like I've never felt before. Maybe I can sleep it off. I take a few more sips of my Gatorade and put the bottle on my nightstand. I have a few hours to spare.

Hayley

"Yeah, he's home. He's sleeping. He only stayed at his first job for about an hour...said he doesn't feel good."

I hear banging coming from Peter's bedroom.

"Tristian, I have to go," I whisper.

"Do you need me to come there?" he asks.

"No. Just let me go. Bye." I hang up the phone.

I walk down the hallway and into Peter's room. He's sitting on his bed, shirtless, and holding a small garbage pail. His face is inside of it. His chest and arms are shiny with sweat.

"Are you throwing up?"

"Yeah..." He gags into the bin. "I feel better right after I vomit, but then I start feeling sick again...even worse than before. It's so strange." He picks up the Gatorade bottle and chugs.

"Yeah... That's weird."

"I'm feeling okay right now, so I'm going to work." He tries to stand. He stumbles a little but doesn't fall.

"I don't think you should do that."

"I don't care what you think." He walks slowly over to his closet.

"So, what? You're just gonna throw up all over everyone there?"

"There's a bathroom." He puts on a black shirt.

"Well, you're just gonna get everyone sick then?"

"Look, I said... I said I'm feeling a little better. Maybe it's food poisoning or something?" He tries to walk toward me, but he trips over nothing, landing on his hands and knees.

"What the fuck?" I hoist him up and help him onto the bed.

"It's like...the room is really hot...and spinning. Is it really hot in here?"

"Maybe you should drink more of this Gatorade." I hand him the bottle. He needs to sleep right now—a deep, deep sleep. I don't want to see him suffer. I just want this to end.

He tries to hold the bottle, but he drops it. His eyes can hardly focus on me. I push him against the backboard and prop his head up. I untwist the cap and hold it up to his mouth. I'll help him along. He cannot make it to work. He has to stay home. I can't get caught. I want to be a part of my baby's life.

"Swallow it," I demand.

He drinks it, but after a little while, he tries to push the bottle away from his mouth.

"Hayley, stop," he says. "I need—" He grabs the garbage can and vomits into it again.

This is not going to work if his body keeps rejecting it! I knew Tristian wasn't smart enough for this. Fuck!

"I think you're dehydrated," I say.

"How the fuck could I be...be dehydrated? Look how much of this, fuck...Gatorade I've had?" He stands back up. "Okay...I can do this. Where're my keys?"

"You're really about to drive to work? Are you fucking serious?"

"Yeah, I am. Sean said... He said if I miss one more night, I'm done," he slurs. "I had to take almost an entire week off to deal with all this court crap."

"He also said if you show up drunk—"

"I'm not drunk, and you know that!"

"Okay, well... FYI, you seem drunk. Are you sure you haven't been drinking?"

"I HAVE NOT BEEN DRINKING!"

"What's really in that bottle, hmm?"

Tristian and I have a plan. I'm going to tell the investigators he was really drunk. It must have been alcohol poisoning. It's believable, right? They won't bother to do an autopsy, I don't think...right?

"It's just Gatorade! You can fuckin' smell it!"

I pick up the bottle and untwist the cap. I sniff it. "Yeah...I don't know."

"Taste it if you don't fucking believe me!"

"No, no. That's okay." I twist the cap back on and put the Gatorade down. He picks it up and takes it with him.

"I'm going to work." He stumbles out of the room. "I just have to take deep...breaths and tell myself I feel fine. I can get through tonight. Mind over...over matter."

"You're not driving anywhere!" I follow him into the living room.

"Then you drive me."

"What? No!"

"You can't st-stop me from leaving the apartment. Either you drive...drive me, or...or I'll drive myself."

"I'll hide your keys, you drunk bastard!"

"Then I'm gonna start...start walking."

I quickly snatch the keys. He stares at me blankly for a few moments.

"Here... Here I go, then." He walks down the stairs to the door. He holds tight onto the banister.

I'm going to get caught. I'm going to get caught.

"Okay! I'll drive you!"

"Thanks." He sits on the stairs clutching the bottle.

Fuck... Maybe he'll drink more and die in the car? I don't know what to do. I'll have to make sure he's definitely dead before I call nine-one-one. I'll drive really slow.

CHAPTER TWENTY-SIX

Danny

It's Friday, and I'm dragging ass. How bad would it be to lie to Matt? To lie to Peter? I just want to go home after school and sleep. As I stare at my math test, I realize I actually know this stuff. Maybe if I get a good grade, Peter won't be so mad about me sneaking home this afternoon.

"All right, everyone. Take out a red pen and switch tests with the person next to you," Mrs. Roland says.

"Here." I hand Matt my test.

"Put your red pen away. I definitely got a one hundred." He hands over his test.

Show-off.

"Let's start with number one," Mrs. Roland says.

She begins to review the first question, eventually writing the final answer on the board. Matt got number one wrong. HE GOT NUMBER ONE WRONG!

I turn and Matt puts a check near my answer. I got it right, and he got it wrong. Maybe today will be a good day. Matt looks over his shoulder as I put a big fat X on his answer.

"Are you serious?" he asks.

"I mean, you wrote the wrong answer."

"Okay, but that's a really big X!"

Mrs. Roland continues to go through the answers. At the end of the review, Matt hands me my test. I look at it and smile. I got an 85 in math. Matt still did better than me, but I'm proud of myself. We pass our papers forward, and Mrs. Roland collects them. When the bell rings, I pick up my notebook and stand.

"So, I'll meet you at your locker after school? My mom's gonna pick us up today," Matt says.

"No, actually."

"Really? You're supposed to be coming to my house every night."

"Peter took tonight off. I'm going to go home on the bus, but tell your mom Peter said thank you."

"All right. That's cool, I guess. I'll see you on Monday, then?"

"Yeah. I'll see you Monday."

"Okay. Later."

"Later."

Butterflies and a sense of excitement fill me. I got an 85 on my math test. I get to go home after school. I did something bad, so why am I smiling?

★★★

After school, I head into the kitchen and put my phone on the table. I find a package of fruit snacks in the cabinet. Why do I have an Eminem song stuck in my head? I don't really know the lyrics, but I bop my head to the music.

Hayley's not even home. Maybe she already left. Maybe she's gone for good. That'd be sick.

I hear the car horn outside.

Spoke too soon, she's home.

I peek out the kitchen window and see Hayley sitting on the hood of the car, smoking a cigarette. She's getting kinda chubby. Probably all the soda she's been drinking.

Another car pulls up next to her. A man gets out of the backseat. Oh shit, it's Tristian. He's not supposed to be here at all. He's holding a black backpack. He slams the door of the car, and it drives away. Looks like...they're fighting?

Tristian swings the bag onto his shoulder, and they walk toward our apartment door. Hayley fumbles and drops her keys. I can hear what they are saying through the window.

"Why did you bring him to work?" Tristian asks. "Are you stupid?"

"It's fine!"

Are they talking about Peter?

I clutch my fruit snacks and run into my bedroom. I close my bedroom door behind me, just like Peter said to do. I hear the front door open. I'll just stay in my room. I close my eyes and breathe.

The door shuts, and they're walking up the stairs. Oh my God, they are definitely fighting. They're screaming, and Hayley's crying...again.

I turn off the lights and press my right ear against my closed bedroom door.

"It's going to be okay. Listen! He just looked drunk. His boss is just going to think he's drunk again. That's it, Tristian!"

Hayley's coughing and sniffling.

"I'm going to vomit." She runs down the hallway, probably toward the bathroom. She's puking loudly in between cries.

My heart starts to race. What did they do to Peter?

"Just let me think a minute!" Tristian yells.

Hayley flushes the toilet.

"He said he wasn't feeling well. He took this bottle of Gatorade with him. When he was in the bathroom, I poured a bunch of it out and filled it with that stuff you gave me. He's going to drink more of it—hopefully, all of it. He won't make it to a hospital or home. Even if he did, they'll just think it's alcohol poisoning. I'm going to say... I'm going to say he was drinking before I took him to work, but that he still demanded I take him. Then, for emphasis, I'll say he hit me! There's no way they'll be able to resuscitate him, right? He drank too much of it, right? Right? Holy shit. I need to take something. I can't—"

Now I'm really panicking. I'm going to be sick too. I'm dizzy. Where's my fucking cell phone? I have to call Peter! I have to call McAlister's! I have to call the police! I have to call someone!

I pat my pockets. My phone isn't there. I crawl over to the bed and start feeling around for it in the dark. SHIT! Where is it?

Hayley's phone rings, and she yells. "It's Peter. He's calling me!"

"Stop crying! Stop crying, and pick it up!" Tristian responds.

"He-Hello?"

Hayley

"Ca-Can you come... Please, come get me."

"You just got there." I sniffle, pacing around the living room. Tristian's sitting on the couch.

"I just... Come g-g-get me. I'm real sick."

"It's not my fucking job to come get you." My voice trembles.

"I s-should have stayed home t-t-tonight."

"Yeah. I fucking told you." I sniffle again.

"Hayley..."

Tristian's looking at me. He's shaking his head.

"You have to go get him. This is fucked!" Tristian whispers.

"Okay, okay! You know what? Give me a few minutes. Just... Just stay where you are," I say to Peter.

"I-I can't wait. P-P-Please."

"JUST WAIT WHERE YOU ARE!"

I hang up the phone.

"Clean yourself the fuck up, and go get him! It's going to look suspicious as hell if you show up to the bar crying," Tristian says.

"I'll splash my face with some water."

My whole body is shaking. I walk into the bathroom and look at myself in the mirror. What have I done? I can't back out now. Can I blame this all on Tristian? I can say it was his idea. Maybe I'll get less time. But I'm the one who carried it out. I'm the one that poisoned him. I'm completely fucked. This baby is going to grow up just like I did, with their mother in jail.

I take short breaths in between sobs, turn on the sink, and start splashing my face with water. I take a nice long breath in.

My phone starts ringing. It's him again.

"What? Hello?"

"K-Kara is...c-coming to get me."

FUCK.

Kara

It's dark. It's cold. Why am I doing this again?

You're stupid. This guy means nothing to you. There are so many men out there. Why are you wasting your time with him? Why did you agree to pick him up? He's not worth your time!

I turn my blinker on. I'm done talking to myself about this. I'm done talking about this, in general.

The road is clear. I turn left into the McAlister's parking lot, already looking around for him. He's not in front of the bar. I turn left at the corner by My Tokyo.

There he is, sitting. No...laying? Laying on the curb by the dumpster? It just gets better and better, doesn't it?

I pull over sharply against the sidewalk. I must've nearly run over his hand because he flinches fast. What reflexes for a drunk!

He's sitting up straight now, grasping onto a mostly empty bottle. I get a better look at him. His long, wavy hair is matted into a bun. His black apron, which is normally tied neatly around his waist, is hanging off of his body. Was he using it as a blanket? His clothes are stained with...dirt?...vomit?

I reach across the center console and fling open the door with all my might. It hits into his knee. He rubs it, slowly, then he looks up at me. I turn my face toward the windshield. I refuse to look at him. I refuse to give him that.

"Th-Thank you." He climbs into the car. He chugs down what's left of his drink, drops the empty bottle accidentally, and picks it back up.

"Peter. This is the last time. I hope you realize that." I start driving before he can close the door. I feel bad for him, but not bad enough. He finally gets a grip on the handle and shuts it quietly. Too quietly. I'm not sure if it is really closed. Maybe I should...

Nope. I will not. I keep driving.

"You're r–right, it is last time...because...Sean let me go," he says. "Just what I... Just what I...n–needed..."

I see him out of my peripheral vision. He's looking at me, expecting a response. He expects pity or acknowledgment, but I'm enraged. I clench my jaw.

"I meant the last time you'll be seeing me...ever." I tighten my grip on the steering wheel, readjusting myself as if it will help me gain some sort of strength, but I don't look directly at him.

"What do you mean?"

He continues to gawk at me. He knows fully what I mean.

I refuse to look at him. It's the one bit of power I have left. I can't fall for the "deer in headlights" look. I can't do this to myself. I shouldn't be looking at him, anyway. I have to keep my eyes on the road. I'm not getting into an accident because of this fool.

"I told you, if you wanted this to work, you would stop drinking. Here we are again, and this time... This time, you got fired for it! How did you expect I would react to this? You think I would forgive you, give you another chance? Unlimited chances?"

"And I told you I am not d–drunk! I'm sick, Kara. I—"

"Oh, stop it," I interject. "You know what, you are sick. You're an alcoholic, and you need help. You—"

"Mary, Mary, Jesus, and St. Joseph, I had nothing to drink, n–n–nothing! I need someone to...someone to believe me."

"You smell like vomit, Peter. You look disgusting, you—"

"How would you know, for Christ's sake, you won't even... You won't even l–l–look at me."

His eyes are stuck on me, but I would look anywhere else other than at him right now. My eyes dart around the road, then I see it. We're passing by the blue sign with the white "H" on Woodside Avenue.

Perfect opportunity. Perfect retort.

"If you're sick, I'm taking you to the hospital." I flash my blinker as we approach the turn for the medical center.

He moves his head in toward his lap and cradles it as if he is going to vomit. Finally, he's not staring at me.

"Oh, hell n-n-no. I'm not going to no hospital. I have enough drama—"

"So, you're willing to risk your life because of 'drama?' What fucking 'drama?' I don't believe you. You're drunk. Just admit it!"

"I d-don't care anymore. Just take me home. I just—"

"You're a liar, and you're never going to change." My eyes start to get watery. Why am I giving him the satisfaction of crying? "I don't know why I put myself through this! I don't—"

"TAKE ME THE FUCK HOME!" He sits up straight. I can still see him in my peripheral vision. He's angry. I won't take this crap. I don't have to take this.

I slam on my brakes in the middle of Woodside Avenue. I don't care. No one's on the road. He nearly flies into the windshield. He protects his body with his hands as he hits into the dashboard. Oh well, should have put your seat belt on. I look right at him for the first time, with resentment.

"Why? So you can be with your BITCH? GET THE FUCK OUT OF MY CAR!"

He laughs. He has the audacity to laugh.

"Yeah," he says. "So I can...go be with my b-bitch. Fuck you, Kara. Think you, you know all of...everything, but you don't know s-s-shit."

He opens the car door and nearly falls trying to get out. He somehow stands up straight and slams the door behind himself, stumbling down the road in front of me.

I drive away, but slowly. Tears are running down my cheeks now.

Don't look back, Kara, don't look back.

But I look back. I see him on his hands and knees, vomiting on the side of the street. I keep driving.

CHAPTER TWENTY-SEVEN

Hayley

I'm sobbing. I'm sitting on the couch sobbing. Nothing can fix this. Not even the Oxys. They didn't help at all. Now I'm just extra paranoid. My tears feel hot like flames burning down my face.

"Stop it!" Tristian says.

He doesn't understand, and I don't have the strength to tell him now.

"I can't."

"You want the neighbors to call the police? You want the police to show up here?"

"You think that's what I want?" I stand. "You think that's what I want? You talked me into this. YOU!"

"But you're the one who actually did it. Now, shut the fuck up! I'm just here to help you cover your own ass. I have something in mind."

I pace around the living room. I'm making myself dizzy, but I feel like if I walk faster and faster, I could float, take off...be anywhere but here.

"Where is he?" I fall to the floor. "It doesn't take that long to drive home. What if she took him to the hospital? What if they run tests? What if they find poison in his blood? We're so screwed! Oh my God!"

"Calm down. Who knows why it's taking so long? What time is the kid supposed to be coming home?"

"Not until Peter's normal end of shift." I sniffle.

"Perfect."

We hear a banging noise coming from outside. Tristian walks to the front of the apartment and peeks through the blinds.

"He's home!" He turns to look at me. "There's no car, though. Looks like he walked. He's got a bottle in his hand, and... He just threw it out." He laughs. "It's empty."

"Okay, okay... Just let him go to bed. I don't want to do this anymore. I changed my mind. Tristian..." I start crying again, "I'm so scared."

"Oh, no. You're not backing out. Plan B is much more fun, anyway. We just have to figure out where to hide a body."

"What the fuck do you mean? You failed. It's over. There's no Plan B. Let's get out of this while we still can!"

The door opens, and I hear Peter trip up the steps. Tristian darts toward the front door.

"No, Tristian. NO! What are you thinking?"

I chase after him, looking down from the top of the stairs. Peter's face first on the floor. Tristian yanks him up by his arms.

"What ... What are you d-doing?" Peter asks groggily.

"Get the fuck up."

"Tristian! Put him down. Help him get into bed!"

"You sorry fuck." He drops Peter on his side and kicks him in the chest, hard. Peter gasps for air. It's nothing like the powerless punches I gave him just a few days ago. The kick literally knocks the wind out of him.

"TRISTIAN! NO! NO!"

I run down the stairs and try to help Peter up. Tristian pushes me away. My head bangs against the opposite wall. I slide down the steps and land at the very bottom. I push myself back up and lean against the door.

"Too late," he says to me. "You already committed to this. You committed to this the moment you poisoned his coffee this morning."

Peter looks directly at me. He's still trying to catch his breath.

"I don't want to be committed to this anymore!" I sob and cover my face with my hands. I claw at my own skin like I want to rip it off, free myself from my own body. "I'm done!"

Tristian pulls a wheezing Peter up by one wrist. He drags him up the stairs that way. Peter tries to use his other hand to claw at Tristian's fingers, but Tristian doesn't care. I hear Peter's body hit each and every step. Tristian lets go of Peter's arm once he reaches the top. He leaves him on the floor and walks away.

I crawl up the stairs on my hands and knees, but it's like climbing a mountain. I'm dizzy as fuck. I don't know if I'm really high, or if my head hit the wall too hard, or both. I don't care. When I make it to the top of the steps, Peter is curled up into a ball, vomiting. Is that blood? I think that's blood. I think he's throwing up blood. Fuck!

Tristian

"Peter! Peter!" She's on the floor with him now, holding him in between her legs. I knew she was a weak-minded bitch. Not like me. Once I'm in my zone, I'm in my zone...and I'm there.

I dig through my backpack and pull out my Bluetooth speaker. I shove it in the pocket of my sweatshirt, turn on my phone, and click shuffle on my playlist. I crank the volume up as loud as possible. Some heavy metal shit starts playing. That will work. Hayley normally has the TV blasting in here, anyway. I doubt the neighbors will think twice about it.

"WHAT ARE YOU DOING?" she yells.

"HUH? CAN'T HEAR YOU!"

"TRISTIAN!"

I take the rope from my backpack. Now I'm ready.

I walk toward them. Hayley's eyes look like they might pop out of her skull. She scoots backward on her ass, holding onto the little fuck.

"Tristian, no! Why do you have rope? What are you—? It wasn't supposed to be like this!" She cries and cries.

"Nothing's ever the way you expect it to be. That's why you have to adapt."

"Please, stop! Please leave him alone!"

She puts him down and lays on top of him, almost like they're about to fuck or something. It only makes me angrier...but this is an easier position for me to rip her off of him, anyway.

I grab her by the waist. She's stuck on him. I tear her off like Velcro.

"NO!"

She kicks me while I drag her toward the kitchen. She grabs onto anything she can. She's clearly on his side now. I need to get her back on mine.

"It's okay, Hals. It will be over soon, and then we'll have the money to get a place of our own. You'll never see me like this again. I'll be the Tristian you know again, and we'll have a set of keys of our very own."

"What are you talking about? Keys? I don't know you! I don't know who you are!"

"Just calm down—"

"I can't calm down. PETER!"

"Stop saying that asshole's name, and let me take care of this. We're almost done here."

I push her toward the cabinets. I didn't want it to come to this, but I'm going to have to tie her up. It's the only way to get the job done.

"Hayley? Hals?" I snap my fingers in her face. She whimpers a little. Maybe the Oxys are finally kicking in. She doesn't move. Guess I don't have to tie her up, after all. This works too.

I go back over to ass-face. He's still struggling to breathe, but he hasn't moved from the spot where I left him.

"You know what she thinks of you?" I ask. "It's actually a funny story. She's the one that poisoned you, not me." I kick him directly in the forehead. The back of his skull smashes into the corner of the wall. He doesn't make a sound. "What else did she say about you...? Oh yeah! Big teeth, crooked nose. Let me help you with that." I kick him in the nose.

He flips over and tries to push himself up. He can't do it. I'm sure this isn't what he pictured when he said he'd fight me. He didn't realize how powerful I really am.

I bend down to look in his eyes. "Where is it?"

He's not focusing on the question. I grab his face.

"WHERE THE FUCK DID YOU PUT MY KEY?"

He still doesn't answer.

I drop him again so that his head hits the ground. I kick him. I just keep kicking him in the chest and stomach, and I don't stop. I don't see, I don't think, not about anything other than the key he took from me. The hundred thousand dollars that will get me a key of my own...

I kick him until his shirt looks like a used maxi pad because of the blood pouring from his nose. He's still breathing. Time for the grand finale.

I pick him up and lean him against the wall, looping the rope around his neck three times. He looks like he's fallen asleep.

I pat his cheek. "You awake there? Wouldn't want you to miss this."

I take hold of the end of the rope. Then the music changes.

Huh?

"Come All Ye Faithful" starts playing.

When the fuck did I download this?

Peter

God, I'm sorry. God, I'm sorry. God, I'm sorry. I know I deserve this, but please let it end. Let me die already. That's what *she* wanted, anyway.

Why this song? Is he taunting me? Sick basturt.

My eyes drift open and closed, then open again. The first thing I can make out is a cloud of knotted red hair. Someone's lying down next to me.

Hayley?

"Seamus!"

It's not Hayley.

"Adair..."

"Seamus? Get up, Seamus! You have to get up. It's get up time!"

"I... I can't do it. Not now, Adair"

He smiles and laughs, but nothing is funny.

"Ding!" he yells.

"Ding?"

"Ding! Ding!"

"I don't understand, Adair."

"Ding! Ding! Ding!"

My eyes open wider now. I'm suddenly, explosively, vividly awake. Adair is gone. *I recognize that ding.*

"Stupid kid left his phone here?" Tristian walks toward me and kneels. He holds Danny's phone in front of my face.

"Where is he? What did you do to him?"

"We haven't even seen him. Shut the fuck up!"

"STOP LYING!"

I push against the floor and try to stand. My elbows tremble and give out. I fall back down.

"He's not home. He's fine, Peter!" Hayley says, speaking for the first time in a while. Tristian looks away from me and toward the kitchen.

"Then why the fuck is his phone here? He wouldn't leave his phone at home, you fucking MONSTER!"

Tristian stares at me, nervous and wide-eyed. Then he pulls my hair and yanks my head back.

"Look at me. Is the kid home?"

"I have no fucking idea!"

Tristian pulls the knife from his pocket and holds it to my throat.

"I'll slit your throat right here, right now. Is the kid in his fucking bedroom?"

"You're such a coward. A fucking coward!"

Tristian pushes me back down and walks toward Danny's room. I thrust myself up with all my might and lunge, grabbing onto his ankle. He stumbles, looks down at me, and frees his leg from my hold with one quick shake.

"Tristian, please," I beg. "Please."

O come, let us adore Him
O come, let us adore Him
O come, let us adore Him
Christ the Lord!

He smiles and pulls his leg backward. He kicks it forward, and—

Danny

I'm dangling out the window. If I let go, I might break my legs. How am I ever going to get help? I have to aim for a bush or something and just hope for the best. It's the only option I have. The music keeps getting closer and closer... Christmas music? It's not Christmas!

Something claws at my hands. I look up. Tristian's staring down at me. He looks like a devil! Fuck! I should have let go sooner.

"LET GO OF ME!" I yell. "HELP!"

He yanks me back up and through the window. I try to run, but he's too strong. I punch him, and he laughs. I punch him again.

"Stop tickling me," he says.

Tickling? I'm not that weak, am I?

"HELP ME! HELP!"

He pushes me against my desk and starts tying me to it. I use all the strength I have, even my back-up strength—my angry strength, my panic strength—but I can't get myself free. I cry and cry. Guess I'm not as tough as I thought.

"STOP! Tristian, leave him alone. Please!" Hayley yells as she falls into my bedroom.

"Why? So he could rat us out? When I came in here, he was dangling out the fucking window. The little mutt bastard almost escaped without us even knowing he was in here at all!"

Mutt? What does that mean? I'm not a dog. Why would he say that?

"There's so much evidence, anyway... Tristian, the living room looks like a fucking murder scene! It doesn't look like alcohol poisoning!"

I stop thinking about what Tristian called me. Now all I can think of is murder. Peter being murdered. I can't breathe. I can't catch my breath.

"WHAT?" I yell. "NO! You... YOU KILLED PETER, HAYLEY?"

Tristian ignores me and grabs hold of my ankles tightly. He starts tying them together.

"Danny—" she says.

"You BITCH! You disgusting BITCH! I HATE YOU! I've always HATED YOU!"

Hayley stares at me. Her jaw is quivering like she's freezing, but it's fucking hot as hell in this apartment. She turns away toward Tristian.

"Such a sweet boy," Tristian says as he finishes the knots around my ankles. "That should hold him for a while."

Suddenly Hayley's on the ground, screaming. She covers her ears. Her screams are way louder than the music playing. Christmas music isn't that intense.

"STOP! Stop it! What are you doing?" Tristian pulls his phone out of his pocket, skipping through songs until something loud and weird starts playing.

She keeps on screaming. She screams, louder and louder, until she chokes. Tristian shoves everything back into his pocket. He picks her up around her stomach and pulls her out of my room. Hayley's shrieking, wailing, and kicking, but she's no match for him either. None of us were. Tristian slams the door behind them.

Hayley

Tristian rips me out of Danny's room. I keep screaming as loudly as possible. Oh, God...my throat. Please, someone, hear my screams already and call the police!

I kick and punch, trying to get free. As I'm dragged into the living room, I see Peter still lying on the ground. His eyes have rolled to the back of his head. He's shaking violently.

No, no, no. no.

"Peter! PETER!" I sob, gagging on my saliva. "No!"

"Don't look at him. Shut up!"

"You didn't say this would happen. You didn't say any of this would happen! You let it get to your head. You got your revenge. Let me go. I can't breathe!"

"I'm sorry that you thought a murder was going to be rainbows and roses, you dumb bitch!" He drops me onto the floor.

The room is getting smaller and smaller. My ears are ringing. Tristian is saying something, but I don't know what. He's

313

holding his head. Suddenly, the ringing stops and my hearing comes back. In fact, I hear sirens! I see lights. Cop car lights! We're going to jail! We're going to prison forever! I feel relieved. Maybe someone can help Peter. I wouldn't be a good mother, anyway, and everyone knows he's a good dad.

"The police are here! HELP! HELP!" I scream.

"What are you talking about?"

"The sirens! The lights! HELP!"

"There's no one here! There's no sirens! There's no lights!" Tristian says, but he's wrong. I see them through the window. I run over and start pounding on the glass.

"HELP!"

Tristian grabs me around the waist again. I turn to look at him. Snot is running into my mouth. It tastes salty on my tongue. I try to break free from his hold, shimmying and shaking. I claw and bite his arms.

"I can't do this! I can't fucking do this! You're making this harder than it has to be!" Tristian says.

"Tristian, the police are HERE!"

"You're losing your mind! Stop screaming!"

Through all of this, he holds onto me and covers my mouth.

"PETER!" I hear Danny yell, banging from his room.

"There's no way that little shit untied those knots. How could he?"

Tristian is panicking. He's finally panicking. He shoves me away, grabbing at his head and pulling his own hair.

"I'm getting the fuck out of here," he says. "You can't handle this. You can't do this. I'm not going down with you. I'm running." He sprints to the sliding glass door.

I look back over at Peter. I really, *really* look at him.

I think it's too late.

He's still convulsing violently. He's covered in blood. He's gasping for air and clutching onto life...

This is it. Peter's dying, and Tristian's leaving me to take responsibility for his murder. Then what? What will our baby do? A dead father, an incarcerated mother...

A sudden rush of adrenaline hits. I jump up. I have to live. I have to go. I need to run and hide. Someone will untie Danny, eventually.

"Tristian!" I follow him through the sliding glass door. I fall but get back up. I use the railing around the balcony to help me. I look below and see Tristian running through the woods behind our apartment. I sprint down the stairs and chase after him. My tears dry from the wind beating against my face. I run as fast as I can.

"Tristian? TRISTIAN! Don't leave me all alone!"

I can never come back here.

CHAPTER TWENTY-EIGHT

Danny

I've cried myself to sleep a lot of times, but this time's so much different. I'm tied to my desk. The sun's just starting to shine in through the window. Peter's dead on the floor outside my bedroom. I choke up at the thought of it. When will someone find us here? Why didn't anyone call for help? I've been yelling all night. I guess Peter was right about the neighbors... I guess Peter was right about a lot of things, *especially* Tristian.

"Help me! Someone help me! Please, someone help!" I kick the floor with my legs as hard as possible. Don't the people downstairs hear me? Aren't they home? I feel very, very angry. All I can think of his Hayley and Tristian living out the rest of their lives in prison.

"Help!"

Something bangs in the living room. Someone's here. They must've already found Peter. I hope they pull his body out of the apartment before they untie me. I can't see him dead. I can't...

"I'm in the bedroom! I'm in the bedroom! Help me!"

My door opens slowly. No way...

"Peter? Peter! Peter!"

"Danny..." He walks over to me. His shirt is covered with blood. There's blood in his hair, all over his face, even behind his ears. His nose looks broken. His left eye's swollen almost shut.

"I thought you were dead! I thought they killed you! You're covered in blood! Your head! Your face!"

"I'm okay. It doesn't hurt anymore."

He stumbles over and sits beside me, examining all the knots tying me to the desk.

"Holy shit. He tied you good. I need a knife."

He slowly makes it back to his feet.

"You have to call the police, Peter. Call the police right now!"

"Let me get you off of...off of the desk, Danny." He leaves the room and comes back with a kitchen knife. He walks over and starts cutting away at the rope. "It's j-j-just you and me for now on. No one else. No one, just us. Just us. I promise you."

"Are you okay? You sound terrible."

"I don't feel great."

"Once you get me off of this desk, you have to go to a doctor."

"I'm getting better. I'm fine. I just need to r-r-rest...okay?"

The rope snaps completely. I pull my hands in front of my body and roll my wrists. Peter starts cutting the knots around my legs.

"You're not going to go to the doctor? Peter, what did you drink?"

"I have no idea, but I'm feeling better than I was yesterday. It's passing out of my s-s-system."

"No, you have to go!"

"If I start feeling really sick again, I promise I'll go...b-b-but for now... I just need to...rest."

The rope snaps off of my ankles. I'm free.

"But you're going to call the police? You're going to report what they did to us? Right?"

"Yes."

"Okay. Do you think she'll come back? Do you think *he'll* come back?"

"I don't think either of them are that stupid... Danny?"

"Yes?"

"Will you be all right if I...lay down? Just for a little bit. It's m-mostly heartburn."

"I'll be okay," I say.

He hugs me tightly for a long time. "Nothing, and no one, is more important to me than you. Got it?"

He pulls away from our hug and looks me in the eyes.

I look straight back at him. Now that I know Peter is alive, my mind goes back to what Tristian called me. *Mutt...Like a dog?* I think of that Snapchat filter. I never want to see it again.

I want to ask Peter what it means, to be a mutt, but he looks so bad. He probably feels bad too. Maybe later...but it hurts, though. A lot of things hurt right now. Maybe I feel as bad inside as Peter does outside. Maybe we both hurt a lot.

Do we get revenge? Do we ignore it? I don't know what we do.

"Okay, Peter," I say. There is no more to say.

"I love you."

"I love you too."

I'm scared, and I'm sad. Hayley is gone, and she's not coming back. I've finally won, but I feel so confused.

Peter

Just let me sleep...

My cell phone's vibrating. The sound of it hitting the top of the end table...ugh. It might as well be vibrating on my forehead. My chest still burns. It's been days. I must have an ulcer. My stomach feels hollow. I need to eat something, but that only makes it worse.

I reach over and grab my phone.

Private name, private number. Okay...

"Hello?"

I hear nothing on the other end beside the echo of my voice. I close my eyes again and push my hair out of my face.

"Hello?" I ask again.

I hear breathing. What the fuck.

"Who is this?"

I sit up and shift my legs over the end of my bed.

"I..." a woman responds.

"Hayley?"

"I'm so sorry. I'm sorry."

The phone disconnects. I stare at the wall for a while. I put my phone down, stand, and stretch. It's time to try to start my day.

I feel bad for her. I know how it feels to run from something very, very bad. I wonder where she is...if she's safe. Does she need my help?

Seamus

I draw in the sand with my fingers. Ma stands in front of the ocean with her back facing me. It's windy and hot at the same time. Her hair is blowing wildly, but she doesn't tie it back. We hardly come down to the beach, except for when she feels like she needs to talk with Pop. For some reason, she thinks this is the place where he can hear her the loudest. She says she can hear him too.

I lay down in the sand and close my eyes. I listen to the sound of the ocean and the wind, not the voice of my dead da. Maybe he just doesn't want to talk to me.

"Come here, my son," she calls.

I open my eyes and sit up. She's looking at me and smiling. I smile back. I push up on the sand and get my bearings.

Adair runs toward Ma from behind me. She opens her arms, and he hugs her. When he pulls away, she pokes his nose playfully. He laughs and laughs. She grabs onto his hand, and they both face the ocean again. She points out into the distance as he jumps up and down happily.

I'm still smiling, even though I shouldn't be. She wasn't talking to me. Why would I ever think she was talking to me?

I sit back down. I'm still smiling. It hurts. It burns to smile, but I just can't stop.

LOOK OUT FOR BOOK TWO
RUN AWAY HOME: SHATTERED.

.

ACKNOWLEDGMENTS

Life is a novel. There's a beginning, a middle, and an end for us all. Along the way, you find those who contribute to your story.

There's no way to write a novel alone…and anyone who says they have, simply hasn't acknowledged the people who changed them, encouraged them, and inspired them along the way. I write fiction, so they may not be characters in Run Away Home, but this book could not exist without the people I'm about to mention.

First and foremost, I don't think I'd be a writer if my imagination and wonder wasn't nurtured by my family growing up. Thank you to my mom, who not only allowed me to dream, but demanded I did.

My partner in imagination and pretend, my childhood friend, teenagerhood friend, and forever friend…also the person I reach out to constantly to ask opinions about make believe people…my cousin, Christine Lang.

My dad, who financed my way through private college, and only grimaced a little when I said I wanted to study creative writing.

My husband who not only puts up with my dreams, but truly believes in them as much as I do. A man who has always made me feel good about what I've created and who I am. My husband, Scott.

The two people who I trusted to critique the very first draft of RAH, My best friends who stood by me when I was finding my way in college and life, Trish McLernon and Alex Ross.

The two friends who read the second draft of RAH and let me know they can't wait to read the next two books, Courtney Geraci and Olivier Andre.

The person who may have read this book almost as many times as I have. The professor who told me that the idea for this novel had merit back in 2012, the person who edited the first draft, the second draft, the third draft...Lord knows how many drafts. My professor, mentor, fellow writer, and friend, William J. Mcgee.

And of course, to the entire team at RhetAskew Publishing, who believed in RUN AWAY HOME enough to edit it three times, format it, and publish it: Jennifer Soucy, Dusty Grein, and Mandy Melanson.

ABOUT THE AUTHOR

Catherine Manett is a graduate of Hofstra University where she studied creative writing. Since then, Catherine started a career as a caseworker for Adult Protective Services. In her position, she assists her community's most vulnerable adults with connecting to services that meet their essential needs. Through her work, Catherine has found a passion for helping those who battle homelessness. Growing up on Long Island, it became clear to Catherine that the price of living in New York is unaffordable. Because of this, Catherine has volunteered with many nonprofit organizations including Habitat for Humanity.

Catherine has always had love for writing and was inducted into Sigma Tau Delta, an international English honor society, in 2015. RUN AWAY HOME: TEMPERED is Catherine's debut novel and passion project. It will be the first of a series of three.

In her spare time, Catherine enjoys competing in pageants, and has held the titles of Miss Long Island Teen 2012, Miss Queens America 2015, and Mrs. New York American Women of Service 2021. Catherine also enjoys bowling, spending time with her husband and cat, and of course, drinking Riesling, Corona, and Sour Apple Martinis.

FIND CATHERINE ONLINE

Twitter: @CatherineManett

Instagram: @CatherineManett

Facebook: @OfficialCatherineManett

Website: https://catherine-manett.mailchimpsites.com

WWW.RHETASKEWPUBLISHING.COM

Made in the USA
Monee, IL
29 July 2023